Put Beginning Readers on the Right Track with
ALL ABOARD READING™

The All Aboard Reading series is especially for beginning readers. Written by noted authors and illustrated in full color, these are books that children really and truly *want* to read—books to excite their imagination, tickle their funny bone, expand their interests, and support their feelings. With three different reading levels, All Aboard Reading lets you choose which books are most appropriate for your children and their growing abilities.

Level 1—for Preschool through First Grade Children
Level 1 books have very few lines per page, very large type, easy words, lots of repetition, and pictures with visual "cues" to help children figure out the words on the page.

Level 2—for First Grade to Third Grade Children
Level 2 books are printed in slightly smaller type than Level 1 books. The stories are more complex, but there is still lots of repetition in the text and many pictures. The sentences are quite simple and are broken up into short lines to make reading easier.

Level 3—for Second Grade through Third Grade Children
Level 3 books have considerably longer texts, use harder words and more complicated sentences.

All Aboard for happy reading!

For everyone at the
Grace Opportunity Project,
especially
William Zhao and Victor Lun
—K. McM.

To the Harris family —A.D.

Text copyright © 1993 by Kate McMullan. Illustrations copyright © 1993 by Anna DiVito. All rights reserved. Published by Grosset & Dunlap, Inc., which is a member of The Putnam & Grosset Group, New York. ALL ABOARD READING is a trademark of The Putnam & Grosset Group. Published simultaneously in Canada. Printed in the U.S.A.

Library of Congress Cataloging-in-Publication Data
McMullan, Kate. The biggest mouth in baseball / by Kate McMullan ; illustrated by Anna DiVito. p. cm. — (All aboard reading) Summary: William becomes a better baseball player when he concentrates more on the game and less on his joke telling. [1. Baseball—Fiction. 2. Jokes—Fiction.] I. DiVito, Anna, ill. II. Title. III. Series.
PZ7.M47879Bi 1993 [E]—dc20 92-24467   CIP   AC

ISBN 0-448-40516-4 (GB)   A   B   C   D   E   F   G   H   I   J
ISBN 0-448-40515-6 (pbk.)   A   B   C   D   E   F   G   H   I   J

ALL
ABOARD
READING™

Level 3
Grades 2–3

The Biggest Mouth
in
BASEBALL

By Kate McMullan
Illustrated by Anna DiVito

Grosset & Dunlap • New York

When I was little, I went to all the Junior Champs baseball games. I watched my big sister Anna slug home runs for the Drills.

The Drills were sponsored by Dr. Payne. He's our town dentist. Get it? Dentist...Drill? And let me tell you, Dr. Payne's name fits. That man is as mean as a toothache.

Still, I dreamed of being a Drill someday. I dreamed of the crowd cheering, "Drill 'em, William!" I dreamed of walking off the field a hero. All grass-stained and dirty.

So, the second I was old enough, I signed up for the Drills. I got a sparkling new uniform. I was all set.

At our first practice, all of us
new Drills huddled together by the
backstop, talking.

"I only have to stay on the team
till I lose ten pounds," Justin told us.

"My dad hopes baseball will toughen
me up," said Tori. "But I don't think
it will."

6

Victor looked up from his book. "My mother thinks I need fresh air," he said.

What a team! I was the only one who wanted to play.

All of a sudden, Tori's lip started trembling. She looked scared. "Oh, no," she said. "Look who's coming."

I turned around. Across the field marched Dr. Payne. He looked like a short, stocky old bulldog. A red baseball cap shaded the top half of his face. We could only see the bottom half. It needed a shave.

"Looks like he's in a foul mood," I whispered as he came closer. "Get it? A baseball coach in a <u>foul</u> mood?"

"Ooooh," said Victor. "Rotten joke."

"Thanks!" I said. "They're my specialty."

"Line up!" barked Dr. Payne. Then he walked back and forth. He came to me and stopped. "So, you're Anna's brother?"

"The one and only," I said.

"Can you hit like your sister?"

"I can hit like Darryl Strawberry," I said.

So he pitched me a few. I was so
nervous, I didn't hit one.

"Today I'm hitting more like
strawberry jelly," I said. It was a little
joke.

But Dr. Payne didn't laugh. The other Drills didn't turn out to be so hot, either. But by the end of practice, Dr. Payne had made up his mind. He'd decided I was the worst player on the team.

Every practice, Dr. Payne would frown at me. "Are you sure you're Anna's brother?" he'd ask. He hardly ever put me in a game. Halfway into the season, my uniform still looked brand-new. It didn't have a single grass stain on it.

The last Saturday in July, the team from Terry's Truckers ran over us Drills 26-0. Pathetic! Afterwards, I was sitting on our front steps reading a joke book to cheer myself up.

"How did it go, William?" Anna asked me.

"Great," I said. "I was so great I was on television."

"Wow!" said Anna.

"Then Mom made me get off," I said. "She was afraid I'd break the TV set."

"Aw!" groaned Anna. "What a terrible joke!"

I took a bow. Then I plopped back down on the steps. "I wasn't really great. Unless you call sitting on the bench great."

"You just need practice," said Anna. "Come on. I'll hit you a few."

We went to the park.

Anna slammed the ball over my head.

"Watch me! I catch fly balls the way other kids catch colds!" I yelled. But I missed by a mile.

"Keep your eye on the ball!" Anna tapped a grounder. It rolled between my legs.

I threw down my mitt. "Aw, I stink!"

"No offense, William. But you kid around too much," said Anna. "Forget the jokes. Just think about your game."

Forget the jokes? I couldn't believe my ears. Me? Forget the jokes? Never!

The next week, the Drills met at the field. We were playing the team from Betty's Bridal Shop. Everyone looked as if we'd already lost. And the game hadn't even started.

"Let's walk those Brides down the aisle of doom!" I tried to pep up my teammates.

"Ha!" said Justin. "They'll cream us."

Then Dr. Payne showed up. "Here's the batting order," he growled. He put me sixth. I was thrilled! Even if it was because three kids were out with the flu. Maybe today was the day I'd come home with a dirty uniform.

Tori was up first. She was chewing gum so her lip wouldn't quiver. But she still looked scared. She closed her eyes and swung at the ball. Three times. One away.

Justin stepped up to bat next. His gut hung over home plate. He glared at the Bride pitcher. Crack! He hit the ball—right into the shortstop's glove. Two outs.

Victor usually struck out. But not today. And neither did the next two batters.

Here was my big chance!

I stepped up to the plate with two outs and the bases loaded.

My hands started sweating. My legs felt like rubber bands. Was I nervous! So I did what I do when I'm nervous. I cracked a joke.

"Know what this is?" I held up the bat.

"Duh! A baseball bat!" called the pitcher.

"A fly swatter!" I called back. "Get it?"

Did the pitcher laugh? No.

Did he strike me out? Yep. One, two, three. I'd blown my chance. I'd let down my team. Boy, did I feel like a flop.

The Drills took the field. Most of them, that is. Yours truly sat on the bench beside Dr. Payne. We watched the Drills get creamed just the way Justin had predicted. We ended up 19–0.

Dr. Payne shook his head. He muttered, "The game of baseball is decaying before my very eyes!"

"Seven days till the next game," Victor said with a big smile as we walked home together. "No baseball for 168 hours. Or 10,080 minutes."

"Great," said Justin. "Let's go get some ice cream to celebrate."

I felt bad. I still liked baseball, even if I stunk. It was supposed to be fun. I tried cheering my friends up some more. "Hey, know what you call a dog that stands behind home plate? A catcher's mutt!"

Tori groaned. "Where do you get these awful jokes?" But at least she was smiling again. Arm in arm, we headed for the ice cream parlor. We all drowned our sorrows in banana splits.

4

The next Saturday, we played the team from AAA Burglar Alarms.

"Try something different today," Dr. Payne said in his pep talk. "Try winning!"

But did Dr. Payne try anything different? No. As usual, he had me warming the bench.

Tori pitched the first ball over the batter's head. The next pitch was even higher. Her lip was shaking so much she could hardly chew her gum. She needed to loosen up.

"Hey, Tori!" I called. "Put some ice cubes in your pocket. And keep your cool!"

Tori smiled. She took a deep breath. Then she snapped her gum and pitched a strike.

"This batter is so nice," I called. "He wouldn't hit a fly!"

Tori pitched again. Strike two!

What do you know! It looked like me and my big mouth were helping Tori. She struck out three batters in a row.

On his way to the plate, Justin punched my arm. "Keep those jokes coming!" he said.

So I did. I told Justin to take some string to the plate to tie up the score. I told Victor how to hold a bat—by its wings! With me as a one-man cheering squad, the Drills started having a good time playing. And, slowly, we caught up with the Burglars.

Dr. Payne couldn't believe it. His mouth was hanging open. He looked as if he was waiting for <u>his</u> dentist to start drilling!

When we were just one run behind, I tugged on Dr. Payne's shirt. "Put me in, Coach! You've got to! It's the rule!"

"Rule, bah!" said Dr. Payne. But he sent me to left field.

From the outfield, I kept the jokes coming. I was hot! I was cooking! Too bad I didn't see a fly ball soaring toward me until it dropped at my feet. By the time I picked it up and threw it in, two Burglars had crossed the plate.

"Victor!" Dr. Payne yelped. "Go to left field. William! Get over here!"

I slunk back to the bench. Dr. Payne was stomping on his cap.

27

The Burglars won. By three runs.

I walked home with my friends again.

"We weren't that bad today," said Victor.

"Plus it was kind of fun," said Justin. "Let's go get some ice cream to celebrate."

"Not me," I said. "I was awful."

"Your jokes really helped," said Tori.

"Yeah?" I said. Helped <u>them</u> maybe. Not me.

"Come on. Cheer up, William," everyone said. Then they all chipped in and bought me a chocolate sundae.

When I got home, Anna was sitting on the front steps. "I watched your game today," she said. "You must be the biggest mouth in baseball."

"The cleanest player, too." I hadn't even spilled chocolate syrup on my uniform. It still looked as new as the day I got it. "Think more practice would help?"

"Couldn't hurt," said Anna.

After dinner, we went to the park. Anna pitched to me.

"Hear about the new baseball movie?" I called as I sliced the air with my bat.

"Keep your eye on the ball," said Anna.

"It's <u>The Umpire Strikes Back!</u>" I missed the next pitch, too. "Know what kind of umpires you find at the North Pole? Cold ones!" I laughed so hard I forgot to swing.

But Anna wasn't laughing. "What do you want to do? Tell jokes or play ball?"

"Hey, is this a riddle?" I asked.

"No," said Anna. "It's something to think about. 'Cause you can't do both. Not at the same time."

"But my team needs my jokes," I told her.

"Fine," said Anna. "But when it is your turn at bat or when you are playing in the field, get serious."

"Me?" I said. "Serious? Ha ha ha!"

"Hey," said Anna. "Did you hear the joke about the fast pitch?"

"No," I said. "What?"

"Never mind, William. You just missed it." Anna looked fed up. "Come on. Let's go home."

"Hold it," I said. The season was almost over. There were only a few more games. I wanted to prove I wasn't a total dud. "Okay. I'll get serious."

Anna helped me every night that week. All I thought about was baseball. No jokes. No riddles. Just baseball. I hit fast balls, slow balls, high balls, low balls. I caught flys, grounders, line drives, bouncers. By Friday night, I still wasn't headed for the Hall of Fame. But I was better.

Saturday, our game was against the toughest team in the league, Papa's Pest Control.

I sat on the bench in my spanking clean uniform. Dr. Payne sat beside me. He twisted his cap and muttered, "I'd give my eyeteeth for one good slugger."

Tori's two little brothers led the crowd in a cheer:

"Drill 'em! Drill 'em! Never stop!
Drill those Pests until they drop!"

"Go Drills!" yelled Anna from the stands.

Papa's Pest Control had real cheerleaders. They stood in front of the bleachers wearing little cockroach suits.

They shouted:

"Two, four, six, eight!

Who shall we exterminate?

Eight, six, four, two!

We're gonna kill the Drills, that's who!"

The Pest pitcher stood on the mound grinding her teeth. The first baseman cracked his knuckles. The catcher spit halfway to third base. This was one scary team!

Tori stepped to the plate. She was chomping her gum about ninety miles an hour. She sure had the jitters.

"Don't put the bat in your mouth!" I yelled. "You'll get bat breath!"

Tori blew a bubble and hit a single.

That inning, we scored two runs. But the Pests knocked in four. And they scored three more two innings later.

Next time Tori was up, I called, "What do you get if you cross the king of beasts with a baseball?...A lion drive!"

And she got one! A line drive for a double!

"Why did the ump kick the chicken out of the game?" I called to Victor. "For using fowl language!"

Victor hit a single. And Tori got to third.

"What did the baseball player with big feet get?" I shouted to Justin. "Big shoes!"

Justin hit one over the fence. A homer! Three Drills crossed the plate! Now it was 5-7! I jumped up and down! I cheered!

We were still only two runs behind when the Pests had their last at bat.

I hadn't played yet. So Dr. Payne had to put me in. "Take right field," he said. "And try to stay awake out there."

I stayed awake. I didn't goof up. And the other Drills kept the Pests from scoring.

Now it was our turn at bat. If we could get three runs, we'd beat the Pests!

The first Drill flied out to center field. The second batter went down swinging. Two outs. Things looked grim. And I was up.

But Dr. Payne had other ideas. "Justin," he shouted. "Pinch-hit for William."

I couldn't believe my ears.

But then Tori spit her gum into a clump of bushes and said, "That's not fair! It's William's turn to bat!"

"Yeah!" said Victor.

"You'd better let him bat," said Justin. "'Cause I'm not batting for him!"

Hey! What do you know? I wasn't the only one on the team with a big mouth.

Dr. Payne closed his eyes. But he waved me into the game.

Very slowly, I walked to the plate. I had a baseball-sized lump in my throat. The Pest pitcher stared at me. She growled and pitched a high fastball. I swung. Strike one!

"Look 'em over, William!" my friends shouted.

Oh, boy! It was one thing to keep my mind on baseball in the park with Anna. In a real game, it was something else. I felt sick. I felt dizzy. I felt a joke coming on. "Know why Cinderella was a bad pitcher?" I called out. "She had a pumpkin for a coach!"

The ball zoomed by me. Strike two!

The pitcher gave me a wicked grin.

I couldn't seem to stop myself. "What baseball player wears the biggest helmet?"

"The one with the biggest head!" came Anna's voice from the stands. "Now use yours, William!"

Hearing Anna did the trick.

I shut my mouth. I looked hard at the ball. My eyes never left it. The pitcher wound up.

CRRRACK!

I got a hit! I raced to first. My friends were cheering! It sounded even better than when they were laughing at my jokes.

The next Drill drilled one to right field. I ran. When I stopped, I was safe at third. Me! Safe at third! Then Justin slammed one out to center field.

"Home it, William!" cried Tori. "Home it!"

I started running. The Pest catcher held out his glove. The ball whizzed by my ear. I slid into home plate. The catcher and I were lost in a cloud of dust.

The fans were quiet. The dust settled. Then the umpire shouted, "Yer...out!"

It was all over. The Pests had won the game.

Tori helped me up. "Don't feel bad."

"You did your best," said Justin.

I spit out a mouthful of dust. Dirt was caked on my uniform from my neck down to my socks.

8

I put my arm around Tori and Victor as Anna came up and snapped our picture. It shows me wearing the dirtiest uniform on the team. Maybe even the dirtiest uniform in the history of baseball.

This was the last picture ever taken of the Drills. After the game, Dr. Payne started yelling, "Turn in your uniforms! I'm retiring to Florida. I'm taking up shuffleboard. I never want to hear the word baseball again."

"But our team just got going," said Tori.

"Tell it to the tooth fairy," snarled Dr. Payne. "Your baseball days are over."

"Oh, I don't know about that." A tall woman with yellow hair stood behind Dr. Payne. "I'm Ms. Cornblatt, owner of Cornblatt's Canned Corn. I watched your game. With good coaching, you could be a fine team. I will sponsor you next season. But only if…"

"What? What?" we asked.

"Only if you don't run out of corny jokes."

Everyone looked at me. "No problem!"

"Good!" said Ms. Cornblatt. "A corny team is perfect for Cornblatt's. Your uniforms will be ready in two weeks. You can wear them in our next TV commercial."

And so all of us Corns got to be on TV. And this time, no one made us get off.

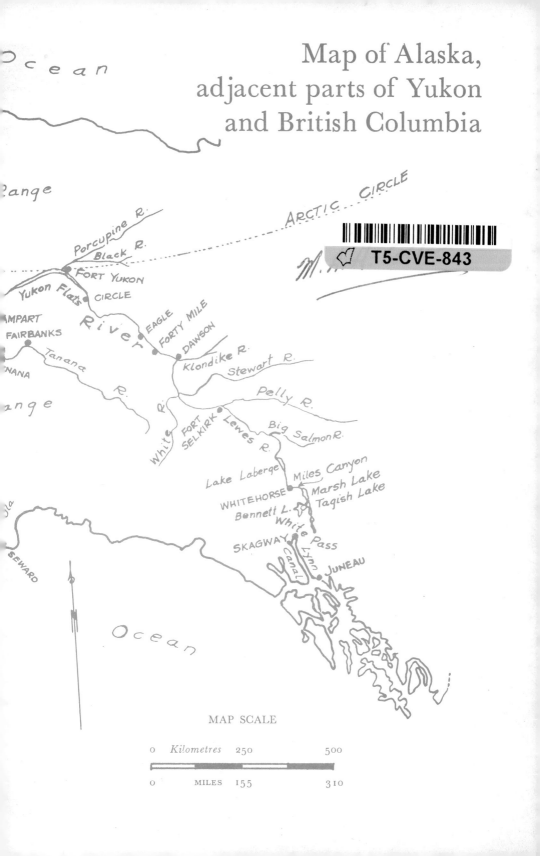

Map of Alaska, adjacent parts of Yukon and British Columbia

Ocean

Range

Porcupine R.

Black R.

ARCTIC CIRCLE

FORT YUKON

Yukon Flats   CIRCLE

River

MPART

FAIRBANKS

EAGLE

FORTY MILE

DAWSON

Tanana

NANA

Klondike R.

Stewart R.

R.

Pelly R.

ange

White

FORT SELKIRK

Lewes R.

Big Salmon R.

Lake Laberge

Miles Canyon

Marsh Lake

WHITEHORSE

Taqish Lake

Bennett L.

la

White Pass

SKAGWAY

Lynn

Canal

JUNEAU

SEWARD

Ocean

MAP SCALE

| 0 | Kilometres | 250 | | 500 |
| 0 | MILES | 155 | | 310 |

WAYS HARSH & WILD

○ ○

Doris Andersen

J. J. DOUGLAS LTD., VANCOUVER, 1973

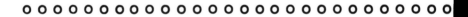

○ ○

HARSH & WILD

ISBN 0-88894-027-0

73 74 75 76 77 5 4 3 2 1

J. J. DOUGLAS LTD.
3645 McKechnie Drive
West Vancouver, British Columbia

Designed, printed and bound in Canada by
MORRISS PRINTING COMPANY LTD.
Victoria, British Columbia

Jacket design by Jim Rimmer

To my husband GEORGE C. ANDERSEN

Contents

Introduction

THIS IS THE STORY OF MY UNCLE, Bill Walker, of his adventures on the Black, the Yukon and the Innoko rivers in the northern wilderness three quarters of a century ago. He came to live with me in West Vancouver and every evening for a year, I listened enthralled while he spoke of his early life in British Columbia, the Yukon and Alaska in gold rush days.

Bill was a gentle, reticent man, and I was fascinated by the contrast between his quiet personality and his wild, hair-raising adventures. Not only were the stories exciting, but they were a first-hand account of a rugged, lawless period of history and they involved, besides the famous Yukon River, several other lonely, rapid-ridden waters about which little or nothing has been written. It seemed imperative that a record be made of Bill's experiences, and the evening conversations soon gave way to hours of diligent questioning and note-taking. Bill took a great interest in the book's progress but did not live to see it completed; he died in Hawaii in July 1972, a month before his 90th birthday.

Bill's life of adventure was interwoven with that of my father, Ted Crompton and the navy deserter, Jock Weir. Partners for nearly 20 years, they trapped, traded, searched for gold and raised families in the wilds. Ted married Bill's sister Maude and lured her to a tiny, isolated Indian village on the Yukon River. Maude, a product of an Eastern finishing school, hated the wilderness as

9

fiercely as Ted loved it. Bill's young wife Alice strove to cope with the hardships of life on the upper reaches of the wild Innoko River, finding it a strange mixture of comedy, tragedy, kindness and cruelty. Jock and his Meg struggled to wrest a fortune from the Innoko creekbeds and paid a fearful price for the gold they gained.

My sister Margaret supplied me with much material drawn from memories of her three years as a child in the trading post in the Indian village at Mouse Point, and her husband, Thurston Taylor, discovered among my father's boxes of books the diary of Ted's trip up the Innoko River. I am indebted also to Frank Mowat of Quadra Island who lived for many years with Ted and Maude and was able to remind me of several of Ted's Alaskan adventures.

I wish to thank Rev. Wilfred P. Schoenberg of Crosby Library, Gonzaga University, for permission to quote an extract from the report of Father Jetté; J. O. Kilmartin, Chief of the Map Information Office, U.S. Department of the Interior, for maps and information regarding Mouse Point and the Innoko creeks, and Ron D'Altroy, curator of the photo archives of the Vancouver Public Library, for his help in locating several prints to supplement Ted's personal collection.

DORIS ANDERSEN
August 1973

From their folded mates they wander far,
Their ways seem harsh and wild;
They follow the beck of a baleful star,
Their paths are dream-beguiled.

RICHARD BURTON

Youngster in the Yukon

ONE

WE WERE RELAXING one autumn evening in our log cabin on the bank of the Yukon River, my brother-in-law Ted and I, after a hard day spent hunting in the Kokrine Hills. Suddenly we heard the sound of running footsteps approaching the cabin and got up hastily to answer a pounding on the door. Ted threw it open to disclose a small, trembling Indian boy.

"Charlie here! Charlie got knife," the child gasped. "Come quick!"

Charlie was an outlaw Indian who had taken to the hills. He was a mean, vicious fellow who raided his village at Mouse Point regularly when the men were away trapping and terrorized the unprotected women and children. I wouldn't have cared to meet him myself on a dark night, especially when he was high on hootch. Ted and I were the only white men for miles around, and Ted as fur trader stationed at Mouse Point was sought out by the Indians whenever trouble came to the 10 cabins that comprised the village, our own being last in the line that straggled along the river bank.

Our boots scrunched the first snow of the season as we ran, led by screams and drunken shouts coming from one of the cabins. Telling the child to stay outside, Ted shoved open the door. Charlie had cornered several women and children at one end of the room and was threatening them with a knife. He turned as the door was flung open, his face flushed with rage and liquor and his eyes bloodshot and savage.

13

"Ted," I whispered, hovering at his heels, "he's crazy with drink. I'll run back for the shotgun." I thought we, too, were mad to have come unarmed.

Before I could turn away, Ted stepped into the room and walked slowly and calmly toward the outlaw. "All right, Charlie, hand over the knife."

Ted was a trader, not the law, but he had the voice of authority. Charlie staggered about, swearing mightily and waving his knife at the cowering women, then made a run at us, brandishing his weapon. Ted held his ground, hand extended, and Charlie, with one last fierce oath to establish his toughness, suddenly capitulated, gave up the knife and let himself be locked up in a shed for the night while he sobered up.

"The fight'll be out of him by morning, Bill, when he wakes up with a splitting head," Ted told me. "The women can let him out then, and he'll take to the hills again as usual with a fresh stock of food from their supplies." He led the way back to our cabin, whistling nonchalantly. It had been a small incident to him, nothing unusual in his daily life in the wilds.

Why does a man seek the wilderness and its hardships? I was down on my luck when my chance came; Ted spent his youth in his father's big home in Devon, England, with a corps of servants to cater to his needs. Yet both of us sought the wilds when still in our teens, and neither of us regretted a fate that had brought us together to share the turf-topped, abandoned cabin of a woodcutter which Ted had taken over for a temporary home and trading post. We found wilderness life a challenge that we welcomed, and that was lucky, for we were to tread ways harsh and wild for many years to come.

I was a kid of 17 when in March, 1900, I was offered the job of escorting a team of horses from Victoria to Lake Bennett in the Yukon. I went, expecting an exciting but brief look at the goldfields before returning to my prosaic task of fattening an ornery bunch of mules for the Alaskan trade. Instead I stayed in the far north for 18 years and came out at last a grown man — grown in confidence that I could lick the wilderness any time, any place. But the wilderness has its own subtle way of winning out in the end. You may think you have licked it and have escaped, but it is always there, in your heart and in your mind.

My family had fallen on hard times after the death of my mother when I was four years old. Something also died in my father then. He was still jaunty, prone to joking and singing comic songs; yet for him, life had lost its zest and no undertaking seemed worthy of completion. No longer interested in his thriving wholesale business in Victoria where he represented the John Macdonald Company, linen and woolen importers, he sold out, placed his children in boarding schools in New Westminster and bought the Queen's Hotel in the same city.

Maude, my older sister, was sent to St. Ann's Academy, a big brick convent on Albert Crescent, described by the Colonist newspaper in 1882 as "a sanctuary fit for these innocent young ladies." We seldom saw her. We heard she was a restless pupil; the nuns were forced to seat her at a desk on the platform beside her teacher where a watchful eye could be kept on her. But Dad remembered that Mother had held great hopes for their eldest daughter, and he was determined to make a "lady" of her. Beyond this he had little ambition, leaving his boys (Bob and Harry and me) free to run wild on the weekends.

My brothers and I called the Queen's Hotel our home for several years, and Harry and I (both of us much younger than Bob) would spend our free time playing hide-and-seek in the lobby or searching out Joe Fortes the bartender and begging him to take us boating.

Joe Fortes was a big, lovable black man, hard of muscle and soft of heart, and he stands out in my memory as the chief source of consolation for Harry and me during those unstable days. He would tell us stories of his adventures that made our eyes pop.

"Born in Trinidad, I was. Sailed on a windjammer to Liverpool and won a gold medal when I got there. The Lord Mayor's little girl handed that medal to me!"

"For winning a race, was it, Joe?"

"That's right, Little Billy, a swimming race on the Mersey River!"

Joe was a great sportsman, and he liked to show us the awards he had won. He was a faithful lacrosse fan. Our hotel lobby was often full of players who were idols of the day, lounging about as they waited to play in the tri-city games. Joe would point them out to us by name and describe that fierce and bloody sport — first played officially by the early French settlers who had learned its techniques from our native Indians.

Joe Fortes could always be persuaded to use a part of his free time to take Harry and me for rowboat rides. He loved to be either in the water or on it. Many years later, I met Joe again on the beach at Vancouver's English Bay where he was then the lifeguard, a local celebrity who had taught generations of children to swim. "Little Billy!" he exclaimed, pumping my hand and beaming radiantly.

When Joe died, they honored him by singing "Old Black Joe" at his funeral and erecting a monument to him in Alexandra Park near the beach. It is there yet. The inscription reads:

LITTLE CHILDREN LOVED HIM.

I was still a small boy when I had my first taste of wilderness country. My father gave up the hotel and moved us 40 miles up the rugged west coast of Vancouver Island to Port Renfrew, known to early traders and explorers as Port San Juan. He planned to homestead on wild forest land between the San Juan and the Gordon rivers. There were six of us there: three boys, my little sister Edith, our father and our stepmother. My father had married an honest, hard-working woman who had been caring for Edith, and he hoped that once again we could live together as a family. But homesteading would never do for his Maude. He sent her to Toronto to visit our well-to-do grandfather, John Green, governor for 28 years of the massive white brick jail on the bank of the Don River.

As Dad had hoped he would, John Green took a fancy to his granddaughter. Maude was no patient Little Nell, but she had the cajoling tricks of a kitten when she set out to please, though she could spit and claw like a little cat too. Grandfather enrolled her in in a small but select finishing school run by two daughters of the portrait painter, Theodore Berthon. Berthon, a pupil of the French classical artist, David, painted most of the city's notables, and today many of his portraits hang in Osgoode Hall in Toronto and in the art galleries of Canada. He had further distinguished himself by his timely birth in the Royal Palace of Vienna where the elder Berthon, court painter to Napoleon, was executing a portrait of the victorious Emperor. Maude was content in her new school. Her infrequent letters were full of her new friends and her first love, René Berthon, the 19-year-old son of Theodore. She wrote happily that René had given her a silver jewelcase, a locket with their initials entwined, and a spoon that he had won for marksmanship in the prestigious Queen's Own Rifles.

All this sounded mighty dull to us boys. We were beside ourselves with excitement at the prospect of living in a log cabin, hunting and fishing and, best of all, enjoying a year-long holiday from lessons (for there was no school at Port Renfrew).

When we reached the mouth of the San Juan, we saw something that put the crowning touch on our raptures: an Indian village and real Indians paddling about in their big cedar dugouts.

My father and brother Bob felled trees, cleared a bit of land and, with the advice and help of neighboring settlers, built us a log cabin. Harry and I were free for most of the day to do as we liked; and hour after hour we explored the woods near the shore, gawked at the Indians in their village, or fished in the river. It was on the bank of the San Juan that we first ran into Ted Crompton, who was to lead us into a life of adventure in the Alaskan wilderness.

We had wandered farther than usual down the riverbank while looking for a likely fishing hole when we spotted a young, bearded white man making an Indian canoe. We were beside him in a minute, circling the cedar log that he had burned out and adzed into shape and peppering him with questions as he heated stones in a fire to steam and spread the water-filled canoe in the traditional Indian manner. He answered our questions about his work good-naturedly, and when the stones were sizzling in the water he stood up, hands on hips, and inspected us.

"Well, who may you be?"

Harry spoke up, for I was still shy, solemn, and tongue-tied.

"I'm Harry Walker, and this is my brother Billy."

As Ted Crompton sized us up, it was easy to guess his conclusions. I was known then as an obedient child, while Harry, a handsome

Map of Vancouver Island

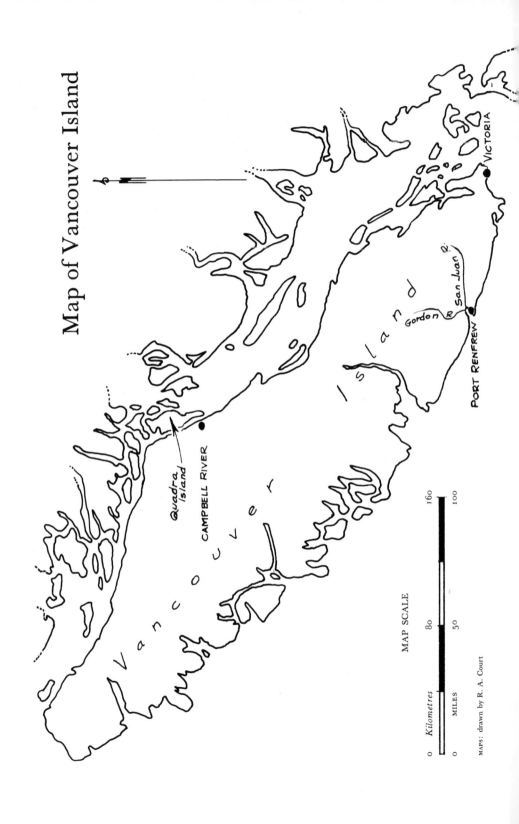

Quadra Island

CAMPBELL RIVER

Vancouver Island

Gordon R.

San Juan R.

PORT RENFREW

VICTORIA

MAP SCALE

Kilometres   0   80   160

MILES   0   50   100

MAPS: drawn by R. A. Court

youngster with dark, lively eyes like Maude's, was generally conceded to be a handful.

"I have a big brother, too," Harry volunteered. "He's at home with our father and stepmother."

"No sisters?" Ted asked hopefully, winking at Harry.

"Yes, there's Edith. She's seven."

"Seven?" His face fell.

"And my sister Maude is fifteen."

"Fifteen? Now, that's more like it." He leered comically. "Tell me about Maude."

"She's away at boarding school in Toronto."

"Oh! Well, I won't be seeing her then, will I?"

Ted led us down-river to where a huge rock jutted out over the water and advised us to do our fishing there. We went home with a fish apiece, and that of course raised him still more in our estimation.

Much like myself a few years later, Ted had struck out on his own at an early age, searching for freedom from restraint. He had abandoned the chance to study a profession, unlike his older brothers who had chosen law and medicine, for confinement irked him whether it entailed restriction within scholastic walls or the limitation of exploratory thought imposed by his fundamentalist English parents who shuddered at the current writings of Darwin and Huxley.

Ted, an amiable, easy-going youth, had no wish to distress his parents by taking a rebellious stand. He was the odd pup of the litter and felt that the best solution was to get out and search for some place where he could be free and independent. So, at the age of 18, he left England and sailed to Canada, then drifted across the country to British Columbia. There he fell in with two lighthearted Englishmen who had bought themselves an old whaler, fitted her with masts and sails, and defied tradition by giving her a sturdy, masculine name: *John Grant*. They took Ted to where she lay at rest in the slough beyond Victoria harbor. One look and he lost his heart to her, seeing her in his mind's eye skimming over the waves with the wind in her sails. Here lay freedom personified. To him, their invitation — "Will you join us, Ted? We need another hand." — was a clarion call to liberty.

Harry and I never tired hearing Ted recount his 10 adventurous years as the three carefree young men cruised where impulse led them among the San Juan Islands and up the rugged west coast of Vancouver Island.

"Did I ever tell you how I shot a buck and then he shot me back?"

"No, how did he do that, Ted?"

"Well, I followed that buck for miles through underbrush and fern, down into gullies and up steep inclines. I saw his tracks leading into a little lake and got on a log at the lakeside and crossed over. Paddle? Why, I used a flat board ripped from an abandoned trapper's cabin that was rotting away beside the lake. I stalked my quarry, shot him down, hoisted him on my shoulders, and started back. I was climbing down a steep bank when that old buck overbalanced me with his weight and I slipped and fell. My gun discharged and ripped a great hole in my shoulder as the buck and I bounced and rolled over each other like a pair of wrestlers to the bottom of the gully. I was bleeding like a stuck pig, so I tore rags from my shirt and stuffed them into the hole. It was a miserable ordeal to crawl over that rough terrain to the lake. I paddled one-armed to the broken-down cabin and lay inside it for five days, raging with fever. After that I forced myself up and climbed, slid and shoved my way through savage country until at last I reached the sea and the *John Grant*. I thought that buck had finished me off, for sure, but they took me down to the hospital in Victoria and sewed me together, and look at me now, as good as new."

Ted brought tears to our eyes with his story of a little white dog — "Best dog I ever had" — which a panther once snatched from his doorstep in Port Renfrew and devoured in the night, leaving the bones under the trees as grisly evidence for its master to find in the morning. Ted told me how he had staked out a small, squealing pig as bait and lain in wait, shooting the predator as it sneaked up on its prey and then burying it beside the dog's remains with the grim satisfaction of justice triumphant.

"That little dog comes to me often in my dreams," he added. "I see him looking up as me as plainly as I see you now." Ted was a romanticist, and that appealed to us, too.

One day, Ted and his companions had anchored in the mouth of the San Juan and observed the little settlement of Port Renfrew which was struggling to carve itself out of the forest. Here was a new game for them. They set about building a log cabin and clearing the land, all in a leisurely manner with frequent time out to hunt and fish; and, for Ted, time to study the Indians and their methods of smoking fish and shaping cedar canoes.

Work was half play for them, not to be taken too seriously, a principle that Ted followed all his life. It drew raised eyebrows and tongue cluckings from my father and the other settlers when they saw the unorthodox method of land clearing adopted by the crew of the *John Grant*. The young men made a practice of boring two holes at right angles into the trunks of the trees, then filling the holes with shot and letting fires smoulder there until the trees, gutted by flame to hollow shells, crashed down untidily in all directions. But I have no doubt that more than one man shared Harry's and my yearnings to lead the free and easy life of those three Englishmen.

A few years of stump ranching were enough for my father, who turned his back on the wilderness and brought us all back to Victoria. Clearing the trees and the heavy underbrush from the land had been backbreaking work, and the roads promised by the government never materialized. Besides, Maude's boarding-school days would soon come to an end and he wanted a town house made ready for her. He opened up a real estate business and did his best to keep the wolf from our door — but with no great success.

One morning I was leaning on our garden gate, idly watching a horse and wagon approaching down the dirt road. Suddenly I gave a whoop and a holler and pushed the gate open:

"Ted! Hold on! Ted!"

He hauled on his reins and grinned as I panted up to him. It was our old friend from the San Juan valley, driving in to market with a wagonload of vegetables. He, too, had left Port Renfrew and was now running a market garden in Saanich, just outside Victoria. He was proud of his vegetables and picked out a fine cucumber and a huge head of cabbage for me to take to my stepmother. Ted had a green thumb. Flowers and vegetables thrived under his care in every climate and in any soil.

I was taken aback at first to see our adventurer settled down to such humdrum toil, but after talking with him that day and on other mornings when he let me ride to town with him, something of the wonder and enthusiasm he felt for the miracle of growth from seed to fruit rubbed off on me. When my father was forced to admit that he could no longer hold the wolf at bay single-handed and that my brothers and I would have to leave school and find jobs, I was quite content to start work at $12 a month in a nursery garden on Carey Road operated by a neighbor of ours, a German gardener named Layritz. Bob found work in a grain store, while Harry worked a little and played more. He revelled in what he called the "high life," his good looks and quick wit making him popular with wealthy friends who let him indulge his tastes. Much of the time he was off sailing on somebody's yacht while Bob shoveled grain and I shoveled dirt; but we bore Harry no grudge, since we felt that he and Maude were a different breed from ourselves.

Maude was back now, her school days ended. With her pretty face and stylish clothes, she seemed sadly out of place in our plain household; it was a drab contrast to both the home our mother had made for us as children and Maude's fashionable boarding school in Toronto. Her romance, too, had come to a tragic end. Young René Berthon died suddenly, collapsing one day as he strolled down Yorkville Avenue. Two days later he was buried in St. Michael's cemetery. Shocked and bereft, Maude had come home with her locket, her jewelcase, and her silver spoon packed in her little straw suitcase. She was wild with bottled-up energy for which she could find no satisfactory outlet, and we all suffered from her sharp tongue.

I poured out our troubles to Ted.

"Wish I knew something that would please her. She's good fun when she's happy, but life's not worth living when she's miserable. We're desperate, Ted."

"Don't worry," he consoled me. "I'll fix things up for you." A week later, Maude received an invitation to take tea with Ted's brother, Dr. Ernest Crompton and the doctor's wife, Madge.

Ted's glowing letters about the delights of life in Canada had inspired his brother to leave England and set up a practice in Victoria. Ernest married his partner's sister, became city coroner as well as private physician and surgeon, and was leading an active professional and social life. Maude came home with eyes sparkling as she described the good-natured doctor, his charming wife, and their home that was to her a symbol of Victorian gentility, crammed with pots of ferns, antique chairs, oriental rugs, pictures, photographs, porcelain ornaments and a grand piano. We all sighed with relief; and a little later, when Maude accepted the invitation of the childless Cromptons to live with them as companion and adopted daughter, we felt our problem had been solved.

"I wish her mother could see her now," Dad would say contentedly when Maude dropped in to tell us about her new life. The Cromptons spoiled and petted her, bought her clothes that delighted her, and took her with them to balls, receptions, and teas. She was soon engaged to a young Englishman with a dashing black moustache, who was starting a modest career in real estate. He would be in no position to marry for some years to come, but he was an affectionate, dependable fellow, always at hand to squire her to picnics and regattas.

Maude quoted her new friend Madge like a well-trained parrot. Madge took charge of her education with enthusiasm, teaching her to embroider and to crochet delicate lace. She impressed on my sister two vital maxims: humdrum labor was the monopoly of the working class, and an English gentleman was God's greatest creation. This last, by the way, was a tenet firmly held by many Victorians.

Our small capital in those days was unlike any other city in Canada. Its mild climate resembled that of England, and this, coupled with its situation in a province reassuringly titled British Columbia, attracted an influx of expatriated English who rebuilt their new home into a caricature of the old country: policemen in bobby helmets, flower baskets strung from lamp posts, and houses of pseudo-Tudor architecture surrounded by gardens fragrant with roses, daffodils, and mignonette. Up and down the streets, tweed-clad couples strode briskly, the English and their imitators. There were many of the latter, for the English formed a sternly insular set which dominated the social life of the capital; if one could not be English it was best to be a reasonable facsimile. So Maude bicycled

23

with Madge about Beacon Hill Park under wide-spreading Garry oak trees which closely resembled British oaks, and took tea on green lawns as she watched young men in white flannels playing England's national game of cricket. The two Canadians considered themselves Englishwomen, living in a corner of a foreign field that was forever England. It was fine training for Maude if her destiny was to be a lady, as my mother and father had planned. None of us dreamed she would end up in the Alaskan wilderness, in a primitive Indian village on a bank of the Yukon River.

Into Victoria's quiet English atmosphere there burst the rowdy Gold Rush of '98. Victoria was on the direct route to the goldfields, and thousands of prospectors passed through, stocking up with supplies before catching the boat for Skagway. Donkeys and dogteams were a common sight as they were led through the streets to the Klondike boat. We often saw the steamer backing out of the harbor, decks crowded with gold-hungry adventurers eager to be underway to the promised land.

They were a strange conglomeration, drawn from all walks of life to search for wealth and rugged adventure. The Seattle *Post-Intelligencer* had flashed the news around the world one morning in July 1897: the steamer *Portland* had arrived in Seattle from St. Michael in Alaska with more than a ton of gold aboard! Miners had struck it rich on Bonanza Creek in the Yukon and were returning home with sacks of gold dust and nuggets. Reporters played up rags-to-riches stories that were found to be even more fantastic in fact. Here was a golden panacea to end all ills; it seized the imagination of thousands who abandoned families and businesses and begged, borrowed, or sold their possessions to outfit themselves for the trip north. Farmers, doctors, jewelers, merchants, missionaries, dance-hall girls and school teachers, con men and priests, the riff-raff and the respectable, all jostled together in the jam-packed steamers that took them to Dawson, to Nome, to Fairbanks, where a series of stupendous strikes occurred in rapid succession. Many arrived unequipped and totally unprepared for the ordeals ahead; some suffered defeat, others rose to the challenge, learning to feel for the harsh new country a passion they had never known for gentler lands.

To Maude, the sights were oddities unrelated to her life. The news that shattered her was Madge's announcement that she and Ernest were returning to England to live.

Maude was urged to visit them once she was married, but marriage to her young Englishman was still in the distant future. Maude came back to us, and again the fuel of her restless discontent was poured on our miserable heads.

"She whirls through the house like a hurricane, disturbing us all," said our distraught stepmother, breaking into tears.

"I'll send her to Dick and Meg in Seattle," my father decided in desperation. "Her uncle and aunt will keep her busy and happy."

Maude had no sooner left us than Ted Crompton came pounding on our door.

"Bill, where's Maude? I must see her at once."

"Why, she's gone to Seattle."

"Seattle? What ever for? When will she be back?"

"She may stay forever. Oh, if you'd been here, Ted, to see the temper she's been in, you'd be glad to know you've missed her."

"What's her address? Get it for me, Billy, that's a good chap. I've got to find her right away."

He tucked the address in his wallet and was down the steps and out of sight before any of us thought to mention that Maude was engaged.

They came back to Victoria a married couple, Ted beaming as though the whole ton of gold aboard the steamer *Portland* had been transferred to him. Our uncle Dick had decided Maude's fate. "Bert is a fine boy," he had told her, "but Ted is a man. Let him take care of you." Maude was happy with the decision. She was married to the brother-in-law of her beloved Madge and expected to resume the same sort of life she had known for three years in the pleasant home on Gordon Street. As yet, she was unaware that Ted's tastes and ambitions were totally unlike those of his brother.

Harry and I felt sorry for Ted, knowing Maude's moods, and my brother warned him not to let her get the best of him, but nothing dimmed his smile. He had sold his farm and planned to try his luck in Alaska, and Maude, blissfully ignorant of conditions there, had agreed to accompany him. Harry begged to go with them, an idea

25

that Maude promptly vetoed. Harry and Maude were too similar in temperament to be peaceable companions. They repelled one another like positive poles, seeing their own faults reflected. But Harry was 20 now and, like Maude, had neither money, training nor inclination for labor. Perhaps a quick fortune gleaned from gold mining or fur trapping would be the best solution for him. Ted was willing to take him; in the end Maude was overruled and a month later, the three of them waved farewell from the crowded deck of the Alaskan steamer bound for St. Michael.

Poor Maude. No sooner had the steamer reached the open waters of Queen Charlotte Sound than it began to lurch and roll in the choppy waves. Maude took to her bunk, wretchedly seasick.

"I thought I was dying," she told me later. "I was sick every morning, all the way up the coast and up the river to Fort Yukon."

Ted catered to her, bringing trays of hot biscuits and tea to her bedside and coaxing her to eat. But the sight and smell of food had sickened her, and she had shoved the trays away, sending the biscuits flying.

In Fort Yukon, the trader's wife quickly diagnosed the cause of the morning sickness: Maude would be a mother by the following April. "You'd be well advised," the trader's wife had told her, "to take the steamer on its return trip out. No boat can travel after the freeze-up, and Fort Yukon is no place for you with a first baby coming in spring before the thaw." Maude took her advice and left on the next boat.

I sympathized with Ted's plight, to have won and lost a wife in so short a space of time, but Maude's decision must have been music to Harry's ears. The sort of adventures he hoped to have up there in the wilderness with Ted would have been sadly curtailed by the presence of a temperamental sister demanding constant comfort and attention.

"There was nothing in Fort Yukon but a few log cabins and a lot of dirty mud flats," she explained to us when she got back to Victoria. "Thank heaven I escaped in time."

"I'd give my right arm to be there in your place," I said wistfully.

"Oh, you're only a baby," she cried. I was her favorite, perhaps because I never plagued her, but she had little respect for my opinions — least of all for my longing for a life in the wilderness.

Yet she possessed a venturesome spirit. Nothing had daunted her on the long trip back to civilization, not even the ordeal of a shipwreck in Norton Sound. Severe storms sweep over the Bering Sea at times, reaching almost hurricane intensity and increasing in violence until the waves are carried over the low, flat beach at Nome, flooding the waterfront, smashing buildings and driving anchored boats and barges ashore. At St. Michael, Maude had transferred from the riverboat to the ocean steamer which headed first for Nome to pick up more passengers before sailing south. A lighter was lashed to the ship's side to allow a landing in shallow waters. The ship was traveling through heavy seas across Norton Sound when the wind and waves forced her off course into these shallow areas that extend far out from the mainland. Most of the passengers were in the dining room, toying uneasily with their dinners as the ship rolled and plunged, when there was a tremendous crash, the steamer tilted to one side, dishes and crystal slid from tables to floor, and a great wave foamed and surged across the room. Someone screamed: "To the lifeboats!" and there was a stampede up the wide stairway to the decks.

Maude had reached the top of the stairs when she was suddenly seized about the waist from behind by a male passenger who thrust his hand inside the front of her dress. She screamed in outrage and grabbed at his wrist.

"Don't remove it, madam," he begged her. "There's nothing like it to keep out the cold!"

She pulled herself free with a withering look, but while running to the deck she heard an odd crackling sound. A quick check revealed that the stranger was no rapist after all; he had shoved a thick fold of newspaper down against her chest to protect her from the icy wind.

The passengers were transferred to the lighter, the women shrieking as waves crashed over the deck. When the barge, too, was grounded, the men waded and the women were carried through the breakers to the shore, the crew leading them up the bank to the tundra where a canvas was spread out over the damp moss. They were placed in a circle, the women in the center with the men forming the circumference, and blankets were brought from the boat.

Maude recounted with relish her dramatic experiences during the storm, describing the shipboard friendships and camaraderie that catastrophe produces. She planned now to move to Tacoma, near some of the friends she had made.

Five years passed before Ted got her back again.

TWO

It seemed that everyone in the world except me was headed for adventure in the north. Even my employer, the little German gardener Layritz, to whom both mining and wilderness life were unknown quantities, had had his fling at the goldfields. He was a taciturn fellow, and when he appeared at my elbow one morning he merely said: "Bill, I go to Alaska," and departed forthwith. I worked on at the nursery, watching the business decline, until one afternoon in early summer when Layritz suddenly reappeared beside me in the barn. "Well, Bill, how are you?" was all he said as he headed for the house to change his clothes and start the long, hard job of rebuilding his trade. Eventually his nurseries became famous in the west, but I doubt if his Alaskan trip was a success for he never once referred to it.

I lost interest in the nursery now that Ted had abandoned his market garden and felt myself at a dead end with my starvation wages of $12 a month. There was little chance of a raise while Layritz was struggling to build up his business. My only joy in life those days was on Sundays when I went horseback riding. My father had a friend, a hotel keeper named McKeon, who also owned a country place called Clairmount Farm where he kept a stable of riding horses. McKeon took a fancy to me and told my father I was free to ride his horses at any time. So I grubbed all week in the dirt and rode about like a gentleman of leisure on Sundays. McKeon seemed to like the way I handled the saddle horses. When I told him how sick I was of gardening, he was kind enough to speak to a friend who raised horses and mules for the Alaskan trade and persuaded him to take on an extra hand.

I arrived for my first day of work agog with anticipation. I was shown the barns and the long rows of stalls. A few moments later my growing enthusiasm was sadly deflated when I was handed a pail and told to feed the herd of mules that ran loose on the hillside — wild brutes with tempers as ugly as their ungainly bodies.

One evening some weeks later I climbed up the path, a bucket of feed heavy in each hand, my eyes searching the hilltop apprehensively. If only I could get to the trough at the halfway mark and fill it without attracting the attention of the mules . . . but no, luck was against me today, as usual. One mule had come closer. It caught sight of me and uttered its hideous bray which was echoed at once by the rest of the herd, and then the lot of them came pounding down, shoving and pushing each other as they reached the trough and kicking at each other's ribs with explosive thumps. I dumped the feed and eased my way out from among them, my scalp prickling in momentary expectation of a crippling thump on my own ribs.

As I trudged disconsolately down the trail with my empty buckets, remembering the nursery now with a hint of nostalgia, my employer hailed me from the open doorway of the barn.

"Bill! Are you game for a trip to Alaska and the Yukon?"

I nearly somersaulted over my buckets in my hurry to get to him. The expression on my face must have been answer enough; I was a prisoner granted an unforeseen reprieve.

"Call came in for 13 teams of horses and a driver for each team to go to the logging camp at Lake Bennett in the Yukon. I've got 12 men so far. Get in here and pick out a team for yourself if you want to join them. You're young, but there's a chance you'll be kept on at Bennett Lake as teamster."

I dropped my buckets and walked slowly up and down the stalls, frowning as though deep in deliberation, but cocking my ear to hear the comments of the other men. Most of them were cab drivers who had signed up for the job to get their passage paid to the land of promise; they were picking out the breed of light, spirited horses that were best at drawing cabs about the city. That seemed unwise

Map of North Pacific Coast

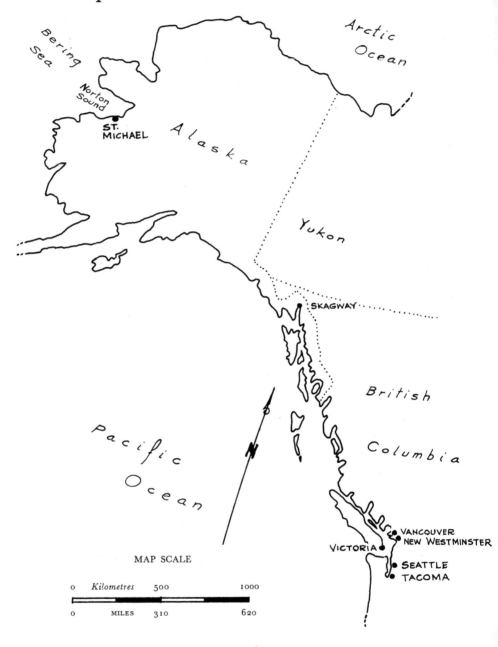

MAPS: drawn by R. A. Court

to me, and eventually I chose two strong, heavy horses, a sorrel and a bay.

I saw my team loaded aboard the boat and made my way below deck where animals, hay, and feed were crowded together for the trip. My sorrel and bay were standing calmly in their places, ignoring the nervous, snorting horses about them, so I went up on deck and leaned on the rail, turning my face to feel the whip of the sea breeze, its salty odor redolent of adventure.

Skagway, the town that marks the start of the White Pass trail to Lake Bennett, lies at the head of a long fiord, Lynn Canal. Three years earlier, Klondike miners had arrived there in crowded boats only to find no town and no wharves. Long mud flats kept the boats from anchoring close to shore, and supplies had to be transferred to small craft, while horses and mules were tossed overboard to sink or swim. The flats swarmed with bony, half-starved animals and frantic men collecting their supplies from the crates and boxes tossed in haphazard confusion on the beach. Hardly one in a thousand of the miserable horses that were dragged over the White Pass survived to reach Lake Bennett. They died of cold and hunger in the snow and in the icy creeks, collapsed in the deep mudholes, or stumbled and fell down the steep ravine which bordered that terrible trail. The men who abandoned them and pressed on after gold were often forced back before reaching the summit by winter snowstorms that blocked their way. Spring was worse, with sudden thaws creating quagmires. Even if they traveled in summer and managed the 45 miles to Bennett, many lost everything in the White Horse Rapids as they headed downriver for the Klondike. Desperately they fought their way back to the coast to squat on land near the mud flats until they could raise their passage fare home again.

So evolved Skagway, a town of transients that attracted the toughest and most unscrupulous characters to batten on innocent arrivals or on those fortunate few about to depart with pockets full of nuggets. Businessmen arrived, smelling out money-making opportunities. Saloons, dance halls and restaurants sprang up. Bogus information offices were set up by "Soapy" Smith, the gangster boss of Skagway, who lured his unsuspecting clients inside and then set his men on them to rob them of their wallets. Skagway became known as the most lawless spot on the globe until, in desperation, the more sober citizens set up an organization, appointed a mayor, and drove the gangsters out of town. "Soapy" himself was shot to death in a gun battle with a member of the posse of law and order.

When our boat reached the head of Lynn Canal, I saw three long wharves stretching out over the mud flats to take the cargo. Corrals of starving horses no longer dotted the beach, but the same icy winds that greeted those first arrivals were blowing down from the mountain pass, making me shiver in my light clothes and blow on fingers that were numb in my thin leather gloves. I had left Victoria on a warm March day, but March in Skagway might well have been mid-winter. The name of Skagway comes from the Indian word *skagus*, meaning north wind, and its full force blasted me as I stood freezing on the wharf waiting to collect my horses. When I led them at last through the town, saw them stabled and fed in a livery barn, and found myself a bed in a roadhouse, a feverish cold and cough laid me low.

The woman in charge of the roadhouse was a kind-hearted soul who was determined to mother me. She brought hot lemonade to soothe my raw throat and tucked me into bed as she would a baby. I was dragging myself up the next morning when she came in with a pot of warm grease to rub on my chest and ordered me back to bed.

"You can't travel that icy pass while you're sick, boy! You stay in bed where you belong."

"I'm not sick," I protested. "It's nothing but a cold. I've got to leave today with the others."

"You stay in bed, dear. You don't know what the White Pass is like."

I lay in my blankets, chafing with impatience and cursing my big brown eyes and guileless features which continually drew down upon me so much humiliation. It was bitterly cold. The woman kept a poker thrust in among the coals in the bunkhouse stove and came in at frequent intervals to take the poker and lay it along the waterpipes to keep the water from freezing. By noon I was desperate, and when she came in once again and went off with the poker, I got up hastily and dressed myself, searching out a warmer jacket in my pack for the trip. When I went to pay my bill, she did her best to dissuade me from going but acknowledged defeat at last. She pressed upon me a pair of woolen gloves, sighed at the folly of youth, and went back to her battle with the waterpipes.

The rest of the teams had left long before my late start. I led my horses up the start of the trail, trying to set a brisk pace, but my big, slow animals were not to be hurried. I never overtook the other teamsters, and except for a brief stop at the summit of the pass to check in at the police post, saw no sign of life on the 45-mile journey through the mountains.

Two years before, there had been a continuous, black, slow-moving line of men and horses climbing the steep trail through the pass. It was said that if a man dropped out of the line to tighten a girth he might wait hours before he could get into the line again. But the first great rush to the Klondike had ended. Nome, on the seacoast opposite St. Michael, was now the magnet that drew the multitudes. And those who still had business in Dawson or Bennett could travel on the new railway built the year before between Skagway and Bennett. Skagway businessmen had buried the hundreds of rotting corpses of horses in the gulch and built a wider wagon road above the narrow, tortuous trail used by the first stampeders.

Along this road I led my horses. Even my heavier clothing failed to keep out the cold as I plodded along, shoulders hunched, clutching the reins but keeping my arms crossed over my chest with my hands thrust into my armpits for warmth. All about me towered snow-clad mountains bordering the trail like gigantic, silent sentinels, and between them peered the summits of other mountains, range after range. To those men who struggled through the pass only two years before me, black flyspecks against the vast whiteness, the mountains must have seemed like icy-breathed monsters blocking the way to the treasure that lay beyond. As for me, I was scarcely aware of them. All my concentration was needed to battle that numbing blast and to place one foot before the other, slowly, steadily, like the big, calm beasts behind me.

Being alone did not distress me. I was buoyed by the thought that here was a chance to prove to myself that I could endure and triumph unaided. As the youngest son, somewhat resentful of the

33

authority of two older brothers, I was eager to show my maturity. The tender concern of the roadhouse woman had implied that I was still a child which was enough to keep me going doggedly all through the night, until finally I was through the pass, the icy wind no longer cutting at my face. And there it was below: Lake Bennett — and a city of tents.

THREE

Lake Bennett only a few years before had stretched out, lonely and still, below the silent hills. But the cavalcade that struggled through the White Pass found it a natural resting place and an essential stop for those who must build boats to take them down the Yukon to Dawson and the goldfields. They set up tents along the shores of the lake, felled trees, and then whipsawed the logs into lumber for scows and boats.

A good many partnerships dissolved during the whipsawing, a tricky business that frayed tempers and occasionally roused furious rages. To whipsaw, a scaffolding framework was built and the log hoisted up and laid across it. A line was drawn down the butt of the log for the saw to follow. One man stood on the scaffolding above while the other stood below. The sawing procedure caused the trouble, as each accused the other of failing to pull his weight or to keep the saw on a straight path. A variation of a quarter inch would result in uneven boards that could make a boat unseaworthy. Frustrated builders chopped their boats in two rather than share the source of their quarrel. Goods were divided, even stoves were chopped in two, bitter men preferring to destroy them rather than to use anything jointly.

A logging company came to Bennett to supply the tremendous demand for logs and scows. Businessmen followed to supply other needs. Big tents dotted the shore and extended up the hillsides, some with signs labeling them: Saloon, Bakery, Barbershop, Restaurant. One of them bore the dignified name: Lakeview Hotel. The Victoria-Yukon Trading Company had a large tent that could accommodate 20 to 30 men. It worked in conjunction with the logging company that had hired our teams to drag logs to the mill

34

and used the lumber mostly for building big scows to take supplies downriver to Dawson. Once in Dawson, the scows were broken up and sold for lumber, which brought a good price; thus there was a steady demand for logs in Bennett.

I came into the VYT tent feeling mighty pleased with myself for having made that long, cold journey alone in comparatively good time. I was sure the test had matured me noticeably, but the loggers and teamsters were strangely undiscerning. They glanced up from their dinners and gave me the once-over, seeing only an ingenuous boy who was fair game for old hands.

"What's your job, kid? Cook's flunky?"

"They've just taken me on as teamster," I said proudly.

"Go on! A green kid like you? You won't last a day."

"Who took you on? Not McGuire, I bet. Wait 'til he sees this! Old McGuire has the devil's own temper. Pull a fast one on McGuire and he rages like a maniac."

"That's right," cut in another. "I've seen him take an iron peavy to a man. I'd sure hate to be in your shoes, sonny, when McGuire finds out some joker hired a kid still wet behind the ears."

"Aw, let the kid eat his dinner," chimed in a sympathetic type. "Even in jail, they give a fellow a good meal when his number's up."

They made room for me at the table. "Eat hearty, boy. You'll need strength to duck that peavy."

There was still nine to twelve feet of snow at Bennett. The first months of early spring had been spent in shoveling it from the four-mile trail between the mill and the logging area up in the hills, clearing a roadway that ran between high banks of snow. Now that the trail was partly cleared, we drove our teams of horses over it, the poor beasts floundering to their knees in the soft snow that remained. Two days of steady marching by each of the teams was enough to pack this down into a hard roadway for the logging operations higher in the hills. Piles of logs waited there, cut and stacked through the winter, and we teamsters were called on to haul them out to the mill. A dozen big bobsleds were joined and loaded up for each team of two horses, and one after the other they would start down. In some places the trail was so steep that the

35

horses came down with legs straddled out, almost in a sitting position, and chains had to be attached to the runners to prevent the
sleds from overrunning the horses.

Even my slow team hit a pretty fast clip on the trail, and it was
fine sport to guide them down between the high snowbanks with
the bobsleds snaking out behind as we whipped around the curves.
As the weeks passed, I grew overconfident. One day, as I turned
too sharply on a curve and hit the side of a snowbank with the
reach, there was an ominous crack. I halted the horses and jumped
down with a sinking heart to find the reach broken — and my head
now vulnerable to McGuire's wrath. "Watch out for the peavy!"
the men warned me darkly in the tent that night.

For the next few days I was nervous as a cat, driving my team
with painstaking care. One morning I drove into the millyard,
halted my team, and glanced back at my loaded sleds. I was surprised to see the figure of a man hunched on top of the logs on the
last of the twelve bobsleds. Then, with a chill of apprehension, I
recognized McGuire, who must have scrambled to his perch as my
team pulled out of the logging camp and traveled the four miles
quietly observing me.

I jumped down and stood quaking as he hopped off and
approached me. But he only touched his cap in greeting, walked
past me and into the mill. Nothing was ever said to me about the
broken reach. It was a blow to realize that I had been made the
butt of a joke, but in time I decided this was preferable to a blow
from the peavy of the maligned McGuire, who no longer would
haunt my dreams.

In the summer, I got back my own to some extent. When the
snow melted from the trail the sleds were inoperable, so the logs
were hauled to the bank of the swift Snake River that runs down to
the lake. The logs were shoved down the steep ravine with peavies,
the rushing water carrying them to the mill. Often the logs would
jam in the narrow river, and a logger would crawl gingerly over
the tangled mass, attach a hook and chain to the key log and carry
the chain back up the bank.

My moment of glory came as the call sounded for my big sorrel
and bay, the heaviest horses in the camp. Up we proudly marched,

36

the big slow horses and the young greenhorn who had been the only driver with enough foresight to choose a team suited to the job. The horses were hitched to the chain. "Take her away!" As the big beasts dug in their hoofs and strained ahead, the key log was suddenly whipped out and the tangled pile collapsed into the water to continue its journey downstream.

It was while we were loading logs up in the hills that I saw Klondike Kate, the dance-hall girl who was the toast of a generation of miners and a gold mine herself for newsmen who kept her colorful career in the headlines for almost sixty years.

Kate Rockwell started her career as a soubrette in a Coney Island variety hall. She was performing in a sister act for the Savoy Theatrical Company in Victoria at the turn of the century when tales of fortunes in the Klondike prompted her to cancel her act and buy herself a ticket to Skagway. Someone had told her that entertainers were needed in Bennett and that miners were free with their money. She traveled through the pass over the newly built railroad only to find herself, much to her dismay, in a tent city whose theatre was a dark saloon with only a tiny stage on which she was to sing to the accompaniment of a battered piano. She stuck it out for two months, winning hearts with her youthful beauty but making little money in a town where prospectors had still to reach their El Dorado.

Kate returned to Victoria and joined a group organized by the Savoy Company to travel as a burlesque and musical show to Dawson. Here she found lasting fame. From the moment that she stepped on the stage in Dawson to sing a sentimental number in her warm and intimate voice, the miners went wild. By the time she had finished her spectacular flame dance there was bedlam in the theatre. Her youth, her vivid blue eyes, her red-gold hair and slender figure made her a startling contrast to the general run of dance-hall girls who were attractive enough but whom the men labeled with affectionate disrespect: Nellie the Pig, May the Cow, the Grizzly Bear, the Oregon Mare, and Box Car Annie. Their name for Kate — Flower of the North — put her in another class. She was quick to assess the appeal of her youth and apparent innocence and though still in her early twenties, she lowered her age to

37

nineteen. Many of the miners were a strangely innocent lot, credulous and romantic, ready to do battle if a slighting word should be uttered against Kate by skeptics who wondered about the nightly haul of nuggets and diamonds that she collected in addition to her large salary.

I first met her in the woods above Bennett while helping to load logs. One of the loggers pointed to a man and woman approaching on horseback. Even from a distance, Kate was recognizable by her red-gold hair. The two had ridden down the trail from Dawson to Bennett so that Kate could see the tent town again and revive memories of the two months she had performed in the Bennett saloon. She rode her horse among us, laughing and talking and enjoying our gaping admiration. Before turning to rejoin her companion, she opened her saddle bag and tossed out packets of cigarettes, shrieking with laughter as the loggers ran to catch them. Seeing me hanging back, bashful as usual, she pointed at me and then tossed one directly into my hands, causing me to blush and giving the men fodder for months of joshing. Then she rode off down the trail, the sunlight glinting on her auburn hair, turning often to blow kisses as the men cheered and whistled.

"Well, kid," one of the loggers said to me as he pocketed his cigarettes, "you've seen Klondike Kate, the best-hearted girl in Dawson City. And I'll tell you something else. If a miner goes to Dawson for a blowout, he'll head for Kate every time and get her to mind his poke. Those boys trust Kate a damn sight more than they trust the bank."

Boatbuilders were busiest during the summer months, and the continual noise of hammering and sawing was deafening. There was a huge pile of sawdust near the mill which extended out to the shoreline. The dogs of Bennett were idle in the fine weather, with no sleds to pull, and they gathered daily on top of the pile, over twenty of them at a time. There they lay sprawled, sleeping in the sun like elderly men relaxing in their club lounge. Somnolent in the warmth, they had no energy for antagonism despite the variety among them in size, breed, age and sex. But let one of the lake steamers approach, sounding its whistle, and every dog would rear up, throw back its head and howl long and dismally, each in a

38

separate key. Combined with the noise of hammer and saw, it formed a weird, discordant theme song of the tent city.

I felt like joining the dogs in their dismal howling as the summer drew to a close and no word came from my family. I was homesick, and tired of the good-natured baiting of my fellow workers whose teasing was endless. I wondered how Ted and Harry were faring and wished I could be with them. Then, in early September, a letter was handed to me. It was from Ted and had been mailed in Dawson. He and Harry planned to go up the Black River in the fall to trap and trade. "Why don't you join us?" Ted suggested.

That was all I needed to make me pull up stakes. It was the right time to leave. The camp at Bennett would be closing down for the winter, and there would be months of shoveling snow before teams could be driven again. By leaving at once, I had a good chance of making Black River before freeze-up. The company was about to send five big grain scows down to Dawson. "Jump aboard!" the men said when I went down to the lake and asked for a lift. Ted and Harry would be gone from Dawson by the time we reached there, but perhaps I would overtake them farther along the way.

FOUR

Our scows drifted easily down the twenty-five miles of Lake Bennett, canvas sails hoisted to catch the breeze. From there we went into a narrow waterway called Caribou Crossing, a river that stretched for about two miles, where they told me herds of migratory caribou were sometimes seen to cross from one bank to the other. The crossing led into Lake Tagish, famous for storms near Windy Arm but docile enough while we sailed its length, and continued on to shallow, boglike Lake Marsh, or Mud Lake as the miners called it. It was all easy going, with no cause for alarm, until we reached Miles Canyon and tied up to wait for the pilot.

While we waited, one of the scowmen gave me a hair-raising account of the rapids. I could see the beginning of Miles Canyon, but the worst dangers were hidden by the curve ahead.

"Around the curve," the scowman told me, "the walls of the canyon are a hundred feet high. They close in suddenly, choking

39

Arctic

Brooks

Siberia

• CANDLE

Koyukuk R.

NOME

NULATO

KOKRINES
MOUSE

KALTAG

Yukon

Norton Sound

Stuart I.

ST.
MICHAEL

Innoko R.

Nowitna R.

ANVIK

Iditarod R.

OPHIR

HOLY CROSS

TAKOTNA

Kuskokwim R.

ANDREAVSKI

Bering Sea

Alaska

Bristol Bay

N

Pacific

MAPS: drawn by R. A. Court

Map of Alaska, adjacent parts of Yukon and British Columbia

Ocean

Range

ARCTIC CIRCLE

Porcupine R.

Black R.

FORT YUKON

Yukon Flats

CIRCLE

RAMPART

FAIRBANKS

River

EAGLE

FORTY MILE

DAWSON

Klondike R.

Stewart R.

NANA

Tanana

R.

Pelly R.

ange

White

R.

FORT SELKIRK

Lewes R.

Big Salmon R.

Lake Laberge

Miles Canyon

WHITEHORSE

Marsh Lake

Bennett L.

Taqish Lake

White Pass

SKAGWAY

Lynn Canal

JUNEAU

SEWARD

Ocean

MAP SCALE

| 0 | Kilometres | 250 | 500 |
| 0 | MILES | 155 | 310 |

the river to one third of its width and speeding it up to a racing torrent. You'll see the waves splashing up the sides of the canyon and falling back to form a hogsback in midstream that's a yard higher than the sidestreams. The hogsback is easier riding than the sidestreams, but there's a giant whirlpool in the middle and a big rock just beyond it."

"Do we stick to the sidestream then?" I asked, swallowing hard.

"We'd get nowhere if we did that. It's all wild water and cross currents. Oh, we'll make it through. But some don't. And others take a look at the rapids and decide to send their boats down un-manned. They run along the trail on top of the cliffs and pick up their boats down below in calm water."

"The boats make it down, unmanned? They don't get sucked into the whirlpool?"

"Some do, some don't. The rock gets a lot of them. I heard of one fellow that turned his boat loose and was running down after it when he saw it swept onto the rock and smashed to pieces. He hiked all the way back to Skagway, packed his goods over the pass for a second time, built a new boat at Bennett with the last of his savings and sailed to the canyon again. He launched the boat and saw it swept onto the same rock and demolished. He grabbed his gun and shot himself to death beside the rapids that had ruined him."

I had a few qualms by this time, but I was told that Miles Canyon was only a warm-up. White Horse Rapids, below the canyon, were known as one of the greatest perils encountered on the trip to Dawson. A huge reef of rock thrust itself into the river at one point, narrowing it to one half its width and boiling the water into waves two feet high. Beyond were shallows and sandbars where the hulls of wrecked boats lay rotting, and all along the right bank were the graves of travelers who had drowned in the wild waters.

None of the scowmen looked perturbed as they listened to these tales, and I wondered if my informant was pulling my leg, as had the loggers and teamsters at Bennett. I thrust my hands into my pockets and clenched my fists in an effort to look nonchalant. Reflecting on the size of the five big grain barges, and noting the confident air of the pilot as he climbed aboard carrying his own large sweep for steering, I felt reassured. But my eyes widened as we slid into the current. We were caught at once and shot into the canyon, the pilot fighting the pull on his oar to keep the scow on the high crest of water in mid-channel. My jaw dropped when I saw the whirlpool ahead, but the pilot swerved to the right, close to the rock walls where the water was dashed against them by the sudden narrowing of the course and thrust back to form the central hogsback. The scow wove and plunged in the wild current, then we swerved again to the safer hogsback, another swerve to avoid the rock, then a final fight through the roaring waters to regain the hogsback and the ride was over, leaving me breathless and sweating.

Next came Squaw Rapids, out of which the scow shot like a cannonball. We saw the high, pale cliff that warned us of the White Horse Rapids ahead; and then we were into them, half a mile of raging water with the rock reef at the end that would funnel this torrent into a 60-foot wide hell of towering white waves and treacherous cross currents. I was confident now that the pilot could get us through, but as we neared the reef a current caught us and whirled us toward the rocks. The pilot's face was wet with sweat and spray, his teeth clenched with agonized effort as he fought the pull of the current with his sweep. It was like the pitting of two wills against each other — one struggling for control, the other, infinitely stronger, dragging us into chaos. Then our bow veered; in an instant we were past the reef, plunged through the remaining rapids, and were tossed out to calm water.

The tension broke and we all laughed shakily, looking about us at the wrecked boats on the sandbars and the wooden markers on the graves that dotted the bank. The scow slid over to the landing and the pilot jumped ashore.

"We made it! Pretty close, eh, pilot?"

"Too close for comfort. Those devil rapids, I've been down them hundreds of times and they still play new tricks on me. A hundred and fifty boats smashed up in them in '98, and plenty more since then. I tell the fellows that try to make it alone, if you get through White Horse Rapids you can tackle anything in Alaska or the Yukon."

The pilot pocketed his $10 fee, shouldered his sweep, and trudged off up the trail to bring down the rest of the barges, one by one.

I was on the barges for over two weeks, traveling roughly 600 miles from Lake Bennett to Dawson. We drifted through treacherous Lake Laberge, named for the high cliff that lined its eastern shore and which offered no landing spot for travelers caught in sudden storms. These squalls often rose without warning, capsizing boats and hurling men into glacial waters so icy that death came quickly. Early maps refer to the lake as Lebarge, as did early travelers who were unconcerned with French translation or correct gender. Robert Service, poet of the Klondike, used the early spelling, too, when he wrote *The Cremation of Sam McGee*:

> The Northern Lights have seen queer sights,
>   But the queerest they ever did see
> Was that night on the marge of Lake Lebarge
>   I cremated Sam McGee.

We had an uncomfortable ride down Thirty-Mile River, following a twisting, torturous course that was shallow and studded with rocks, but then Big Salmon joined in and the river widened and a few islands appeared. At Five Fingers I looked for more excitement. Ahead I saw a reddish lava dike stretching across the river which had cut through it in five long streamers of swift rapids. Jagged, tree-topped rocks four miles long jutted up between them like narrow islands.

"We're off! Hold onto your hat!" The steersman grinned at me, but when he saw me tensing up he took pity on me. "Don't worry; it's safe enough so long as we take the right-hand channel." Even then, it was no joy ride. We were swept through at terrific speed, dragged close to the rocks and then, just as I gave a yell and ducked my head, whirled away and spewed out into calm water. No one showed concern so perhaps this current, unlike those in the White Horse Rapids, was predictable and could be depended upon to toss us to safety after having its fun with us.

After all this suspense, it was a welcome relief to come to the broad and pleasant Lewes. Our five scows drifted serenely and we sprawled out on deck, dozing in the sun. Only one man at a time was needed for lookout, to avoid the steamboats that swept up and down the river and the rowboats and skiffs that carried solitary prospectors or trappers.

The lookout called to me when we came to the junction of the Pelly. "Right here, the Yukon proper begins," he explained. He pointed to the site of old Fort Selkirk, first built half a century before. "Robert Campbell sailed down the Pelly and set up the fort. He started a trade with the Stick Indians and ran into trouble with the Chilkats who'd cornered all the Stick trade up to then, packing in goods from the coastal ships and trading them for furs. The Chilkats wiped out their opposition in a hurry one night, swooping down on the fort and burning and looting it, but Campbell and his men got away to Fort Yukon, God knows how. For a good many years, I understand, you could see three solitary chimneys rising out of the grass like ghostly gravestones. They were all that remained of Fort Selkirk."

As I learned more of the history of the northland, then and in years to come, it seemed to me that the Yukon River was peopled with ghosts, tragic ghosts that sighed in the treetops and murmured their stories in the lapping of the waves. The lookout's tale had shaken me out of my lethargy, and I got up and stared at the changed appearance of the water. We had passed the White River which discharges glacial silt and volcanic ash into the Yukon, and the crystal clear waters we had sailed in up to now, with every pebble on the river bottom visible, had turned cloudy and opaque. Farther down, the Tanana River brings in more silt, the crumbling river bank muddying it still more. It stays a dirty river all the way to the Bering Sea where it drops its burden like an excretion to form dark mudflats along the shoreline.

We passed the mouth of the Stewart where Jack London spent a year and made the frontier town of Stewart famous as the setting of several of his stories. We had traveled over 600 miles from Bennett Lake when we rounded a broad curve of the river, and there, at the junction of the Yukon and the Klondike, we came to Dawson.

45

Dawson was still a rowdy frontier town in the fall of 1900, even though the stampede to the Klondike had petered out and boatloads of prospectors were heading down-river to the new discoveries at Nome. On Front Street near the bank of the Yukon, Klondike Kate was packing them in with her songs and dances, and saloons and restaurants stayed open all night. Across the Klondike was Louse Town, noted for one muddy street with a narrow boardwalk on each side that gave access to rows of close-packed cabins. Here the prostitutes of Dawson plied a brisk trade. They had been banished from Dawson, not for moral scruples, but as a fire precaution after a Dawson dance-hall girl had thrown a lighted lamp at a rival and half the town went up in flames.

Our scows tied up on the shoreline along with a huddle of row-boats and barges. The grain was unloaded and the scows were sold for lumber.

"They won't be knocked down for a couple of days," the men told me. "You can sleep aboard for a night or two and pick up any supplies you need here in town. We aim to buy a few things ourselves and see a bit of night life. Come on, kid, we'll show you the sights."

We walked along Front Street, pushing our way among men, dogs, and laden packhorses that crowded the muddy road. The boatmen pointed out spots to avoid. "Keep out of there, kid. That card game is set up to fleece cheechakos."

There was no need to warn me. I kept a tight clutch on my wallet and did most of my sightseeing from the safety of the street. Prices in Dawson dismayed me. Some items cost 50 times the price charged in Victoria. After I had bought new work clothes and boots and eaten a few meals in restaurants, there were too few dollars left in my wallet to take me by steamboat to Fort Yukon and hardly enough to pay for a secondhand rowboat. I walked up and down the waterfront, trying to strike a bargain with one of the newcomers, but no one showed interest. Already, lumps of mush ice were forming in the river and soon travel by water would be impossible for eight long months. I was in despair. Had my journey to adventure ground to a halt so soon?

"Better come back to Bennett with us, kid," urged one of the scowmen. "Fort Yukon is a mighty long way from here and it looks like you're never going to make it."

"I'll try awhile longer," I said, and let them go without me. It was unthinkable to turn back, having come so far. I kept up my patrol of the shoreline, offering my modest price to every arrival who pulled in and growing more and more discouraged as one refusal followed another.

There was a gloomy looking fellow pacing the shoreline near me, taking out his watch every few minutes and then peering up river for a sight of the steamboat. Having heard me offering my price again and again, he finally beckoned me over.

"You want a boat, do you? Well, take mine — over there, see, pulled up on the beach. It's no use to me now, I'm catching the steamer outside today. I've had my fill of the north, nothing but bad luck from start to finish."

I took out my money, but he waved it away. "The boat is nothing but a cockleshell. Take it, you're welcome to it."

I ran to the boat, overwhelmed by sudden good luck. It was a cockleshell, all right, a little flat-bottomed dinghy big enough for only one man, but it was light and I had it in the water in a jiffy. The Porcupine River was a few miles below Fort Yukon, and the Black River flowed into the Porcupine some 20 miles from its mouth, so if I kept going, the Yukon would take me there. I grasped the oars and began my 200-mile journey to Fort Yukon.

It took me a few minutes to get the hang of my awkward little boat, but after experimenting I did best by seating myself facing the bow to be ready for what lay ahead. The river was calm and smooth here, and the gentle current bore me along slowly and easily. I was a tiny, audacious speck riding that gigantic river like a dot of plankton on a great blue whale, undismayed by the lonely vastness about me. Already the spell of the wilderness had captured me, as though it had all been waiting, silent and lovely, for me to come to it and grow familiar with its ways and moods.

I recognized Eagle by the swath cut through the timber above the town to mark the boundary between the Yukon and Alaska. It was necessary to stop now and check in. There was a fort here, Fort Egbert, established during the gold rush, and the place was full of uniformed soldiers. But once I had passed on and rounded the curve in the river, I was alone again as though Eagle had been a mirage glimpsed briefly in a lonely landscape.

It was a long journey, but I found no part of it monotonous. Here in the upper ramparts there were steep cliffs and mountains rising on each side of the river, and often there were creeks that tumbled their waters into the Yukon. The sandbars were thick with driftwood, formed by trees torn from the banks by the undercutting of the current. In one spot a black bear, not yet holed up, picked its way over the logs; and further along a moose, feeding on willow shoots on the bar, scented my approach, snorted, and splashed its way up a creek and into the bushes.

When Alaska was bought from Russia in 1867 for two cents an acre, a disgruntled congressman referred to Seward's purchase as an "inhospitable, wretched, and God-forsaken region," but as it slowly spread itself out before me in all its immensity, it seemed to promise a wealth of adventure and romance. It promised, too, something that I valued still more: a chance to prove myself beyond all doubt a man of independence and fortitude.

Eager to get to Harry and Ted, at first I traveled steadily, night and day, nibbling cold snacks while rowing, and letting my boat drift downriver in the dusk while dozing a few hours, curled up on the floorboards. There was next to no traffic here on the upper reaches of the river, and it was reasonably safe to trust my boat to the steady pull of the current. After awhile, though, it picked up speed. The river began to tear round the curves, dashing under the undercut banks. No more sleeping while I traveled; it was important to stay alert, to keep my dinghy on course and out of the treacherous pull that might thrust it under the bank and shatter it against the dying trees as they hung, half uprooted, with their branches trailing in the water.

When my head nodded and my eyes shut in spite of myself, I pulled over reluctantly to a sand bar, wrapped myself in my blanket and slept fitfully for awhile on the floorboards. The nights were very cold now and my single blanket could not keep out the chill. I woke often and lay looking up at the stars and listening to the hooting of owls and the howling of dogs tied to stakes on the river bank below the occasional straggle of Indian huts. Except for these, and once in a long while a woodcutter's cabin standing close to cordwood stacked up to sell to passing steamboats, there was scarcely a sign of life for the hundred winding miles between Eagle and Circle.

Not much life at Circle, either, when I passed by. It had a population of over 3000 around 1894 after gold was discovered in many of the nearby creeks, but the Klondike strike lured nearly everyone away, and now the cabins stood empty for the most part. Only a half dozen Indians and white men came to the doors of cabins to watch me drifting past. The miners named the place Circle because they thought it was on the Arctic Circle. They were wrong about this, but still it was mighty cold on the river, and I stood up to put more pressure on the oars and give a bit of relief to my legs which were cold and stiff.

Suddenly I came upon a startling change in the landscape. A turn in the river had brought me to open, level land, with the river spread out all over the flats, its width concealed in part by a network of islands. The cliffs and mountains were gone; there were only the flats, with the waterways secreting themselves between the chains of islands. The water spreads and retreats on these flats, causing new channels to come and go. Every trip through the flats may involve an unfamiliar route, with new sand bars in the shallows, or an unexpected dead end slough. Sand and gravel cut by the swift current from the banks farther up are carried down and settle here to form unsuspected bars. More than once they blocked my way and it was necessary to backtrack and choose a new channel.

It was dreary on the flats in late autumn. The trees on the winding banks were white with the first snow, which lay on the long moss that trailed over the bank into the water and on the driftwood heaped on the sand bars. I rowed over 80 miles through the flats and then, when the river made a curve above the Arctic Circle before flowing south and west to the sea, at the crest of that curve I came to Fort Yukon.

Hunger Up The Black

ONE

FORT YUKON looked just as Maude had described it. Wide mud
flats greeted me first, smelling abominably. Dilapidated log buildings housed the church, three stores and a small hospital, and Indian
cabins were strung along the river bank. Half-starved Indian dogs
fought for scraps of garbage that had been dumped along the
waterfront. There was no longer a fort. The buildings, once the
pride of the Hudson's Bay Company, had been torn down 15 years
before, to supply wood for the Yukon steamers.

James Murray's fort, the second that the factor built there, was
a showplace completed only a few years before the Americans took
it over. All the buildings were strongly constructed, and the com-
mandant's house boasted glass windows, highly polished plank
floors, white plastered walls and huge fireplaces. When the United
States bought Alaska, boundary lines were revised and Fort Yukon
was claimed as American. Murray moved his men up the Porcupine
across the borderline and the fort declined steadily. Eighteen years
later the buildings were demolished. The site was marked on some
maps: 'abandoned.'

When I arrived, Fort Yukon was a stopping place for steamers
too large to navigate the flats during summer low water and a
tying-up spot for boats when the river freeze-up came. There might
be 300 men at a time holed up in Fort Yukon, many of them
drifters and wastrels who passed the time preying on the Indians

and then sailed off, leaving the natives disorganized and diseased. The missionaries tried to help the Indians. Fort Yukon had an Anglican mission which became Episcopalian after the transfer. The church workers did their best to persuade the natives to conform to the moral code of the Protestant religion; but this alien code was not the complete answer to the complex problem, and Fort Yukon remained an unhappy, unwholesome spot.

However, it looked good to me as I beached my dinghy beside a big poling boat and walked up to the trading post. I went over to the counter.

"I'm on my way to Black River to join Ted Crompton and Harry Walker," I announced to the clerk. "Were they here? I'm Harry's brother, Bill. Did they leave a message for me?"

"Crompton and Walker? Let's see, now. Yes, those were the two fellows who left here on a freight scow several weeks ago. No, no message." He turned to his wife. "No message for this boy, was there?" She shook her head.

My heart sank. How was I to find them? Did I dare set off on what might be a wild goosechase, up the Porcupine and the Black in my cockleshell, with the freeze-up due any day now?

"Seems to me they were heading for the junction," the clerk recollected. "How are you traveling?" He and his wife went to the window with me and looked out at my dinghy which was dwarfed by the poling boat alongside it. The woman exclaimed:

"You're traveling alone in that flat-bottomed skiff? Why, you'll never get up the Porcupine before freeze-up, child. Talk to Dan Cadzow in that big poling boat. He's going up the Porcupine himself and I daresay he'd take you along."

I thanked her and hurried down to where the sturdy Russian and several other men were loading supplies.

"Sure, sure, come aboard," Dan Cadzow greeted me cheerfully. "These trappers are headed for the Black, too. What's one more? My boat'll hold you. I'll put you all off at the fork."

So I met the four trappers who later would share our cabin and the hardships of the terrible winter that lay ahead.

I took to Campbell Young at once. He was a big, good-looking fellow with a fine swing to his walk, due perhaps to his years with the Northwest Mounted Police. He said he'd left the force to try a life that promised him more freedom and adventure. He was intelligent and well read, friendly and unassuming, and he had an easy, hearty laugh. His choice of partner surprised me: a rather dour Scotsman named Adams; maybe the law of opposites made them congenial. The other two partners were Ed Brush, who had been a hospital orderly in Edmonton; and Harry Anthony from the same city, a temperamental fellow quick to take offence. Anthony had been an opera singer, so perhaps his moods came naturally to his artistic nature. In the group was an Indian named John Englishshoes who would travel the whole distance with Cadzow, to return to his village 100 miles up the Porcupine.

We entered the mouth of the Porcupine through a narrow, crooked slough and met a rush of water speeding down to join the big river. John Englishshoes stayed in the boat to pole, the rest of us stringing out along the gravel bar, holding a series of loops tied in a long rope. Each of us thrust an arm through a loop and strained against the current, slowly dragging the boat upstream. Gravel bars lined the river, alternating sides as the curves of the river varied. We would haul along one bar, then pole across the river and haul the length of the opposite bar.

Twenty-five miles up-river on a gravel bar close to the mouth of the Black, we pulled ashore for a meal. It was tinned beans for all of us. We had had more than our fill of beans during the past few weeks and were eating with no great enthusiasm when an Indian came down the Black. He landed, walked over to our campfire, sat down without speaking and stared at each of us in turn, his features expressionless. We were all tired and in no mood to talk either, so we went on eating in silence. Finally, that fixed stare was too much for Anthony's nerves. He jumped up and went from one to the other of us, scraping the remains off our plates onto a pot lid. He handed it to our silent visitor. "Here you are. Beans for you."

The Indian's impassiveness gave him an air of dignity. I was sure he would resent such a disparaging gesture, but he showed no offense. We had shared our meal with him; that was all it meant to him. He finished the beans and looked up at Ed Brush, the former hospital orderly.

"I sick. You give medicine." His voice was as expressionless as his face.

"How in the world did he know I had drugs with me?" Ed muttered in amazement.

Dan Cadzow chuckled.

"Indians expect every white man to carry medicine. They think any sort of white man's medicine is a sure cure for whatever ails them."

Ed appeared unconvinced. He was certain the Indian had used some kind of shaman's magic to pick him out. Shaking his head, he went over to his first-aid bag and took out a couple of pills.

"These won't hurt him, even if they don't help."

The Indian swallowed the pills trustfully, got to his feet, walked silently to his canoe and drifted off down the river.

At the junction of the Black and Porcupine, we parted from Dan Cadzow and John Englishshoes. Cadzow became well-known as a trader at The Ramparts, far up the Porcupine. A quarter of a century later, he was still there, living with an Indian wife. He was host to Amundsen in 1905, when the explorer found his post the last point of civilization before setting out to cross the vast wilderness of the Brooks Range to rejoin his ship.

I wanted Campbell Young to meet Ted and Harry, so the trappers walked with me along the bank of the Black to find Ted's cabin. It soon showed up among the trees near the river, fully completed, with smoke billowing a welcome to us from a tin smokestack.

Bursting with impatience, and anticipating the surprise I would give my brother and Ted, I ran the last few steps and pounded on the cabin door. Ted looked out, with Harry peering over his shoulder.

"Bill! How in hell did you get here?"

"Just thought I'd drop in to see how you were making out," I grinned.

They had missed the letter I had sent to Dawson and had never expected that I would set out alone to travel 600 miles from Bennett to the Black in response to Ted's casual invitation.

We all trooped in and Ted gave us tea and chunks of johnnycake studded with raisins. I could see that my brother Harry took to Campbell Young as readily as I had. When Campbell suggested that Harry and I come up some time and help him with his trapping, we agreed that we would, for sure.

"I'll keep in touch with you," Campbell promised. "I'll let you know when my partner and I get settled in."

Ted's cabin consisted of a single large room with double bunks on one side and shelves along another wall that held the goods they had brought down the Yukon: daily staples such as beans, bacon, cornmeal, raisins, dried potatoes, flour, canned butter and sugar; and, for trade with the Indians, a supply of rifles, powder and shot, traps, leaf tobacco and tea. Ted had been fortunate enough to buy up these items cheaply from two cheechakos who called in at Fort Yukon en route from Dawson to Nome (cheechako is the term that Alaskans use for anyone who has not suffered through a northern winter and earned the title of sourdough). These two had stocked up with supplies to sell in Dawson, only to find that the big stores got their deliveries directly by steamboat from St. Michael and had more orders on the way, or so they thought. Disillusioned and sick of their unwanted goods, the men were glad to sell out to Ted; and they agreed in the bargain to ferry the supplies, along with Ted and Harry, down the Yukon to the Porcupine and up as far as the Black.

This was an opportunity to resell at a profit, but money-making was always the least of Ted's interests. A few weeks after the trappers left us, a number of Indians came to the cabin to trade, and Harry and I exchanged amused grins as we watched Ted's informal method of storekeeping. He invited the natives inside, admired the skins they spread out for inspection, seated himself on a lower bunk, and began to question them about their village, their families, the type of trap they used and what their opinions were of the large trading companies.

The Indians stared at him suspiciously. Something was amiss, for white men never traded like this. They pointed to their furs. "How much?"

"How much?" Ted eyed the furs. "Maybe a dollar and a half. What you think?"

The procedure was all wrong. The Indians were accustomed to

dealing with traders who sold a rifle by standing it upright and stacking their furs beside it until the pile reached the tip of the barrel, this being the value the trader then put on the rifle. Ted was deep in talk again, and the Indians asked him several times for powder, shot, and tea before he rose reluctantly and went to the shelves, still talking to them over his shoulder. He spooned out the supplies into separate little bags, which he left standing open on the counter while he leaned on it discussing the duck season.

The Indians moved about restlessly. Finally one of them pointed to the bags and said in exasperation: "Look at bags! Why you leave bags open? Store man always shuts bags!"

Ted shook with silent laughter as he folded down the tops of the paper sacks and tied the packages with string. This was all play-acting for him and he was delighted to be instructed by the Indians that a genuine storekeeper must always shut his bags. Fortunately, his reputation as an eccentric trader was soon counterbalanced for the Indians when they discovered he would mend any rifle they brought him. Ted was good at that. He could make a broken stock look like new. And Harry and I were to discover that Ted's hunting skill meant the difference between starvation and full bellies.

Intense cold came on suddenly. Neither the stout cabin nor the stove that was kept glowing night and day could conquer the chill entirely. On the Black River we were above the Arctic Circle. The three of us slept together in one bunk to keep warm, under blankets and a bearskin robe. Ice was thickening now in the calm eddies and along the edges of the river. Ted made a trip down to the mouth of the Porcupine to see if his supplies had arrived and came back looking grim.

Miners in those days were bitter against the big commercial trading companies which, they felt, did not take seriously enough their responsibility to get supplies to customers in the far north. The chief concern of the Alaska Commercial Company was to supply its own personnel, who were there to carry on the lucrative fur trade. When food arrived for independent stores, or was dumped off at the river mouth for miners in the days before 1900, the men complained of mouldy flour, yellow bacon, green fruit and beans full of rocks and gravel. Some boats arrived carrying only shot and poison to kill the furbearing animals and whisky to ensure a profitable trade with the Indians.

Soon all the rivers were frozen solid. No supplies had reached the Porcupine and we faced the fact that we were dependent upon the scanty provisions in Ted's larder and what game could be taken from the land.

"We'll have to get busy and do some hunting," Ted told us. "We'll have to stock up with meat for the winter." This sounded like good sport to us, and Ted looked pretty confident too. He could not know at this time that it was to be one of those terrible winters when all game, from rabbit to moose, seemed to vanish from the country.

Ted took us down to the bars and showed us how to set rabbit snares among the willows. He pointed out the marks of a rabbit trail in the snow, showing us how to recognize the little tracks. Then he cut a crotched stick and a long willow pole which he laid over the crotch. He attached a thin wire noose to one end of the pole and held the noose to the ground with a tiny whittled toggle.

"When Mr. Rabbit comes down the trail," he explained, "he'll be blind to this fine wire. His head will go into the noose, the toggle will fly loose, and old Mr. Rabbit will swing into the air and hang by his neck until he is dead." He rolled his eyes at us ghoulishly. "Then we feast on rabbit pie."

The next morning we went out to gather up our haul of rabbits. The first snare held one, but the second was empty. So was the third. Every snare except the first was untouched and unsprung. It was the same story when Harry and I set up snares of our own. Such scarcity was unprecedented in Ted's hunting experience, and at times we saw a look of apprehension in his eyes as he counted over our supplies and planned the rationing of staples for the winter months.

"Well, if you can't catch rabbits, I'll teach you how to make money catching marten," he said, trying to keep us occupied and content. He took a steel trap and led us in among birch trees and stunted spruce. Then he cut four sticks several feet in length and stood them up, two to a side, in front of a tree. Brush was laid over the sticks to form a roof on the little house, which could be entered

56

only from the front. Bait on a stick would lure the marten inside, but a trap hidden under moss in the doorway would snap shut its steel jaws on the animal's paw.

"Get yourselves traps and bait," he urged us, "and set them up in places like this one, a good distance apart. Mark your trail with blazes on the tree trunks with your axe."

We set a line of traps and rolled out from under the bearskin early the next morning to check them. We were elated to find a marten in the first trap. It was snarling and biting at the cruel steel teeth that held it, and leaping up and down the trunk of the tree in a frenzied effort to free its paw. For a moment I turned sick at the sight and held back.

"Kill it! Kill it!" Harry commanded, as loath as I was to make the first move. A smart rap on its nose with a stick stunned it, and a blow on the back of its neck ended its misery. Ted's instructions were to avoid striking the head or a blood clot would form and injure the skin.

Harry ran on ahead, and when I caught up to him he had just taken a beautiful silver fox from the trap. On returning in triumph, we were told by Ted that the foxskin would get us $150. In the following weeks we collected a fair number of marten skins, while Ted scouted the countryside with his rifle. He sighted no large game and our food supply slowly dwindled.

Ted showed us how to skin our marten, cutting the skin loose around the feet and ripping down the back of the hind legs to the vent, peeling the skin first from the back legs. A forked stick was clamped at the base of the tail to hold the skin, the body was pulled quickly, and the tailbone slid free like a finger from a glove. For drying and stretching, we carved flat boards slightly longer than the skin and tapered to a point at one end. The skin was then drawn over the board, flesh side out, and flesh and fat were scraped from it. Tacked flat on the board, the skin would shrink as it dried. To prevent a tautness that would make removal difficult, a stick was run under the skin against the board. When this was slipped out, the skin came away easily.

Word came from Harry Anthony that Campbell Young and his partner were settled in their cabin near the headwaters of a creek some distance up the Porcupine. We were eager to keep our promise to help them with their traplines, now that we prided ourselves on being experienced trappers and outdoorsmen. Ted had said we could use his sled and had pointed out two sacks of flour we could take with us.

"You can't go visiting around Christmas without a gift for the trappers," he cautioned us. "They won't welcome two more mouths to feed if they're as short of game as we are."

We had planned to start as soon as Ted got back from one of his hunting trips, but we grew impatient and decided to leave him a note and start out at once. It was now December, close to Christmas, and very cold, but Ted had supplied us with gloves and moccasins. The soft, fur-topped mooseskin gloves reached to our elbows and were worn over our woolen gloves. Our feet were loosely wrapped in several squares of flannel, which was less constricting and thus warmer than socks. We had wound linen puttees around our legs under our high, laced moccasins. We set off confidently, ignorant of the dangers that such a winter trip might hold for two inexperienced travelers in the wilds.

Ted had put a gee pole on the right side of the sled, running from the first stanchion through a ring fixed at the right of the bar joining the up-curved runners in front. This was a trick often resorted to by Alaskans, who found it a help in controlling the flat, heavy Yukon sleds which were awkward to steer. Harry pulled the sled, the rope over his shoulder, and guided it when necessary with the gee pole. I followed behind, as befitted a younger brother, shoving from the rear with a pole attached to the back end.

The first part of the trail ran over the river ice, down the Black and then up the Porcupine, and the runners slid easily over the frozen snow. We hauled the sled past a few Indian cabins and then for nearly 20 miles beyond Anthony's cabin before the short winter daylight drew to a close.

Tired and cold, we paused to rest.

"Do you think we missed the creek?" I asked. "I thought we'd have reached it long before this."

"Harry Anthony said the cabin is miles up the creek and then overland a way," he recalled. "We'll never make it tonight. We'll have to camp here by the trail. Shall we light a fire?"

"By golly, we forgot to bring an axe," I exclaimed. "Have you got the matches?"

"I thought *you* had them. I didn't think we'd need matches, anyway. I thought we'd be at Campbell Young's before dark."

"That wind blowing down the ice sure cuts your face like a knife," I said.

"We'll freeze to death if we sit here," Harry agreed. "What shall we do?"

Harry had always taken command, exercising his right as my elder. If he asked my advice, he must be desperate.

"I wish we'd never come," I grumbled miserably. The icy air had nipped my ambition to brave the elements and prove my manhood. Warm, living creatures seemed anomalous in this vast, silent, frozen world; ourselves an error which the north would move quickly to erase. We sat shivering on the river ice, no longer "experienced trappers and outdoorsmen" as we had thought ourselves, but only two very cold, frightened kids uncertain of their next move.

"What's that, Harry? Did you hear something? Listen!" We both strained to catch the sound I had heard from the distance, around the curve of the river.

Faintly, then more clearly, the murmur of voices and the tinkle of harness bells came to us from far off through the still, icy air.

"Someone's coming!"

We staggered to our feet, clumsy with cold.

Dimly through the dusk we watched a party of natives coming round the bend of the trail. As they approached, we could make out the leader — a tall, broad-shouldered Indian wearing a caribou skin parka trimmed with white fox. He stopped in front of us, looked us over and then thumped his chest with a big, mittened fist.

"Name John Herbert," he said proudly. "Big hunter ... me!"

Harry grinned at me.

"We're no slouches at trapping, ourselves," he boasted, cocky

59

again now that help was at hand. "Big hunters . . . us! We catch many marten, and I catch fine silver fox."

We told the Indian our names and where we were going, and he invited us to join his party at their camp that night. Several families had come from far up the Porcupine, traveling down to trade at Fort Yukon. It was because Ted had heard that Indians from the far north made these annual pilgrimages during the winter, following the rivers down from the headwaters of the Porcupine, that he had built his post near the fork of the Black and Porcupine to intercept them as they passed by.

In the shelter of a grove of trees, the natives dug away the snow down to the thick, foot-high moss, clearing an open patch. Down the center they built a long, narrow fire so there would be room for everyone in the party to gather in a big oval to warm themselves. The Indians heated and ate their food and fed fish to their dogs. Harry and I toasted ourselves first, front and back, reveling in the warmth, and then unpacked our beans and bacon. Ted had cooked and frozen these together in large pans, then broken them into chunks like bits of peanut brittle so that we could carry them in little bags. Since they were precooked, they needed only to be melted and reheated.

When the Indians finished their meal, they rolled up in their blankets and fell soundly asleep. Their huskies slept apart from the fire, curled together in a heap, their long hair white with frost. We stayed wakeful, our bones still aching from the bitter cold — we learned later that the temperature dropped to 50 below that night. The sleeping Indians shivered in their blankets as the fire died down, but none of them woke. Harry and I twisted and turned, getting colder and colder. (I have read somewhere that the early Russian explorers declared that sleeping outdoors in Alaskan winters could be endured only when foxskin blankets were used together with bearskin bags for the feet.)

Harry poked me, shaking like an ague victim and stammering, "I can't stand it! I'm going to chop more wood for the fire."

"We don't have an axe, remember?"

"I'll borrow that Indian's, there on his sled." He rolled out of his blanket, crept to the sled and got the axe, then moved away quietly to a spot some distance from the camp where he could chop without disturbing the Indians. In a few minutes, however, he was back, looking chastened.

"What happened?"

"Axe broke." He showed me the pieces. The extreme cold had made the axe handle as brittle as glass and Harry's first blow had shattered it.

"Golly! I hope it didn't belong to that big fellow!"

"I'll put the pieces back on the sled. Maybe he'll think one of the Indians broke it."

Harry had no conscience when the safety of his own skin was at stake. Quietly, he placed the broken axe on the sled and we sat up the rest of the night, inching ourselves close to the red embers and shivering with cold and apprehension.

At dawn the Indians woke. There was a great outcry when the broken axe was discovered. We jumped up, clutching our blankets. Big John Herbert turned on us fiercely, and the rest of the group drew near. All eyes were turned on us, the faces hostile and resentful. I was about to make a run for it when Harry, marshalling his wits, stepped forward confidently.

"Don't let that worry you," he said, talking fast in the persuasive tones that never failed to win him backing in future years for the schemes that he would dream up. "Take your axe down to the trader at Black River. He can join these parts so smoothly that you won't be able to find the spot where it's mended. He'll make your axe look like new — better than it looked before it was broken — and he won't charge you a cent if you tell him Harry Walker sent you."

John Herbert was mollified. The Indians were curious to meet the trader. They parted from us cheerfully and headed downstream for the trading post.

Big John Herbert, our host by the Porcupine, became a familiar figure to white men in later years. Roald Amundsen, the Norwegian explorer who was first to sail through the North West Passage, in his sloop *Gjoa*, met John in his village on the upper ramparts of the Porcupine when he made his overland trip in 1905 from Herschel Island to Fort Yukon. Having heard the name phonetically, he gave 'Herbert' a Scandinavian twist in his book, *The North West Passage*, spelling it 'Alvert.'

Amundsen had taken his dangerous 42-day trip through the gigantic Brooks Range and across Alaskan wastes to send word to Norway of his successful discovery of the passage. He traveled with two Eskimos and an English sea captain named Mogg, who announced that he must be considered head of the party since he was delivering mail from boats at Herschel Island to Fort Yukon. The mild-mannered Amundsen made no protest when Capt. Mogg insisted the explorer replace time-tested pemmican provisions with frozen pork and beans, nor when the captain rode on the sled while Amundsen ran ahead on skis, nor yet when Mogg slept late in the tent while the explorer rose early to prepare breakfast. Amundsen comments charitably in his report that Mogg was "an elderly man unused to long trips." However, en route they met a party of Eskimos and Mogg was moved to hand out gifts from their provisions with a generous hand. The natives praised him, calling him 'an angel,' but Amundsen could not resist recording: "I did not say how far I agreed with this opinion."

When they reached Fort Yukon, there was no telegraph station to send out Amundsen's triumphant announcement. He had to travel another 200 miles up-river to Eagle, where the message could be sent from Fort Egbert. Fort Yukon provided an Indian guide whom Amundsen heartily disliked. The fort still had its bad name as a harborer of undesirable whites and Indians. Amundsen called his guide 'impertinent' and 'conceited,' and put blame for the Indian's attitude on the missionaries, "showing that good teaching may sometimes turn out badly." The missionaries taught the natives that all men were equal in the sight of God; and, as with other Christian beliefs, this one confused them. Some who had shown a satisfyingly humble respect for the white man's wisdom now questioned his superiority, expressing their resentment with the impertinence that Amundsen deplored. The natives awoke as well to the fact that few whites treated them as equals. No longer able to take pride in their own heritage which they had been instructed to reject, they grew hostile and aggressive toward the white culture that denied them equality.

The rude or inconsiderate individual, Anglo-Saxon or Indian, was offensive to Amundsen, but he had only praise for 'brave' John Herbert, from whom he had bought some dried salmon. He describes him as "a very fine fellow, six feet high, with dark hair and a full moustache." Perhaps it was because John Herbert dwelt at this time by the far northern waters of the Porcupine, his native dignity unimpaired, that he was able to speak with a natural courtesy to Amundsen, as one man to another.

The extreme cold broke on the day we parted from John Herbert. Traveling became a less painful ordeal, but we lost our way shortly after leaving the river and found ourselves on a trail that led eventually to a lake with a single cabin beside it. An Indian opened the door and invited us inside to spend the night. He told us his name was John Whitefish.

In this lonely hut in the wilderness, the niceties of introduction were carried out with ceremonial formality. John brought forward first his wife, then his two little girls. Next he led us over to an elderly relative with a lame leg who sat wrapped in a blanket in a corner of the cabin.

"Jesus!"

Harry muttered to me: "What's he cussing about?" But then we realized this was another introduction. Missionaries had evidently penetrated to this remote spot and left their imprint.

The little cabin was dark and murky. The only light came from bits of cloth that had been dipped in fish oil and set burning in a dish. They gave a smoky light, which John called "bitch." The oil came from the whitefish — actually pale silver rather than white — which inhabited the lake and provided the family with its chief source of food and John Whitefish with his name. The soft-mouthed, toothless fish would not bite on baithooks, so John trapped them instead in fine-meshed linen nets.

We were tired of hauling our two heavy sacks of flour, and the next morning we asked if we could leave the sacks cached on the cabin roof so we could get to Campbell Young's more quickly. John Whitefish agreed. It said much for the honesty of the Indians that the bags remained there untouched until we reclaimed them despite the scarcity of food that winter.

We were directed to the right trail but still had a long way to go. We stopped off again en route, this time at the cabin of an Indian named William Yetran. Several families lived together here, with the men, women and children sharing one large room. They were friendly and hospitable, as were all these Indians around the Black and the Porcupine, and insisted that Harry and I share the "liver and lights" of moose they were cooking. They must have had little to spare, for not more than a couple of moose were caught in that region during the entire winter.

My wretched immaturity showed as usual in my bashfulness, and the women gathered around me like a bunch of solicitous aunts and grandmothers clucking over a helpless child. They felt the light weight of my jacket with little cries of dismay and brought me rabbit skins to tuck around my neck to keep out the cold.

Campbell Young and Adams had contented themselves with the most primitive of furnishings in their trapper's cabin. Apart from bunks filled with dried tundra grass, there was only a pile of stones in one corner that formed a rude stove, opening at the back to an outside chimney. Campbell and his partner had collected a stack of furs and had some drying on stretchers and others hanging against the wall, pending shipment in the spring.

The morning after we arrived Campbell got up first and cooked breakfast. "Now then, gentlemen," he shouted at us as we lay immobile in our blankets, "if you will arise from a state of lassitude to one of enthusiasm, we will breakfast on hotcakes!"

We liked Campbell as much as ever, but after a few days we began to miss the warmth of the big range and the variety in cooking at Ted's cabin. The two men worked hard at their trapping and had little time to spare for us. When they left us to go out to their traplines, taking a tent with them so they could sleep on the trail, we soon grew bored. We had been of little use to them in their trapping, since they had no steel traps up here and used deadfalls instead. Campbell left us an axe and a penknife, all that was needed to construct them, but we were not yet adept at whittling the triggers and setting up the logs. Finally one day we hiked to John Whitefish's cabin and brought back the two sacks of flour on our sled. We left a note for Campbell, thanking him for his hospitality, and headed off down-river.

When we reached Harry Anthony's cabin, we stayed for several days with him and Ed Brush, exchanging news and helping them with their traps. One night we were all in our bunks, half asleep, when Anthony's dogs began barking wildly. Then the door burst open and two men came in, one of them singing crazily. Anthony sat up, fumbling for a candle. As he struck a match, we saw to our amazement that the intruders were Campbell Young and Adams. Campbell was dancing about the room like a wood nymph, waving a handkerchief above his head and singing hilariously: "It's all that's left! It's all that's left! Twenty years of work and all I have left is my little pocket handkerchief!"

"Fire," Adams explained laconically. "Burnt out. Everything gone. Came in from the traplines and found nothing but ashes."

"All I have left!" sang Campbell, pirouetting under his handkerchief. We all tumbled from our bunks in a hurry, convinced that Campbell's mind had cracked with the shock; but he stopped when he saw our concern, shrugged and said resignedly, "No use crying. If it's gone, it's gone."

"Someone must have left a fire on the rocks," Adams conjectured. "Wind may have blown a spark to the bunks. Everything went up in smoke: cabin, furs, stores, money, gear. We're finished."

The men all turned to look at us and Harry and I stared back, stricken. We had been warned never to leave a fire burning on the stones, as a spark blown onto the dried tundra grass in the bunks would start up a blaze in an instant.

"But we put out the fire," Harry protested, "didn't we, Bill?"

"I know we did. We raked it over and threw snow on it."

We could sense their disbelief. Harry had the reputation of wriggling out from under blame, and I was the younger brother who usually followed his lead. Evidently there was an unspoken decision among them to leave accusations unstated. Boys would be boys; carelessness was to be expected of them. Certain of our innocence, we were even more chagrined by forgiveness than by condemnation.

"Forget it," said Campbell. "The thing is, what do we do now?"

65

It was decided that we should take our food supplies down to Ted's big cabin, where the seven of us would share our pooled resources until the spring thaw brought relief. All of us were aware by now that lean months lay ahead. While waiting for the thaw, we could combine forces and build two boats to take us to Fort Yukon as soon as the ice broke.

THREE

Ted welcomed us in. If it meant less food in his belly, it promised good nourishment for his mind, with Campbell able and willing to converse on any subject that Ted brought up.

"It's been a depressing month," Ted lamented. "Indians keep coming to my door wanting to trade their furs for food, and I can only turn them away. That bitch of a steamboat, why didn't she leave on time? We're starving here and my supplies sit rotting away, down there in St. Michael."

He had found plenty of time that month to think about his young wife, too, and to wonder how she was managing. He showed me a tiny envelope, only two inches long, which he had made from thin bark peeled from a birch tree. On a folded sheet of birch bark notepaper of the same size, he had written Maude a love letter in minute handwriting with the aid of a magnifying glass. He let me read the three pages through the glass, and I told him I was sure the novelty would please her. He had expressed his love for her and his distress that they were forced to live apart. But I read nothing that suggested he planned to leave his other love — the Alaskan wilderness.

Our combined supplies were placed on the shelves and severely rationed, but with seven hungry men in the cabin they melted away rapidly. Ted told me to take Anthony's dogs and sled and travel the trail over the river ice to Fort Yukon for any groceries the company store could spare. I got there late and spent the night, but the trader at the N.C. Company store told me Fort Yukon was desperate, too, and offered me only a bag of rolled oats.

I ran into excitement on the return trip. Rounding a bend in the river trail, my dogs sighted a large black fox trotting ahead of them.

They were off like a shot in pursuit, the sled careening from side to side behind them. I was eager to get the fox, for a black one is a rarity. Indians were known to celebrate with a feast and potlatch when they trapped a black fox, and I would be famous as well as a lot richer if I came home with one. But the way the dogs were stampeding, it was impossible for me to unstrap my gun from the sled while simultaneously riding the runners and trying to control the dogs. I thrust the spiked brake down into the snow, but nothing slowed them; they were oblivious of everything but the black, fleeing object. The frantic fox turned aside and jumped at the high bank, clawing the snow and then sliding back to the trail. The dogs made for it, yelping insanely. I struggled again to get at my gun and was still clinging with one hand to the sled, having just pulled my gun free, when the fox gave a gigantic leap, its strength reinforced by terror. It gained the top of the snowbank and disappeared, along with my dreams of the $500 its rare pelt would have brought me.

The men cheered the arrival of the rolled oats — more lustily, I daresay, than they would have greeted a black fox pelt, for money was of no use that winter to get us the food we needed to stay alive. Ted mixed up a kind of bannock, and when he served it, hot and fragrant, it smelled and tasted like food for the gods after the dried apples and tea to which we had been reduced.

The plight of the Indians was even more desperate than ours and several died of starvation that winter. Parties of Indians would come down the river trail, their huskies shrunken from their splendid summer condition to mere skin and bones. The Indians would hand over their furs, and Ted would give them money, but they could buy nothing from us but tea. One old Indian, William Ross, sat on a stump all day on the river bank in the early spring sunshine, drinking cup after cup of strong black tea, trying vainly to still his hunger pangs with the warm stimulant.

One day a young Indian girl, no older than 16, came to the cabin dragging a sled behind her.

"Bring her in," said Ted. "She looks half frozen."

She told us she had traveled from far up near the headwaters to sell her furs and buy food for her people. She was a slender girl with a patient face pinched with hunger.

"You're not giving her food?" Harry Anthony protested, as Ted put on the kettle and got out some cold bannock. "If you try to feed every starving Indian around here, our bag of oats will be gone in a day and we'll all starve to death."

"It's little enough," Ted said, pouring out hot tea and watching the girl wolf down the bannock. He paid her for her furs and tried to explain to her why her money would buy no food from us. As she started off dejectedly, Ted cursed the company stores and vowed never again to trust to the last boat for supplies, nor to depend on winter game for his food.

Improvidence, the inability to save for the future, was a trait peculiar to all the Indians. They dried a little salmon for the winter months but depended upon game to carry them through most of the season. They never seemed to recognize that regular cycle of years during which the amount of game slowly increased to a peak and then suddenly vanished, as in this year, with rabbit tracks almost non-existent, no moose or ptarmigan to be seen, and hunger hanging over the land like a vulture waiting for its prey.

Before the Indians ran out of food, they had been so generous to us that we were half ashamed to keep for ourselves the little bag of oats that stood between us and starvation. It rested on the floor of the cabin under shelves that were empty now except for tins of tea and powder and shot. Harry Anthony guarded the bag like a miser hoarding his gold, getting between it and any Indians who came in to sell their skins. One day, an Indian who was familiar with our cabin moved suddenly toward the shelves after getting his money, to help himself to ammunition. Anthony thought he was making for the oats. He grabbed his gun and leapt in front of the poor Indian who nearly died of fright at this unexpected attack.

"Put down that gun, you silly fool!" Ted shouted, jumping up. "He only wants powder and shot."

Anthony stepped back, lowering his gun and looking sheepish. "He was headed for the oats," he said, and though he put his gun back on the rack, he stayed near it until the Indians had gone.

One Indian named Edward called at the cabin every day just as we were about to start our frugal meal of bannock and tea. He sat on the floor beside the door, watching us eat, and always the patient vigil had its desired effect. Even Anthony joined the rest of us in breaking off a bit of bannock for him and Ted would take the pieces over to him along with a cup of tea. Edward would stand up, bow deeply, and say with fervor and a simple dignity: "Tang you!" We chuckled at this little ceremony, but we were all moved by the patience, politeness and dignity that old Edward managed to retain despite the spectre of starvation that hovered over him.

During one meal when a knock came, Ted said: "Let old Edward in." But it was William Yetran, the Indian who had given Harry and me moose liver when we called at his cabin on our way to visit Campbell Young. He came in and squatted at Edward's usual spot by the door. He was surprised to see us all living together, so Campbell explained to him about the fire.

William leapt to his feet with a cry of anguish, striking his chest and calling out, "No good ... me ... no good!" He electrified us by shouting out every oath he had learned from white men, pointing at himself as he uttered each one: "Damn fool ... me! Bloody devil ... me! Go hell ... me!" and other much more colorful phrases. He was no expert at profanity, though, and when his vocabulary ran out, he strung words together which were both innocuous and inappropriate. But none of us laughed. There was agonized self-condemnation in his voice.

Then came his bombshell. He told us he had stopped off at Campbell's cabin to cook a meal (Alaskans always felt free to take shelter in each other's homes in the wilderness) and had neglected to put out his fire. Yes, he remembered seeing the sacks of flour in the room, so he must have come in after Harry and I had left. He alone was responsible.

"I give you all my skins, you take every skin I got. You take my rifle. I give you everything. You take," he pleaded, but Campbell shook his head and tried to downgrade his losses. Harry and I were so grateful for the Indian's honest confession that we broke our oatcakes in two and handed him the larger halves. William was too hungry to refuse, but he went on muttering oaths to himself, thumping his chest with his fist, and shaking his head despondently.

Ironically, a few of the inedible marten still lingered in the district. We collected them from the traps, skinned them, and flung the bodies into the snowdrifts outside. Hollow-eyed Indians came knocking at our door, asking permission to dig into the snow for the stinking carcasses. They carried them off for an unpleasant meal that was possibly better than no meal at all.

Boatbuilding helped to turn our thoughts from the hunger that gnawed at our bellies. We whipsawed lumber from birch logs and put together two large poling boats. Harry Anthony supervised the building of one while Ted directed work on the other. When the boats were finished, ready to launch as soon as the rivers cleared, Anthony asked me to go with him up the Porcupine. We would take his dogs and sled and pack down the gear still remaining in his cabin.

The snow was now beginning to melt in the warmer sun and as we started back along the river trail, we were forced to stop often to up-end the sled and clear the clogging snow from the runners. After one of these stops, we sat down on the sled to rest for a moment, and Anthony's three dogs collapsed and rested too, muzzles on outstretched forepaws. We sat quietly, without speaking. In the utter silence we seemed alone in a motionless world. We stayed rigid and still, compelled to muteness by the frozen land.

Suddenly Anthony threw back his head and burst into song, making the dogs start and jingle their harness as Verdi's aria from *Rigoletto* echoed along the frozen river. Harry sang as if he were facing not me and the puzzled dogs, but one of his concert hall audiences in Edmonton:

> La don-na è mo-bi-le qual piuma al ven-to
> Mu-ta d'ac-cen-to e di pen-sie-ro!

He sang it to the end, listening with rapt satisfaction to the last notes shivering up the bend of the river, perhaps to startle some solitary trapper far up the Porcupine. The following year, Caruso would sing this aria in Covent Garden in London and ladies would clap their white-gloved hands and men would shout 'Bravo!' to bring him back onstage for curtain-call after curtain-call. But only the three dogs and I would know the eerie loveliness of Harry

Anthony's rendition of that warm Italian aria on the frozen Porcupine above the Arctic Circle.

By mid-April the boats were ready — and the bag of oats was empty. There was nothing for us to do but sit on stumps in the spring sunshine, watch the snow melting and the water running over the river ice, and scan the skies for a sight of the first goose. Finally there was a shout: "Geese coming!" and we saw the birds flying high overhead in V-formation up the river. We laughed with hysteria and slapped each other on the back at the prospect of an end to our hunger.

Ted got up early the next morning and slipped out of the cabin while the rest of us were still in bed. He was gone all day. In the first dusk of evening we saw him coming back around the bend of the river, bent over, his figure humped and distorted.

"Is it Ted? Has he got something? What is it?"

He had two fat geese and 18 plump mallard ducks, all plucked and dressed, strung about him. Whistling complacently, he tucked seven ducks into a pan and popped them into the oven before he sat down to rest. An hour later, we gathered round the table with broad smiles of satisfaction as Ted served us a roast duck apiece.

Then with a crack, a grind and a roar, the breakup came in the Black River. Instantly, the ducks and geese were up and away to their summer nesting grounds. Not a bird was seen for two days. The thought of another siege of famine was unbearable. We decided that rather than wait for the river to clear, we would go down at once among the ice floes. The boats were loaded to the gunnels with our combined possessions and when we launched them, we found they were short in the beam and apt to tip and wobble. But there was no holding us back now; we would take our chance with the ice-filled river.

It was a mad, wild and deafening ride careering down the swirling river with ice cakes all about us. Time and again our two boats shot close to the sweeps, the undercut banks at the curves, where ice cakes collected, ready to smash to pieces a boat that was whirled into them. We jabbed at them with our poles, fighting to get across the strong current to the gravel side of the narrow river without bumping one of the great cakes that tossed and bobbed all about us.

71

Then, rounding a curve, we saw an ice jam forming ahead of us at the next bend. Cakes hit into the stalled floes, up-ending themselves and hurtling back to smash on the ice with the sound of a thousand shattering panes of glass. Our dogs, terrified by this grinding and crashing of the floes, cowered down on the floorboards, trembling and howling. We maneuvered our boats to a gravel bar, but the ice jam sent the water spilling over the bar and in among the trees. We were forced to keep our boats in the flooded willows for several hours until the jam broke and we could continue down in the wake of the floes. Progress was slow, but eventually we made it down the Black, down the Porcupine; and then, after a short, stiff pole up the Yukon River, we came to Fort Yukon.

Here we could eat our fill. Trading posts no longer hoarded food for the river was full of steamboats bringing supplies now that the ice was out. We disposed of our furs and made new plans. Ed Brush, Adams and Anthony went their separate ways. Campbell and my brother Harry reloaded their boat with fresh supplies and headed up the Porcupine again to Ted's cabin on the Black. Harry won himself fame the next winter by shooting a moose. There were few moose at any time in this region, and these were usually picked off by the Indians, who depended on them for meat and for skin moccasins, mittens and parkas.

After this, wilderness living palled for them. My brother took off for Fairbanks, newly arisen that year after the gold strike and Campbell, turned prudent by middle age and misfortune, forsook adventure entirely and went outside to a job with the weather bureau in Edmonton.

Men of Independent Mind　3

ONE

TED AND I DRIFTED down through the Yukon Flats from Fort Yukon to Steven Village in our cranky, whipsawed poling boat.

"Take a look at the game, Bill!" Ted pointed to ducks and geese that we flushed from the marsh grasses as we passed, and the occasional moose or bear on the sand banks that lumbered away if our boat came too close. "No more empty bellies for us. We'll eat well this year."

It was late spring now, and the islands and the river banks were rainbow bright with many-colored flowers. Alaska has more than 700 kinds of wildflowers. I never did learn all their names, but every year I would marvel at the brilliance that so quickly replaced the colorless whiteness of winter, just as the flowers and vegetables we planted would shoot up and mature like magic in a few weeks.

Suddenly the river narrowed radically, twisting and turning at right angles, flowing east, south, west, and south again as it reached the lower ramparts — 100 miles of steep hills bordering the winding river as far down as Tanana.

The town of Rampart was spread along a bench on the south bank, at the foot of mountains rising abruptly behind it. Rampart was a stopping off place as well as a gold-mining site. It was always full of miners, trappers, Indians, and local tradesmen and their families. There was a commissioner, a post office and a few stores and saloons.

"Come on, Bill," Ted suggested as we beached our boat, "let's make the rounds. Maybe someone will give us a tip on the best place to start up a trading post."

First we went to the post office for mail. Ted ripped open a letter from Maude and grinned as he pulled out a snapshot. Maude smiled triumphantly out at us, a bright little baby face pressed close to her own.

"A girl!" Ted announced excitedly. "What a cute little toad she is! Bill, we've got to get busy and build a home for them. I want them up here with me."

We made some inquiries and were told that the Indians of Mouse Point, 200 miles down-river, went trapping far up the tributaries of the Yukon during the winter months and brought back their furs to sell. There was no trading post at Mouse Point, so it might prove a strategic site for Ted. What decided him was the added news that a woodcutter had abandoned some log huts close to the Indian village and they would be ours for the taking. We would have shelter and space for Ted's stock, while we worked on larger quarters.

Ted rented a small cabin for me to stay in while he made a quick trip to Fort Yukon to collect his long-delayed supplies — supplies that would have saved the lives of starving Indians up the Black if the steamboat had sailed from St. Michael on time. The cabin would serve later as a halfway storehouse while we looked over Mouse Point and made sure that the woodcutter's huts were habitable.

I wandered about Rampart and went to see some of the placer mines close by. As yet, we had felt no urge to go mining. For one thing, we had no idea how to go about it; also, there was no charm for us in the thought of burrowing underground to "drift," or working with sluices in the mud. For every man who struck it rich, hundreds suffered discomfort — misery in many cases — and got nothing for their pains. No, we would stay above ground and live where we could smell the spruce and see the open sky, where we could hunt and fish and grow familiar with the wilderness. But the frenzied atmosphere in the mining town drew me out to watch.

A letter had come to me from my father, telling me that even he had succumbed to the lure of gold. He was nearly 60 at the time, but his imagination had been fired by news stories of the second big strike and he caught a boat to Nome, transferred to the lighter that was hauled in by cable through the shallow water, and finally rode over the surf to dry land in a cage dangling from the cable. Reading his account, I smiled at the thought of him, neat and dapper, picking his way through the mud among the thousands of men working at fever pitch, some actually standing in the surf, panning the wet sand; others making the beach hideous with their ditches, wooden sluiceboxes, rockers and piles of dirt and sand; while above them on the low tundra hills big dredges were at work. He soon learned that all the gold-bearing sites had been staked, many of them being restaked by claim jumpers, and that some latecomers — frantic for a share of the riches — had stubbornly staked beyond the paying claims and shot themselves to death in despair when their labor produced no sign of gold. Weary though he had been with real estate, my father decided that Nome was no place for him. He threaded his way back among the tents, swung over the surf in the dangling cage to the lighter, boarded the boat as the whistle sounded and sailed back to Victoria.

All in all, I felt safe for the present from the gold fever. It was another fever that struck me down in Rampart. I had been alone in the cabin for almost a week when I woke one morning feeling hot and nauseated. A walk along the waterfront failed to clear my head and the dizziness persisted. The next day I couldn't eat and came back from my walk with arms and legs aching and head throbbing. Soon I was too weak to get out of bed and lay on my cot burning with fever.

The cabin door stood open, and a miner passing by looked in and saw me.

"What's wrong, boy? Are you sick?"

"Yes, my bones ache and I'm hot and thirsty. Can't get up, either; I'm too dizzy to stand."

"No one looking after you, eh? Wait a minute! There's a fellow hangs around the saloon says he's a doctor. I'll get him to come down here and take a look at you."

He was back in a few minutes with a bleary-eyed alcoholic who

75

weaved his way to the cot and sat down heavily at the foot. The joggling sent waves of pain shooting through my skull.

"Don't worry, sonny," he said, breathing whisky fumes into my face. "I've got what you need, right here with me." He took a small bottle from his pocket.

"Spoonful three times a day. You'll be on your feet in a fortnight. Can you pay me now?"

I struggled to sit up, got my wallet from my pants' pocket and gave him a bill.

"You'll see me again next week," he promised as he heaved himself off the bed and staggered out.

The medicine had no effect on me except to make me splutter and retch, and after a couple of doses I was too weak to lean down and pick up the bottle. Day after day I lay alone, aching and shivering, seeing the walls come close or recede into the distance, seeing the cabin empty one moment and then, in my delirium, crying out in fear at strange shapes that sailed round and round the walls, setting my head whirling with their dizzy pace.

My so-called doctor came again and peered at me closely. His face seemed enormous, his eyes huge and flecked with red.

"You're doing fine, sonny. What did I tell you?"

I thought myself still delirious when Ted appeared in the doorway — gigantic, bearded, demanding explanations. He picked up the medicine bottle, sniffed it and heaved it and the alcoholic out into the road, then came and bent over me.

"Can you hear me, Bill? There's a military detachment in Rampart. They'll have a surgeon with them and I'll get him for you. Hold on."

He returned with the army surgeon, the antithesis of my seedy quack from the saloon: young, earnest and competent, neat and smart in his uniform. I decided I might live, after all.

He looked severely at Ted.

"You should have called me sooner. The boy has typhoid. There's a lot of it about; not surprising, the way garbage and excrement are emptied into the river. He'll soon reach the most dangerous period of the disease, when the fever goes and exhaustion sets in. He needs sponge baths now, plenty of liquids and cool, boiled water; and later you must see that he has a good diet of nourishing food."

"He'll get it." Ted's calm confidence seemed to reassure the young surgeon, but nonetheless he called daily to see me until the disease had passed its crisis.

T W O

Indians straggled from their cabins and gathered on the river bank to watch us as we beached our boat at Mouse Point. Ted helped me ashore and took my arm as we walked slowly to the low log huts built against the hillside. The Indians surrounded us as we walked, looking with childlike curiosity at my thin, pale face.

"You sick? Hey, you sick man?" they demanded persistently, crowding close to me. I was no longer sick, but I was too weak yet to help with any building.

We were fortunate in having the woodcutter's two huts to come to. They had been joined into one with only a partition between them, and we lived in one section and piled Ted's stock in the other. This was Ted's trading post for the first two years, and, though the quarters were cramped, they were adequate to hold groceries and ammunition while he built up a trade with the Indians.

"We'll see what luck we have this winter when they come down with their furs," he said. "It may take time to wean them away from whatever trading posts they've been using. By Christmas, they should be used to the sight of us. It might be a friendly gesture to ask a few of them to come over then for Christmas dinner. I'll take a day off to go hunting and get us a moose, and make a big plum pudding; that should be a novelty for them. Bill, it's good to have food to spare for a change. That winter on the Black still haunts me; I think of those hungry Indians coming to me for food and having to be turned away."

"I'll never forget old William Ross," I reminisced, "sitting on his stump drinking tea and growing weaker and thinner every day. And that young girl — do you remember her, Ted?"

"Where's my rifle? I'll get us a moose now and check on our stock of potatoes and tinned tomatoes."

77

We had our Christmas dinner at noon, to be free to serve the Indians at a later setting. Ted had roasted a haunch of moose meat and cooked a big pot of potatoes, which were hard to come by that year. He had steamed a gigantic plum pudding, made with carrots instead of eggs since none of these were to be had, and the kettle was boiling ready to brew fresh tea.

Ted walked over to the Indian village and spoke to one of the families, telling them that any who did not have a Christmas dinner could come over for a generous helping. As he walked back, whistling, he saw them running over the snow to spread the news.

"How many should we figure on?" he wondered, stacking tin pie plates and tin mugs on the table.

"It's not like last winter on the Black," I reminded him. "You may get half a dozen who've had bad luck in their hunting."

"I told them to send the kids," he said. "Most of them look as though they could stand a square meal."

He took a look out the door to see if anyone was on the way. "My God, Bill, look! The whole village is coming! And what in thunder are they carrying?"

A long line of Indians was approaching, each carrying either a washtub or a gold pan almost as big as the tub.

"Heaven help us," sighed Ted, looking back at his moosemeat that couldn't begin to fill the first washtub in the line. "Do they think I'm giving a potlatch?"

They did. As the natives congregated outside the door, Ted grabbed a tin plate and tried to explain to them that the white man's feast would consist of a slice of meat, a spoonful of potatoes, canned tomatoes, and a helping of carrot pudding — served on this plate — and a mug of tea. There was a muttered consultation among the Indians. They seemed baffled at first and then began to register their indignation and disgust. Finally, the old chief gave a grunt, turned on his heel, and they all trooped off, one behind the other.

Ted flopped on his bunk, mopping his brow.

"Did you hear that, Bill? They expected me to give away all the food in the cabin and all the supplies in the store. That's what an

Indian does when he gives a potlatch. He gives away everything he possesses and that proves he's a great chief."

"Ted, at that rate you proved yourself a pretty small Indian," I said, shaking my head sadly.

"About as small as they come," Ted chuckled. "I don't suppose they ever saw such a miserable potlatch in their lives before."

His friendly gesture was a decided flop. Needless to say, we ate cold moosemeat, fried potatoes and carrot pudding for the next 10 days.

At that, Ted was luckier than another trader 12 years earlier. Because he refused to give them a potlatch, 80 Tanana River Indians arrived at his store bearing a 30-foot log to ram the door so they could make off with his stock. It took the threat of a loaded rifle to dissuade them.

The Indians of Mouse Point were a far less admirable lot than the honest, generous families along the Black and Porcupine Rivers. No doubt our own race was to blame. The human flotsam and jetsam that drifted up and down the Yukon River sold them whisky that drove them berserk, preyed on their traditional fondness for games of chance by tempting them to gamble away their possessions, and passed on to them the diseases that weakened them and decimated their numbers. It was the same story all up and down the Yukon.

Despite their indignation at our niggardly 'potlatch,' the Mouse Point Indians were always ready to accept small handouts from that time onward. They would hang around the store, begging for money. Ted was always giving out treats to the children, distressed to see their sore eyes and thin little bodies. One thing they seemed to crave was raw potatoes, and they would munch these contentedly, sitting on the floor of the store, filling the need for vitamins lacking in their diet. All were poorly clothed, except when the Jesuit priest, Father Jetté, came up from Kokrines with dresses, pants and shirts that had arrived from outside in the missionary barrel. For a few days after this, they looked neat and clean, but soon everything was gambled away or sold and they were back to their rags, many of them drunk and quarrelsome from the whisky they had bought.

Father Jetté's reports around this time tell of "the dirty whites" who were "flooding us from all parts." Referring to the Novakaket River (also known as the Nowi), opposite Mouse Point, he tells of a boat that "went up the Nowi after the Indians with a good load of hootch. Moral conditions are distressing." He spoke of the miners and saloon keepers as "ravening wolves."

Ted and I were drawn into a tragedy that occurred that year to two of the many white men who gambled dishonestly with the Indians of the Yukon. An ex-soldier had found himself a lucrative racket, traveling up and down the river with a mail carrier and setting up a card game with the natives at every mail stop along the route. He was a big, jocular fellow, popular with the Indians. He always won the games and went off with a stack of furs, but no one objected. Their losses only made the Indians doubly eager to save the pelts from their trapping for stakes in the next game which they were sure they would win.

One winter night the mail carrier and his pal arrived late at Mouse Point and went into the little mail shack that stood not far from our cabin. The carrier took his dogs into the shack to doctor their paws, and the card shark stayed with him to help out, since they were behind schedule and planned an early start in the morning. The former soldier lit a candle and stood it, of all places, on a can of gasoline. Then he built a roaring fire in the stove. The mail carrier poured alcohol into a dish, seated himself close to the candlelight and began dabbing the toes of one of his dogs.

Suddenly the wood in the firebox sparked with a sharp crack. The dog gave a startled bounce, striking the can and knocking the candle over. The gasoline exploded with a roar, and in an instant the whole cabin was thick with smoke and fire. Blinded and choking, men and dogs fought to escape. The men clawed at the flaming walls, frantically searching for the door and then for the tiny hole in it through which they must thrust a finger to lift the latch.

We heard their screams and the wild barking of the dogs and ran outside just as the first man fell through the door into the snow. The second staggered after him, his clothes a mass of flames. Behind them the little hut was a raging inferno. None of the magnificent dogs escaped.

We helped the screaming men to our cabin. It turned my stomach to see them under the lamplight, but I helped Ted apply oil to their terrible burns and wrap them thickly in cheesecloth from bolts in the store. Then he set out for Fort Gibbon to get a doctor, leaving me to dose the patients with whisky, the only pain reliever we had. By the time Ted got back, the faces of the men had swollen to a hideous size; and when the doctor unwrapped their hands, we saw they had been burned to blackened bone.

One of the missionaries on the Yukon said to us sternly: "It was a judgment upon them for their deception of the Indians."

THREE

That first winter was very cold. One day the temperature fell to 70 below, we heard later when checking at Rampart. We had no thermometer at Mouse Point, but we learned ways of our own to tell the temperature. Thirty below was reasonable weather in which no particular precautions needed to be taken. The dip in temperature came very suddenly, sometimes lasting only a day and then rising again to a safe 30 below. If we stepped outside and saw our breath steam out and give a faint crackle as it drifted back past our ears, we figured it was 40 below. At 50 below the steam came out stronger and gave a louder crackle as it blew back. At 60 below the sounds were a whoof of steam and a loud snapping crack that were danger warnings we dared not ignore.

It was difficult to breathe in such weather, and men and dogs who were forced to be out in it moved slowly and discreetly. The slightest movement of air was apt to freeze the skin, and we would watch each other for white patches that appeared suddenly on cheeks or nose. "Face frozen!" Ted would warn me and I would stop and rub the spot away with a handful of snow. Our footwear had to be roomy to prevent constriction and chilling, with oversize socks under our boots; better still, several layers of warm flannel cloths were wrapped loosely around our feet, the way we had worn them up the Black, with high moccasins of soft, well-tanned moose-skin laced over them.

The cold spell lasted longer than usual that year and we found ourselves near the last of our supply of chopped firewood.

81

"I'll split us a few more stove lengths," said Ted. As we stepped outside, he warned, "Take it easy. A sudden movement is dangerous in this extreme cold." We walked cautiously to the woodpile, and I stood a big block on end for Ted. He lifted his axe and struck down at the wood. A piece of the blade went flying through the air.

"Look at that, and not a mark on the block!" Ted marvelled.

I turned the chunk over and down came the axe again. Out shot another segment from the blade.

"By God," he cried, "everything's turned topsy-turvy. The block is chopping the axe!"

Even the steel blade of the axe could not penetrate a block frozen by icy air of 70 below zero. We could hear cracking and snapping sounds coming from the grove of trees in the draw; when it grew warmer again we went to investigate and found that many of the trees had split wide open.

Ted was always a great one for stories. He had entertained my brother Harry and me with them when we homesteaded by the San Juan River; here by the Yukon he whiled away the winter hours for me with tales he heard from trappers and miners who called in at his store. One of these was a murder mystery in the Yukon that had been solved the previous spring. It was strange to think of this drama taking place — unknown to us, as we suffered gnawing pangs of hunger up the Black — and coming to its close as we battled the ice floes and made our escape to Fort Yukon.

Two brothers were joint owners of a drygoods business in Skagway. Some of their customers were prospectors, many of whom held off payment until their diggings produced. It was to collect a few of these outstanding accounts from Dawson miners that one of the brothers set out around February when the trail was firm, taking a friend with him for company and for safety too, since despite efforts to clear the country of undesirables, rough characters still hung about the trails waiting to fleece the gullible with the shell game or to rob a miner headed for the towns with his poke of gold dust or nuggets. The two men made their collections in Dawson and started out for home. They never reached Skagway.

The brother who had stayed behind in the drygoods store grew fearful that something had happened to them. They were now long overdue, so he asked the Mounted Police at Whitehorse to investigate. The police checked their posts, which were set up at intervals along the river, and learned that while the missing men had called in at one, they failed to reach the next. The Mounties then searched the trail between the two posts, but heavy snow had fallen and no tracks remained to tell them where in that long expanse of trail the men might have turned off into the trees and disappeared.

The northern wilderness is vast. At any time of the year, a victim or a murderer can disappear in it and never be found. In midwinter, the task of tracking down the missing is doubly difficult. The men had vanished between two points without leaving a clue.

One incident was reported, but it seemed to have no connection with the case. A few weeks earlier, a patrolman making a routine check had noticed trail-marks leading into the woods. He thought it odd that someone should leave the main trail and flounder in deep drifts to make a path which, by all rights, should lead nowhere. And it didn't. The patrolman followed it and found that it merely made a wide semi-circle around the police post and came out again to the main trail. This was not only strange but suspicious, so the patrolman made a quick run down the trail and overtook a big, red-headed Irishman whose sled was drawn by a lumbering, slow-moving St. Bernard dog. Man and sled were searched, but nothing suspect was found except for a police blanket. He was taken to Whitehorse and booked for theft. Whitehorse reported that they could keep him for only a few months and then must set him free, since he had nothing that belonged to the missing men. The Irishman was a troublesome prisoner, demanding that his St. Bernard be tied up night and day. "I can't afford to lose a valuable dog," he complained. "Keep him roped up."

So the clue petered out, and the search was postponed until spring. But the brother in Skagway refused to give up so soon. Someone had told him that a Pinkerton man was in Skagway, waiting for the steamer to take him outside. He looked up the American detective and stated his case so eloquently that the high-priced sleuth agreed to stay over and join in the hunt.

The detective asked to be shown the route the Irishman had taken around the post, and a Mountie pointed out the place where the man and his St. Bernard had turned off the main trail. The weather had turned warmer, the snow was melting now and the trail showed up clearly. At the farthest point he had reached in the woods, the Irishman appeared to have made a halt, judging from the marks of sled and snowshoes. The detective bent over and examined the marks. He scooped up some sodden shavings and stared at them closely.

"Looks like he planned to make a fire," observed the Mountie, squatting and poking among the shavings. "Evidently he changed his mind, because none of these are charred. Maybe he heard me coming along his trail and got out in a hurry."

The Pinkerton man handed the Mountie a damp curl of shaving. "This isn't birch or spruce. Do you have much oak around here?"

The Mountie stared at the wet shaving and whistled softly as its significance struck him: there are no oak trees in the Yukon or Alaska.

Down at Whitehorse they examined the Irishman's sled minutely. It showed no sign of having been tampered with. If he was guilty, there was only one place that he might have hidden the gold. They removed the iron runners of the sled, and out of holes bored in the stanchions poured streams of nuggets. What else could it be but payment made by Dawson miners for drygoods bought in Skagway? But how could the police prove it? Their suspect stubbornly maintained that the nuggets were his own, placed in hiding for fear they might be stolen from him on the lonely trail. His word was as good as theirs unless they could connect him with the missing men. And to charge him with murder they must first find the bodies.

The snow continued to melt, and now old trails were visible everywhere. They led the searchers to cabins of prospectors, woodcutters and mail carriers, some occupied, many vacant. A thorough inspection of the vast area between the police posts would be a monumental task.

The Pinkerton man went back to Whitehorse and harnessed the big St. Bernard to a police sled. After passing the circled post, he and his Mountie co-worker let the dog walk undirected as they followed behind the sled. At a point between the two roadhouses that marked the area where the men had disappeared, the big dog hesitated, turned his huge head to look back at them and then, when they made no sign, headed off into the woods up a faint trail in the wet snow and stopped in front of an empty cabin.

Quickly the men reconnoitred. Off to one side they found spent cartridges that spelled out the method of murder; close by were ashes which contained evidence of the burning of the victims' clothes. Buttons, buckles and fragments of blackened cloth were taken for positive identification. Behind the cabin, tracks led up to the summit of a little hill, from which the murderer had likely watched for his victims to come along the trail. Branches had been lopped from trees all down the slope to permit a clear view. An empty whisky bottle lying in the snow on the hill suggested that he had stiffened his nerve for that deed that was to see him hanged in Dawson. Later the police matched axe marks on trees near the cabin with an axe on the Irishman's sled. Then came the final damning evidence: the bodies of the two victims, which had been pushed under the river ice, were recovered in the late spring.

"No wonder the murderer was so concerned about his dog and his sled," said Ted as he ended his narration and got up to shove more wood into the firebox. "The sled held his loot and if the dog was turned loose he knew it would lead the police to the evidence they needed. It goes to show, Bill, that love of money is the root of all evil and there's no sense breaking our backs to get hold of it." Robbie Burns, he philosophized, had the right words for wealth and high society and all that claptrap:

> The man o' independent mind,
> He looks an' laughs at a' that.

FOUR

Early in May the sun was warm and we went about in shirtsleeves, but the Yukon River was still frozen fast. As the days wore on, water began to form along the edge of the ice. There was perhaps 10 feet of shallow water extending from the shore to the uncovered ice, yet the ice stayed firm with no break in its surface. When the move did begin, it was an eerie sensation. The great mass started to slide past, slowly and quite silently, and still without a split to be seen.

85

"Ice moving!" I yelled to Ted.

A few seconds later the breakup began, first with a crack like a pistol shot and then a roar and a grind as ice cakes piled up at the curves in the river. There was no missing the moment of breakup, heralded by these tremendous sounds of mighty ice floes smashing one into another and shattering with an ear-splitting screech. When the jams came, the water backed up over the river bank and carried some of the huge cakes far up on the shore, leaving them stranded when the jam broke up and the water retreated and flowed on downstream.

The Indians told us it would be summer before the floes on the shore were completely melted, and this gave Ted an idea for an outdoor refrigerator. I helped him dig a tunnel into the hill behind the cabin. We went in for 40 feet, lining the interior with blocks chopped from the stranded ice.

"Now then," he said, "when the salmon come up the river, we'll store them in this ice-cold cave and we'll have spring salmon steaks all year round."

The salmon that ascended the Yukon were still splendid specimens when they reached Mouse Point. As soon as the run started, I set a net in an eddy and later paddled Ted's Peterborough canoe down to check. The floats had sunk below surface, indicating a good sized catch. Sure enough, there were two big fish swimming about in the net. By the time the leaping, thrashing salmon were clubbed and hauled with great effort into the canoe, I was exhausted and well soaked with spray. I staggered while carrying them up the bank to Ted's cabin, admittedly a bit more than was necessary since Ted was coming down and I was tempted to dramatize the size of my catch. They weighed in at 63 and 65 pounds.

Alas, as the summer wore on, the salmon rotted in our improvised refrigerator-freezer. Although ice stayed frozen in the cave, we did not know then that fish and meat must first be frozen before storing it there. While the icehouse would keep frozen food in its frozen state, it was not cold enough to perform the original freezing. After this, we fished for grayling and whitefish just before the freeze-up. I would hold one end of a seine net and walk along the bank, while Ted played out the other end as he drifted downstream. When the floats began to sink and we knew we had a load, Ted would circle toward shore and we would take out our catch, freeze it in the icy air, and store it in the cave. The fish stayed fresh well into spring.

We cured and smoked most of our salmon, adopting the Indian's method of drying them in the sun on tall pole racks, cutting the backbones partly loose and hanging the flesh over one side of the pole and the backbone over the other as a supporting hook. Beneath the racks, we built a slow fire of green branches that sent up smoke to hasten the curing. After the fish had dried out, they were stored in a cache of eight-foot-high poles with strips of birchbark for a roof. We fed our huskies from these caches, staying at the top of the ladder and throwing one fish to each dog, who wolfed it down backbone and all. The Indian dogs went even wilder with excitement at their feeding time, leaping at the ladders and snarling at each other as they fought for their share. All the huskies could tear out chunks from hard-frozen salmon or from frozen slabs of bacon, and we were horrified when the Indians told us that one of their children, who had wandered in among their dogs at feeding time, had been torn to pieces.

For several years Ted boarded over 20 dogs for owners who were making trips outside. Some of the owners never returned to reclaim them. During this time, Ted and I drove a team of 17 sled dogs on winter trips to Rampart or Fort Gibbon. But the animals were expensive to feed. We kept only three of our own: my two, Doon and Williepups, and Ted's surly yellow one which hated Indians and was hated as heartily by all the Mouse Point natives. Ted called him Perroko. He trained him to pull a sled, but Perroko did it with little enthusiasm and much initial protest. Ted talked to him in an odd gibberish intelligible only to the two of them and Perroko would respond with a lazy thump of his tail.

FIVE

With the coming of spring, Ted was ready to make a start on a new cabin and trading post and I felt strong enough to help him. We gained another hand, too, when a couple of men called in at Mouse Point. While wandering about Rampart, we had run into Jock Weir

87

and Harry Lawrence, sailors from a British battleship. Their ship, the *Royal Arthur,* had been in service in the Mediterranean Sea, hunting down Arab dhows (single-masted vessels used in the slave trade), and setting free the negroes destined for a life of slavery. When the *Royal Arthur* sailed north and docked at Victoria, British Columbia, the pair deserted ship and made for Alaska to recapture a little freedom for themselves.

Their first gold-mining venture was at a diggings near Rampart, where there was a placer mine. The method was to thaw a shaft down to bedrock through the frozen muck and gravel with the aid of a boiler and steam points and then to drift below ground. Jock and Harry worked at the bottom of the shaft, first thawing and then digging out the gold-bearing sand. Pay dirt and waste were sent up in winch-hoisted buckets. Their winch man was Rex Beach, a young student lawyer newly arrived in Alaska. They found him to be an exasperating co-worker, his head forever in the clouds as he leaned on the winch day-dreaming of the books he hoped to write about his experiences in the north.

"Wake up, there! Hoist!" they would yell up at him when the bucket stayed motionless after the first signal. "Stop making up those mushy love stories and hoist!" Reluctantly, Beach would drag his thoughts back to the job and he would shout down at the grinning men: "Laugh away! I'll show you yet that I can write!" Jock admitted to me some years later that the winch man had been less simple than they all thought when he let his mind wander from his work. Rex Beach became one of the most popular writers of adventure stories in America and two of his books about Alaska, *The Spoilers* and *Pardners,* were best-sellers of his day.

Jock Weir was the son of a skipper of one of the royal yachts in England. He was no great size, five-foot-eight, but he was a tough, wiry little man and surprisingly strong. He became an expert boxer while serving in the navy, and the part of his seaman's training which included working in the rigging of tall frigates had also given him a good head for height. We confirmed this one day while up at Fort Gibbon, the closest spot to Mouse Point for telegraph communication. We came across several soldiers gathered at the foot of the wireless tower which they told us needed adjustment to some work-

88

ing part at the very top, several hundred feet up. We watched while one of the soldiers climbed into a little seat and was hauled slowly upward. At the halfway mark he signalled frantically to be lowered and when he got out, his face was a sickly shade of green. Thereupon the navy took over. Jock volunteered his services, was hauled to the top, made the repairs, descended, pocketed his fee and walked nonchalantly away. In later years, we took a trip outside and made a stop in Vancouver. We had a swim there in an indoor swimming pool, and Jock startled everyone by climbing to the rafters in the high, curved roof and then leaping into the pool, showering spectators with a gigantic splash.

Jock Weir and Harry Lawrence soon tired of their mole-like existence at Rampart. The take was small working for wages so they left by steamboat for St. Michael to try for jobs as mail carriers. Jock remembered meeting us when we first landed in Rampart to inquire about suitable sites. He persuaded his friend to stop off at Mouse Point so he could look us up and see the post. As we sat over coffee, Ted talked with customary enthusiasm of his plans; and Jock immediately recognized in him a kindred soul with a similar desire for independence and a free life. Jock decided to stay in Mouse Point and help us with the building, whereupon Ted got out a bottle of Scotch whisky to celebrate the new partnership.

"It's the right way to live," said Jock, rocking back on his chair. "Be your own master, that's the way. I've had my fill of 'batten down the hatches!' and 'Aye, aye, sir . . . ' "

"Down the hatch!" said Ted, handing him his Scotch.

"Aye, aye, sir, and that's the only order I want to be hearing now."

Jock parted company with Harry Lawrence, who went on to Nome and became a mail carrier. Harry traveled up to Mouse Point on several occasions to urge his old seafaring chum to rejoin him, but Jock stayed with us all the time we were in Alaska. In his last years, he came out to British Columbia and bought a piece of land next to Ted's on a wild and beautiful island off the shores of the Pacific.

The high, rocky hills of the lower ramparts end just below Tanana, and the river widens again and is full of islands. There were few trees near the Mouse Point Indian village which was shut off from the upper meadows and the thin groves of dwarf spruce by a steep hill. To get our logs, we poled up to the islands where spruce and birch grew thickly. We cut the logs and peeled them, then floated them down the river to the site of the new store. They were dragged up the bank, plumbed to lie straight for the foundation and notched to take the second layer. The foot-high moss was dug up with mattocks and placed, thick and heavy, over each layer to fill the cracks left by ill-fitting logs. Where the logs came tightly together, the moss pressed itself out flat. Poles formed the roof, with lumps of moss eight inches thick laid over them. To hold the moss down, turf was thrown over it, and a large tarpaulin was drawn tightly over all to keep everything dry. We followed the same method when we built the two-roomed cabin to which Ted hoped Maude and their child would eventually come.

The store was finished that second spring, and Ted filled the shelves with stock that the Indians coveted and would trade for with their furs. Ted had a big sign made which he nailed above the door of the post. All traffic on the river could read the proud proclamation: INDEPENDENT STORE. Ted stood looking up at it with a grin of satisfaction.

"See there, Bill. Independent! That's us." He turned and pointed toward a steamboat, white and gleaming, moving up-river, barges clinging to its sides, then towards islands green with foliage and brilliant with wildflowers.

"Look at all that. And think of the game, Bill, moose, bear, rabbit, ducks, geese. What have we left to wish for? All I want now is Maude up here sharing it with me, Maude and that little toad of ours."

Ted had to admit to one flaw in his paradise — the mosquitoes. On the flat by the village they were discouraged somewhat by the river breezes, but thick swarms attacked us viciously as soon as we left the river or the sand bars and penetrated the islands or the interior tundra. Gold pans with smudge fires in them were kept burning by the door of the cabin to prevent them from drifting inside when it opened, and mosquito netting tents were draped over our beds. If too many insects gained entry despite precautions, the pans were brought inside for awhile and a contest ensued to see if the pests or ourselves would succumb first to the smoke.

Along with the mosquitoes came the tiny black flies which the Indians called "no-see-ums" and which raised a welt even more painful than the mosquito's bite. In the fall, when these pests disappeared, gnats came to plague us, descending in clouds and filling our eyes and ears. We wore veils of netting tacked to our hat brims during the worst seasons and puffed on our pipes to try to dispel them with tobacco smoke.

Zagoskin, the Russian lieutenant who explored the Yukon as far as the Novakaket in 1843, wrote feelingly of his acute suffering from the Alaskan midges and mosquitoes which he referred to as "an inevitable evil from which there was no escape." Up the rivers near the headwaters there were horse flies whose bites drew blood. Forty years later, a U.S. army lieutenant, Frederick Schwatka, said of the horse flies: " . . . at the moment of infliction it was hard to believe that one was not disabled for life."

Mosquitoes, gnats, no-see-ums and horse flies were an army that defeated many a newcomer to Alaska, who fled to the outside. But those of us who lasted out the first year learned to live with the pests in the summer just as we learned to live with the sub-zero temperatures of winter.

Struggle for Survival

"BILL, HAVE YOU EVER been up the Novakaket?" Jock Weir asked me one autumn morning.

"Only to the mouth."

"I'd like to go up a couple of hundred miles and stay there for the winter, running a trapline. How about yourself?"

I jumped at the chance.

Jock and I had been trapping up the creeks around Mouse Point during the previous winter, making out pretty well. But both of us were restless in Mouse Point, so comfortably familiar now, with Ted's ample provisions filling the shelves of the store and piled up in cache and ice-lined cave. A challenge was lacking that both of us craved. Ted was anchored to his store for most of the year, but he was content, entertained by his dog, his books and his Indian neighbors. Jock and I decided to leave at once. We would cross the Yukon and pole far up the Novakaket, the river that empties into the Yukon from the south, just above Mouse Point.

On maps of Alaska today, there is a Novakaket Slough and Island but no Novakaket River; however, it appears on some of the old maps drawn in 1898, for interested prospectors. Hudson Stuck, Episcopalian archdeacon and historian of the Yukon, writing of his voyages on the Yukon and its tributaries in the early 1900's, calls it the Nowikaket. He says that "kaket" means mouth and "na" stands for water or river, and that the Nowikaket was actually the mouth of the Nowitna River. But in our day the whole river was always referred to as the Nowikaket or Novakaket.

There were many variations in the early spelling of Alaskan place names, since most of them were known only phonetically. The Nowitna is a prime example. D. J. Orth gives these additional variations in his *Dictionary of Alaska Place Names*: Newicargut, Newikargut, Novikakat, Novi, Nowikakat, Nowikaket, Nowi, Novakakat. Mouse Point village was sometimes called Moose Point and most present day maps show this spelling. The meadows and groves above Mouse Point sheltered many kinds of rodent species. Ted made an ingenious trap from a large oil can topped with a small, baited, revolving can which caught a dozen live mice, and almost every one was a different species. One of the oddest was the long-tailed jumping deer mouse, an athletic marvel that could jump 10 feet, roughly comparable to a man's broad jump of over 100 feet.

Archdeacon Stuck tells a story involving Ted, Mouse Point and the Novakaket in his book, *Voyages on the Yukon and its Tributaries*. He says, writing of a trip downriver: " ... we come to the Nowikaket on the left bank, the river discharging into a bay or harbour. ... On the opposite shore, a little below, is Mouse Point, and I well remember a story told me by the trader at Mouse Point, a man above the ordinary intelligence, on my first visit to the place — a story which illustrates the utter neglect of Alaska by the government of the United States until a few years ago."

Ted's story, which the archdeacon repeats, was that in the spring of 1902 he went across the Yukon to the Novakaket and there on the bank of the river found the remains of an old camp, blackened by fire. Curious to know who had stayed there, he went ashore and rummaged among the debris. To his horror, he uncovered the charred body of a man, its skull hideously crushed. He searched further and found two empty gold pokes of moosehide, a clock with the Dawson dealer's name still legible and several other items, none of which revealed the identity of the man who, he was sure, had been robbed and murdered here the previous summer.

Ted brought over a couple of witnesses to view the body and had them sign a statement which he sent to the United States court at Eagle, telling of his gruesome find. The reply: nothing could be done about it. He sent a duplicate of his letter to the Department of Justice in Washington, but received no reply at all. Finally, in disgust, he dug a hole beside the ashes and buried the remains of the unknown man. No interest was ever shown by the authorities in establishing the identity of the victim or in attempting to track down his murderer.

Despite this macabre discovery, which gave the mouth of the Novakaket a haunted air, Jock and I started up the river to spend a winter in the true wilderness. We traveled in a flat poling boat, pointed at both ends and loaded with stove, traps, tent, guns and food: dried apples, pork and beans, syrup, flour, butter and tea. Cornmeal and tallow and dried fish were carried for the dogs. We made no attempt to take a year's supply. I was a pretty good hunter by now and, undeterred by hardship up the Black, was sure we could live off the land.

Part way up the Novakaket we camped overnight on a gravel bar. While we were eating our supper, a bear suddenly burst out of the willows and almost landed on top of us. We leapt up, spilling beans and tea, and the dogs jumped back, singeing their paws in the campfire and yelping and snarling in mingled pain, fear and outrage. The bear stopped short with a surprised grunt at the pandemonium, then turned tail and lumbered away up the bank.

Jock yelled at me, "Get him!" and to the dogs, "Sic 'im!" I grabbed my gun and plunged through the willows, but the dogs huddled close to Jock, rolling their eyes at him and wriggling ingratiatingly. Our dogs, unlike the Indian dogs, were always wary of all types of bear — black, brown and grizzly. A ferocious barking was the most help we could expect from them.

In this case, their noise served a purpose. It intimidated the bear, and he galloped across an open space to a large spruce tree and climbed fast to a high branch where he stayed perched, quite motionless, playing possum.

Jock came running. "Get him, Bill. He's a sitting duck."

"Jock, it's unsportsmanlike to pick him off like this. Look at him; he thinks he's safe up there."

"For the love of Pete, Bill, do you want to eat this winter or follow Marquis of Queensberry rules with a bear?"

94

"I want to eat."

I sighted, squeezed the trigger and the bear fell with a thump to the ground. We cut him up and packed most of the meat into the boat.

"We're lucky to have bear meat," Jock said, casting an anxious look at me. "It's turning cold, and bears will be hibernating soon."

"Don't worry," I reassured him. "I plan to fill our cache with meat. But that old bear had no idea we could kill him with a gun from the ground. It seemed unfair."

"You be glad he had no idea," Jock chimed in, "or he'd have high-tailed it up to the hills and we'd still be living on pork and beans."

Poling and pulling, we got our boat about 200 miles upriver and came to a little creek that ran out through the willows to the Nova-kaket. As we landed on a bar, we heard an occasional plop and splash from up the creek. We walked up, and found it full of plump whitefish swimming down through the shallow water, flopping into little pools. We built a wooden trap and caught a few. They were migrating downstream, and soon the creek would be empty as they deserted it for the Novakaket and continued on to the Yukon.

"This looks like the right place for us, Jock. Timber's a good size for cabin building, and there's enough of it to attract the marten."

"Here we stay, then."

I hoped we had chosen wisely. Once the snow came, there would be no changing our minds. For better or worse, we would be here for the next eight months.

We worked like beavers to get our cabin built before the snow began. Nights in the tent were already uncomfortably cold even with our stove burning all night while we slept. The birch and fir were smaller here than on the Yukon islands, about eight to ten inches in diameter, but still suitable for building the cabin. We followed the method used by Ted at Black River and Mouse Point, alternating poles and layers of the deep northern moss and roofing it with moss, dirt, and tarpaulin. We set up a framework of poles and whipsawed lumber for our flooring and our door.

Jock and I were still on speaking terms after our whipsawing — always a severe test of friendship. It would have taken a lot more than whipsawing to separate us. In those days, Jock was an ideal partner: daring, independent, generous to a fault, and with a wry sense of humor that made me laugh a dozen times a day. We set something of a record, Jock and I, with the long years spent together trapping and prospecting often isolated in lonely cabins for months on end. This was another cause of split-ups between partners, who grew to hate the sight of a man from whose habits and idiosyncrasies they were unable to escape. We differed in a good many ways, aside from the fact that I was 12 years his junior. I read voraciously whenever time permitted, impelled, as Ted was, to discover all that I had missed by a truncated education. Jock never opened a book but he would listen patiently when I quoted from my volumes of Dickens and Shakespeare, Hood and Gilbert. I liked their robust humor, and so did Jock.

We set up a single trapline extending 10 miles from our cabin, placing each trap where there was a grove of trees, since marten keep away from open land. At the 10-mile point, we threw up a rough little shelter without door or windows. Here we could stay overnight or seek shelter if hit by a sudden storm or a drop in temperature. We could set up our portable stove and be fairly comfortable until the weather cleared.

From the shack, we spread the line out in two directions for another 10 miles each way. We could cover either of these branch lines in a day and get back to temporary shelter or to the cabin without having to spend a night in the open. While setting up the final trap at the end of one of these diverging lines, I spotted a thin drift of smoke coming from a tiny cabin, far away in the distance and up a little rise.

"Jock, it looks like we've got neighbors," I announced when we met again at the shack. "We should take time out to pay a call on them some day."

"Wouldn't mind seeing what sort of idiots besides ourselves want to live up here."

"We're pretty snug here, Jock," I reminded him, being proud of our cabin and shacks and the good location we'd chosen.

"Snug's the word," he agreed. "Everything shipshape."

We made ourselves a toboggan, steaming the birchwood to shape the rounded front. This type of sled can be quickly thrown together for use during temporary stays up the river. Ted kept a Yukon sled at Black River because his goods were all brought there by scow, but normally these six-to-eight footers required too much room in a poling boat loaded with camping gear and food. It was wiser to build a toboggan sled at the cabin site and abandon it when taking to the river again.

There was snow on the ground, now, and freezing temperatures at night. We built a cache that rested on eight-foot-high poles, safe from prowling animals, and placed our supplies there, covering them with canvas. But much more meat was needed for two men and three dogs, and I grew uneasy when we failed to sight game on the days that we took time off to scout. I remembered the winter at Black River, and Jock remembered the tales Ted and I had told him about that time of hunger.

One night in the cabin we were awakened by loud splashing sounds from the direction of the creek. We rolled out of our blankets and ran to the door, peering out into the blackness, but we saw nothing.

"Whatever it is, I'll track it in the morning," I said, anxious to reassure him that I was not prepared to renounce hunting in spite of my sympathy for that trustful bear poised in the treetop.

"If we want full stomachs this winter we've got to fill our cache with meat," I said, thinking of Jock's caution to me then about impractical scruples.

"Yes, we'll do that. I don't fancy a diet of tea myself, like I hear you served yourselves up the Black. Tea's not something that sticks to the ribs, Bill."

Up before dawn and outside at daylight, we noticed that the willow trees near the creek had been stripped naked of twigs and leaves by a browsing animal; and we found fresh moose tracks leading off in the direction of the mountains. We went to the cabin for our rifles, leaving the dogs shut up inside to whine and yelp in frustration. The dogs were more than willing to chase this type of game, but the moose had a good start and barking dogs on his trail would only speed him up and widen the distance between us.

"I'll follow the tracks," I said. "You cut up along the creek. If he

97

turns off for the creek again and stays there awhile you may get to him first."

I shuffled along on my snowshoes at a fast trot for several hours, then settled down to a smooth, gliding walk. Ground was lost whenever the wind shifted and forced me to circle away from the tracks to keep my scent from the moose. The tracks continued toward the mountains, but the sight of occasional big cavities in the snow encouraged me; they told me the moose was taking his time and pausing often to lie down and rest. Stripped branches of dwarf birch and willow shrubs showed where he had stopped to feed, and little scoopings from the snow marked the mouthfuls he had taken to quench his thirst.

By late afternoon it was apparent that I would never get back to the cabin before nightfall. The trail would be obscured by darkness and there was a chance of losing myself and being forced to camp out in the freezing cold. I hesitated, pondering whether to abandon the chase and turn back; but then I spotted another depression in the snow. Pulling off my glove and patting the hollow, I felt a faint warmth and knew my quarry could not be far away. Cautious travel was necessary to get within range without making the big beast aware of my presence.

I was now close to the mountains. Between them was a gulch covered in brush and timber, about 20 feet wide. I slipped off my snowshoes, which would be awkward here, and strapped them on my back, then left the open ground and went into the gulch, working my way up a steep grade. Emerging from the timber, I stopped short.

A huge bull was scrambling up from the flattened snow not more than 25 feet away, near the top of the rise. Eight feet tall, with heavy, widespread antlers and shoulder hump thick with long winter hair, the moose stared at me in amazement. I whipped up my rifle and fired as he lunged away. He kept going, and I staggered after him, my feet sinking deep in the snow. It would be impossible to reach the summit without snowshoes. I stood still, forcing myself to sight carefully. My shot cracked out as the moose gained the summit. He shuddered, collapsed and lay motionless.

What a magnificent trophy! But the size of my kill, desirable for a sportsman, had its disadvantages for a hunter. The moose must be skinned and quartered quickly; the carcass was too heavy to carry back, and a night in the icy air would freeze it hard as a rock, making it impossible to cut into on the following day. Working at top speed, I got it skinned and cut up, put heart and liver in a little bag at my belt and started back along the edge of the gulch, hoping no roaming wolverine would happen on the meat. Once past my landmarks, I used the remaining daylight to head in the general direction of the creek so as to follow its course down to the cabin. Weary and half frozen, I plodded on through the night until at last a welcome sight lay ahead — the faint flicker of candlelight shining through the opaque cellophane-like rolls of material we used in lieu of window glass in our cabin.

Jock was still up, keeping the kettle boiling for my tea while planning a search in the morning if I failed to appear. He grinned with relief to see me stagger in.

"So the creature got away, Bill? I'll make us some tea. Might as well get ourselves accustomed to a tea diet."

"Well, if it's tea you prefer, I'll chuck these out." I dumped the heart and liver from my bag into a cooking pot, casting a sidelong look of triumph at my partner.

At daylight we took dogs and sled and made the long trip to bring back the moose meat. We were lucky. No marauders had stumbled upon it. Before leaving, we set two traps in the gully and threw up another overnight shack.

TWO

With this substantial stock of meat on hand, we decided it was time to pay a visit to that cabin I had seen in the distance beyond the end of our final trapline. We harnessed Doon and Williepups and a young dog named Bungo which we had borrowed from Ted, and loaded the sled with a haunch of moose meat and a supply of bait. We planned to check our lines on the way back, collect our marten and rebait our traps.

The cabin with its thin line of smoke looked lonely and forlorn as we drew near. There was no sign of life until we pulled up in front

99

of it, the dogs barking their satisfaction at the thought of rest and food after their long run. Then the door opened and a lean, middle-aged man appeared, wearing mitts and a parka.

"Hello. We're camped down by the Novakaket. Thought we'd pay a call on you and your partner."

"No partner. Had one once, but he's gone now." The man hesitated, then stood aside to let us in.

When we saw the small room, we understood the reason for his parka. His little stove gave forth only a token heat to combat the freezing temperature. The room was cheerless, furnished with a table roughly made of logs, a bunk filled with spruce boughs and covered with a ragged blanket, and a wooden box on which he seated himself while motioning us to the bunk. There were skins hanging against the wall, and he had been scraping a couple of fresh skins still lying on the table. I put the moose meat beside them and he acknowledged it with a nod and sat staring at the floor in silence. There was no sign of books or playing cards or any musical instrument. Even up the Novakaket, I had a couple of books in my packsack, and Ted had shelves full of books at Mouse Point. To occupy one's mind on the long winter evenings was not only enjoyable but a therapeutic necessity.

"You must find it lonely up here," I ventured, "with no partner to talk to and no one passing by."

The man lifted big, vacant eyes. "Some Indians came by," he said. "Some Indians came by about a month ago and they talked to me. Something strange happened when those Indians were here, something very strange."

"What was that?"

"I've been sitting here thinking every day, how strange it was. One of those Indians said to me: 'You my brother!'"

"Daresay he wanted to show you he was friendly," Jock suggested. "Some miners and trappers are afraid of Indians, you know. They don't trust the natives and they're quick to shoot if an Indian makes an unexpected move."

"No, no, he didn't say he was my friend. He said he was my brother. I've been thinking and thinking how strange it was, and now I'm thinking, why, maybe I am."

"Maybe you're what?" I asked him, puzzled.

"Maybe I *am* his brother." The vacant eyes turned from one to the other of us as we shifted uneasily on the bunk. "Maybe that Indian is my long lost brother, and here I never even knew I had a brother! Isn't that a strange thing!"

We stayed overnight with him, but we got up early the next morning and told him we had to get back to our traps.

"Come down to our cabin if you run out of food or feel the need for company," I offered, but he shook his head and seemed relieved to see us go.

"He's pretty far gone," Jock observed as we headed for our trap-line.

"If he comes out, let's hope he doesn't come out shooting. Wonder what happened to his partner?"

Up north, we called it cabin fever — the sickness that struck at men who lived alone or were isolated for long periods with only one or two companions. We had run across more than one such case. Several Indians came to Ted at Mouse Point one summer and told him of a white man who had barricaded himself in a cabin far up a creek and was shooting at anyone who passed by. Ted went with them and, sure enough, they were greeted with the crack of a rifle shot, a bullet smashing into a tree above their heads. The Indians fled and Ted leapt for shelter. Advancing from tree to tree, he got up close to the cabin and shouted out an invitation to dinner. Food was Ted's major hobby; he always believed that a good meal was a cure for most ills. He described baked salmon and potatoes and tinned tomatoes and blueberry pie with such eloquence that the man came out, unarmed, and let Ted help him pack his few possessions and take him to Mouse Point for the promised meal before he was sent down the river.

I had encountered cabin fever myself the previous spring. A wild-eyed Swede came to the post at Mouse Point and told Ted that his trapping partner had gone crazy and was threatening to kill him. Lying in his bunk at night, he had heard his partner muttering in a sepulchral voice: "Would God be pleased if I killed him? Yes, He would." The Swede said he stayed awake all night and kept a close watch on his partner the next morning until he could sneak outside and run down to the Yukon and across the spring ice to Mouse Point to ask for help.

While we listened to his story, two oldtimers came down the trail and stopped at the Independent Store. The old miners volunteered to go with the Swede and bring in his partner and I agreed to go, too. We crossed over the Yukon ice, went down-river for a distance and then up a creek for about a quarter of a mile, until we spotted a cabin perched high on the bank. We reconnoitered, keeping out of sight among the willow and birch trees. There was no sign of the partner. With guns at the ready, we crept out from cover and up the bank to the closed door. The Swede stayed well back of us. One of the oldtimers kicked open the door and we all whipped out of range with backs against the wall in western style. Not a sound from inside. We peered in cautiously and saw an empty room, clean and orderly.

"He may be out on the trapline," said the Swede. "There's a tent at the end of it, several miles up."

It was too late to go then, so we made ourselves a meal and prepared to stay the night. The two old prospectors slept in one bunk, and the Swede and I shared another.

"Do me a favor," the Swede said as I was about to climb in. "Let me sleep on the inside next to the wall. If my partner comes back in the night, he may creep in here to knife me."

"Go ahead," I agreed, and now it was my turn to lie awake all night, wondering if the mad partner would come back, and if he did, would he stop to identify his intended victim before attempting to please God by killing him.

In the morning the four of us went on a fast hike over the trail to the end of the trapline, but we found no one in the tent or near the traps. As we tramped glumly back to our cabin, feeling deflated at this tame ending to our suspense, the Swede suggested cheerfully that his partner might have fallen through a water hole in the ice.

"The fellow was loco from cabin fever," said one of the old miners as we headed for the trading post. "He never did have a partner."

"Had one and pushed him through the ice himself, most likely," said the other. "He'll have his partner's share of skins now."

"If that's so, he put on a mighty good act," I shuddered. "What a night! Every time a board creaked I thought his partner had come to stick a knife in my ribs."

Shortly after this episode, the ice went out, and any evidence of a murder, if one had been committed, was swept away downstream. The whereabouts of the vanished partner became just another of the many mysteries that remained unsolved during those early Alaskan days.

THREE

We left our unsociable neighbor pondering his Indian brother and set off for the grove of trees in the gully where we had strung out our new trapline. Coming first to the rise where the moose had been shot, we noticed that an animal had been eating the forelegs which I had hacked off and left in the snow.

"Whatever creature it was, it must have been starving to tackle those forelegs," I said. "They were nothing but skin and bone."

"Hope to heaven it wasn't a wolverine," said Jock. "If a wolverine has found our traps, he'll rip up every marten along the line."

We squatted to examine the tracks. They weren't wolverine. They looked like the footprints of a very large dog and the steps were 20 inches apart. We stared at each other in disbelief.

"Can't be a wolf," Jock declared. "No wolves around here."

"We'll soon find out. Those are wolf tracks."

Grimly we went down to our first trap. The tracks led to it, and we found the grouse-head bait gone and the trap sprung. At the second one, the big three-by-four-inch tracks, as well as blood and bits of hair, showed that the wolf had made a meal of the marten. So it went, all down the line. Two days later, back at our cabin, we saw where the wolf had circled our cache, trying to find a way up to it but foiled by its height.

"That's one meal he didn't get," Jock said with satisfaction.

"Yes, but look at the cabin roof. He got the haunch of moose meat we left up there."

We sat down in the cabin to plan our strategy. Unlike the wolverine, the wolf would not destroy in sheer delight of destruction, but much food would be needed to appease the hunger of a big wolf such as the paw prints indicated this one to be.

"He's a mature, wily animal," Jock pondered. "He's learned to rob without getting himself caught. A marten has to step on the trap to bring himself close enough to take the bait, but this wolf knows he's big enough to reach in while he's standing clear. He's familiar now with the complete run of our lines. As long as he stalks them, setting out bait is a waste of time."

"That's right. Those old wolves come to know the tricks of human hunters. We won't get him if we try trapping or shooting. We're stuck with him unless we use poison."

We had brought a bottle of strychnine with us in the event of wolverine finding our lines. This is apt to happen anywhere, as wolverine range up to 30 miles from their burrows in search of food to satisfy their rapacious appetite. Death by strychnine was the usual one meted out to marauders by northern trappers. Jock cut open a piece of moose meat, dosed it well with the poison and impaled it on a stick thrust into the snow. We went to bed hoping our problem would be solved by morning.

The next day we found the bait gone, and signs in the snow showed that the wolf had rolled about in agony before staggering off into the woods.

"That's done it," said Jock. "Our troubles are over."

We spent two days rebaiting our traps, sleeping overnight in one of the shacks and then separating to check the two diverging trails. When we met again at the shack we had a marten apiece. Things were back to normal. The following day we started down the main line, removing a marten from the first trap and rebaiting it. At the second trap there were big wolf prints in the snow and the bait was gone. A marten had been killed and eaten from the next one, and the rest of the traps had been emptied of bait. The tracks went on down to the cabin, circled it, and then led away to the woods.

"That wolf has a stomach of cast iron. He swallowed enough poison to kill him on the spot," Jock grumbled as he filled fresh bait with a double dose to take it up the line again. The next morning the meat was gone and in the snow once more were the signs of a death struggle and the uneven tracks leading into the woods.

After this, we had a week of uneventful trapping. The marten were scarce, but we caught several mink and a few ermine. The ermine skins were counted luxury furs, but the pelt was so small that the individual catch meant only 50 cents compared to three or four dollars for a marten skin. It was early January now. We took off a couple of days to go hunting for game but had no luck. Our cached meat was almost gone; we still had a small supply of beans, some dried apples and tea, and with careful rationing we would have enough flour, butter, and syrup (we hoped) to give us hotcakes for breakfast until breakup time. The temperature plummeted suddenly, but we kept the cabin warm and spent the time repairing traps and stretching skins.

The intense cold abated, and it was time to rebait the traps. Jock stepped outside and gave a yell. "Bill! Take a look at this." All around the cabin and the cache poles were wolf tracks with the same big 20-inch spread of step.

Back in the cabin, Jock reached down the strychnine.

"He's a werewolf, Bill. No ordinary wolf could stomach those two lethal doses." He cut a hole in a chunk of moose meat and poured the remaining crystals into it. "If he comes back after this dose, Bill my lad, we may as well pack up our traps for we'll know we're dealing with no wolf but something from the nether regions."

Wolf or werewolf, it was plain to us next morning that the marauder had been severely affected by the massive dose of strychnine. Besides the first sign of struggle in the snow, he had fallen several times as he staggered away, and his trail showed him headed toward the mountains.

"Jock, I'm going to follow him up. This time I'll make sure we've finished him off. He can't be far. It's a mystery to me that he was able to move at all."

Apart from the desire to end our trouble with the beast, the thought of its three nights of agony had begun to haunt me, but I said nothing of this to Jock, remembering his dumbfounded expression on the first day we had come here, when I had hesitated to shoot down that black bear from the treetop. I took an axe and started off on my snowshoes, calling over my shoulder: "Should be back in an hour's time."

I traveled fast, eager to get the job over with, but the tracks led me on and on, sometimes wavering, sometimes obliterated by signs of a fall, but always continuing toward the mountains. By noon, I had passed our overnight cabin at the forks. My confidence began to lessen. Surely it was impossible for the animal to recover again! By mid-afternoon, weary and disheartened, I was opposite the end of the left fork of the trapline. Ahead lay the wooded gulch that I had climbed through while stalking the bull moose. The tracks led up beside it over the same trail the moose had taken. At the top of the rise, in almost the very spot where the moose had received his fatal wound, I sighted the big gray wolf.

Stretched out in the snow, head on paws as though lying at ease, he looked gigantic. As I hesitated, 10 feet from him, he lifted his head and stared at me calmly with big, golden eyes. For a long moment I looked back at him, and for that moment we were only two living creatures, enmity drained from us by pain and fatigue.

"Old fellow," I spoke softly, "you put up a good fight. You're tough, all right. Don't ever give up, do you?"

I forced my mind back to my own problems. There must be no third miraculous recovery; it was the wolf's life or a profitless winter for Jock and me. Providentially, man condemns the elimination of competition only among his own particular genus in the animal kingdom. Before going closer, I eyed the wolf's length, decided prudently to make sure he was helpless and went to the gully to cut a 10-foot pole. Head on paws once more, the wolf watched me approach. When jostled roughly with the pole, he made no move, so I dropped it and advanced toward him slowly with my axe held ready. His eyes were on me as I raised the axe. Then, with a mighty blow of the butt, I stretched him out lifeless.

I took time to skin him and packed the hide back to the cabin. The big gray pelt was eventually given to Ted and belonged to him for many years. It lay on the floors of a succession of Maude's houses in various parts of the world, and two generations of children played on it, burying their faces in the long, coarse hair and stroking the hard, dry nose. Where the calm, golden eyes had shone there were only empty holes.

The wilderness permits no mawkish sentiment in the stern fight for survival. It was kill or starve for every living thing that winter; and the winter went on and on, long past the time when we expected to see the first signs of thaw that preceded the breakup of ice. Our food supplies, which had seemed so ample in January, had dwindled until only a stock of tea and dried apples remained. Jock, who had always been lean, lost 35 pounds and grew very weak. I had lost weight myself, but though ravenously hungry day and night, I still had energy enough to go hunting for game, but in vain. We cooked up a bowl of dried apples, but found that more than a spoonful doubled us up with cramps.

"Bill, have you ever tried cooking rawhide?" Jock asked one morning.

"No, but I've heard of lost trappers and prospectors who boiled up their leather thong shoelaces or snowshoe webbing, even their shoe leather. Do you think we've come to that?"

"Who said anything about shoelaces? We've still got the hide of that moose you shot. Let's give it a try." He fished up the hide from a snowbank, thawed it out, cut strips from it and set them to boil.

Before long, a sickening stench arose, forcing me to go out for air. Jock persisted until the mixture had boiled down to a kind of evil-smelling glue; then he dipped his spoon in and took a mouthful. He came staggering from the cabin to join me, hawking, spitting and retching.

"Let 'em keep their damned moosehide stew," he spluttered, emptying the rest into the snow. "I'll fast like a monk before I try that garbage again!"

It was late in the spring before the thaw came. Behind our cabin there was a meadow that gradually pooled with water and every day we sat outside our door, shotguns ready, watching for the coming of the ducks. For two weeks, now, our diet had been stewed apples and tea. One morning we saw a duck flying down the river. It turned and headed straight for the pool, and I seized my shotgun and brought it down. It was a skinny little bird, in much the same condition as ourselves, but we plucked and dressed it and boiled it to make a nourishing soup for men and dogs.

After the coming of this pathetic harbinger of spring, we kept our shotguns at hand. Finally, one early dawn, we heard the crying of geese and leapt from our bunks. High in the air, two geese were circling about, looking down at the meadow. Shaking with excitement, I threw back my head and imitated the call of a goose. It sounded more like the croak of a raven, but one of the birds circled closer. I fired, and a big Canada goose crashed down into the wet snow. Calling mournfully, its mate wheeled away over the trees.

Our long fast was over. A few days later, more ducks came and we got three. We lived on these until the ice broke and we were able to pack our gear and furs into our boat and set off down the Novakaket behind the ice cakes. We had 50 to 60 marten skins and a few mink and ermine, as well as the big wolfskin, to show for our winter's work. Our food was gone, and we paddled down as fast as the ice would permit to get back to Mouse Point and a square meal. At one of the forks we met a couple of men coming from the other direction and were given some bacon to keep us going.

We stopped on a bar at the mouth of the Novakaket to fry strips of bacon impaled on willow twigs. Jock stood looking at the mingling waters of the two rivers and the ice cakes, which were fewer now and scattered.

"How about a swim?" he shouted, as he ripped off his clothes and plunged into the icy water.

"You're mad, Jock!" I hollered. But not to be outdone, I stripped and dived in, too, coming up shocked and breathless. I got out fast and made a run for the warmth of the fire, climbed into my clothes and stayed shivering by the flames as I watched Jock dodging with frantic speed among the drifting ice cakes, uttering wild war whoops as he swam.

Maude at Mouse Point   5

ONE

TED WROTE CONSTANTLY to Maude, pleading with her to come to Mouse Point. He told her about the fine home he had for her and of the success of his trading post. She refused to come.

"How does this sound?" he asked me, as he read from the latest letter he had composed after much brain searching for some new attraction to lure her to Alaska. He had described the wonders of the wide Yukon and the beauty of the passing steamboats with their stern wheels churning its waters, of the colorful wildflowers, the fish and game, and the soft, shining furs that he collected from the Indians.

"You won't get her here by writing about flowers and fish and Indians," I said, knowing my sister so well.

"What shall I say, then?"

I hesitated to give my advice, feeling it would make me a traitor to Maude, but Ted's mournful eyes decided me.

"Tell her about the army post."

"Fort Gibbon? Why on earth would Fort Gibbon interest her?"

"It wouldn't. Don't describe it. Just say there's an army post up-river from us. Don't say how far up." I remembered how Maude's eyes would sparkle when she described the military balls to us in Victoria. If she should imagine the personnel of this isolated army post leading the social life of military units in the capital city, could we be blamed for that?

I'm sure it was the army post that did it. Maude wrote back that someone had told her about Fairbanks and Dawson; how there were gay times sleighing in the snow and attending dinner parties and balls put on by various clubs. She even anticipated formal teas and receptions. Maude always needed a stage and an appreciative audience, however small. All in all, she seemed reassured that life in Alaska would be less dull than her brief encounter with Fort Yukon had led her to believe.

We would have to wait, however, while she made herself a new suit with velvet buttons and a velvet collar to match her pillbox hat, and sewed a traveling dress of scarlet serge for little Margaret in the new Buster Brown style with sailor collar and low-slung belt. She sounded eager, now, for the new adventure, and confident that she would conquer hearts and win new friends.

Maude and Margaret were seasick on the 2500-mile trip to St. Michael, but they recovered as soon as they set foot on dry land.

In those days, St. Michael was a treeless island covered with tundra, its only growth a proliferation of company stores, warehouses, machine shops, a hotel and a few of the old log buildings left over from the Russian occupation. Indians and Eskimos were everywhere: paddling about the waterfront in their canoes, trudging single file along the boardwalks, crowding the stores to sell or trade their baskets and carvings.

Outside the trading post, Maude saw a row of Indian babies, strapped to carrying cradle-boards. They had been left propped against the wall like fat little dolls displayed for sale. Their hands were held securely under their blankets by the straps, leaving them at the mercy of swarms of flies that hovered over them and lit in clusters on their noses, cheeks and foreheads. None was crying in protest, but Margaret ran to them and tried vainly to brush the persistent insects from the small, solemn faces.

Maude was always quick to make friends. By the time they left the store to board the river steamboat, she was the center of a group of men and women eager to listen to her lively chatter. She settled herself in the lounge, surrounded by her new admirers and quite content, with no desire to go on deck and watch the steamer progress around Stuart Island to the delta, where the Yukon enters the sea through many mouths. True, the delta is always a dismal sight, treeless and flat, with driftwood piled high on the moss-covered shore. Here the river, dark with silt from the steady undercutting of its banks and from the powdered shale and volcanic ash of glacial streams, deposits its load on the wide flats that stretch out to the Bering Sea. No open-sea vessels can enter these shallows; even the riverboat can only enter by way of Aphoon, the deepest of the fingers that spread out at the tip of the mighty Yukon. But the river widens as the boat passes Andreavski and Holy Cross, and the shores and islands were green with timber and bright with wildflowers when Maude traveled by. Human companionship, however, had infinitely more appeal for her than scenery that, magnificent as it might be, was inanimate and unresponsive.

She was somewhat miffed, we learned, by another small, completely masculine court that had attached itself to an attractive young woman at the opposite end of the lounge. Little Margaret ran over to investigate and was swept into a fragrant embrace. She looked up to see rosy lips that parted to reveal sparkling diamonds set in the center of each of the young woman's two front teeth. Maude called her child back and forbade further wandering to the far side of the room.

"She was a dance-hall girl," Maude told us, disdainfully, but intrigued by her contact with iniquity. "She invested her earnings in diamonds and had them set into her teeth!"

"Sensible girl!" Ted said approvingly, "Bank failures won't faze her and she can flash her wealth around and never worry about someone lifting her roll."

More than one dance-hall girl of the north wore diamonds in this way. The most famous of these was Diamond Tooth Gertie of Dawson, in the Yukon, who won partial acceptance of the town's respectable women when she married a lawyer and was invited to a reception at Government House.

The boat trip sounded no warning for Maude of the primitive life that lay ahead for her. The big river steamboats were far more luxurious than the larger sea-going vessels on the coast. Staterooms, lounges, card and smoking rooms were panelled, painted and furnished as elegantly as the rooms and suites of a first class hotel. The luxury extended into the dining room, with its silver and Irish linen and white-jacketed waiters. It was incongruous transportation, up a river through land that was uninhabited for hundreds of miles at a stretch — transportation used largely by trappers and prospectors bound for the most primitive of living quarters. On the other hand, some of these prospectors were to sail down-river again with vast fortunes in their pokes and the best of accommodation was none too good for them in their hour of affluence and mood for celebration.

Most of Maude's new-found friends were bound for Tanana, or were to change there to a smaller steamer and go up the Tanana River to Fairbanks. But they were all curious to see Mouse Point, and we saw Maude on deck surrounded by them when we came down to the landing spot to welcome her. She was gazing up-river, looking for the town she had expected to find — a town full of sociable people and young army officers eager to waltz the night away. When the whistle blew and the steamboat maneuvered for a landing, she looked down and saw us. She took in the narrow flat with 10 Indian huts straggling along it, backed by a steep hill with the Indian graveyard topping it; and Ted's two modest log cabins, between which about 20 dogs were chained, all of them barking insanely. This comprised the "town." Her bright smile grew fixed and I knew, from the way her eyes flashed, that we were in for a rough time.

Ted saw only the smile and the sparkle as Maude stepped down the gangplank. He lifted Margaret onto his shoulders and carried her, squealing and clutching his head, as he walked beside Maude, swinging her straw suitcase and whistling contentedly. Jock and I followed, lugging the trunk — a vast contraption with a high, rounded lid.

No one could talk while the dogs howled and barked after the departing steamboat. They were a menagerie that Ted had arranged to board during the summer months, and an unfortunate choice as a musical reception committee. As we reached the cabin, Margaret stared in wonder at the jungle of flowers Ted had planted out in front: sunflowers eight feet tall, bright blue bachelor's buttons, larkspur, poppies of every hue, all growing together in luxuriant confusion. But Maude swept down the path, ignoring dogs and flowers, into the cabin and through to the bedroom. Ted followed her in, expecting to hear a delighted outcry when she saw the white-painted iron bed and the Morris chair colorfully upholstered in red flowered material. These he had chosen to satisfy the vagaries of feminine taste. Masculine comfort had dictated the enormous range, the cot, the rough table and the plain chairs which crowded the second room that served as a combined parlor-kitchen.

There were outcries, all right, but not of delight. Back and forth from bedroom to kitchen Maude swept, eyes flashing with fury as she pointed to log walls dripping with moss, to the absence of cupboards, dressing table and plumbing; and through the window to the unkempt Indian huts and a couple of squatter's tents instead of the town full of friendly people she had expected to see. She had been cruelly deceived, she cried, lured into a primitive hovel with false tales of a comfortable home, entertaining neighbors and a life of plenty. When she realized that Ted considered the cabin a comfortable home, found entertainment in the squatters and Indians, and felt his well-stocked trading post represented plenty, she was exasperated to the point of tears.

"I'll change everything, Maude," Ted consoled her anxiously. "You shall have whatever you want. Up in Fairbanks and Dawson the women cover their log walls with muslin and they paste wallpaper over the cloth. How would you like that? I'll bring over boxes from the store to make you a dressing table and cupboards, and I'll get you fur robes of muskrat and bear to spread on the floors and the bed. You won't recognize the place when I'm through with it. See this bed, Maude? You'll sleep in the only bed with a spring mattress within the radius of a hundred miles. And look at the glass in these windows. You won't find many cabins here with glass windows. And these are set with double panes, so that only the outer pane frosts over.

"Besides all these comforts, Maude, you have something that's seldom seen around here: a real door shipped up from Seattle."

He explained the customary procedure of making doors from whipsawed lumber, and we were relieved to see her tears gradually cease to fall and her chin lift up with renewed pride. Social status, after all, is only relative.

By the time Ted had cooked and served us a good dinner, Maude was more cheerful. She was eager to start the transformation of the cabin.

"Come over early in the morning," she commanded me as Jock and I started off for our assigned quarters in the woodcutter's cabin. "I want you to help me choose material." I doubted that she would take my advice, but I imagine she clung to me as a part of the life she had known back in civilization and I felt guilty enough about the false picture of Mouse Point that I had helped to give her, to want to please her when I could.

I turned up obediently in the morning and went with Ted and Maude and little Margaret to the trading post. There were masses of flowers here, too. Ted's flowers were a puzzle to the Mouse Point Indians. One old woman who paused to admire his flourishing vegetables pointed to the flowers, shaking her head.

"No good to eat. Why you plant? Just for look-me-ats?"

After that, whenever Ted brought flowers to brighten the house, he would announce to us happily: "Very nice for look-me-ats!"

Maude failed to see the flowers. She was transfixed with horror by Ted's huge sign.

"Why must it be so large? Why not say *post*? *Store* is so prosaic and plebian!"

"What's wrong with my sign?" Ted protested. "How will travelers on the river know this cabin is a store unless they see my sign?"

"Don't say that word! You have a *post*. No gentleman has a store!"

"I'm a gentleman, am I?"

He hardly looked the part, with work shirt open at the neck and suspenders showing nakedly on top of it.

"Of course you are! Madge says your father never worked a day in his life."

Ted shook with mirth at this English legal definition. By its terms, there were certainly no gentlemen in the wilds of Alaska. "When Adam delved and Eve span, who was then the gentleman?" he demanded, grinning, as he led us into the trading post.

Maude had not spent a winter of near starvation up the Black River or the Novakaket, so the shelves piled high with tinned goods were not a symbol of security for her as they were for the rest of us. But she was pleased when Ted pointed out English jams and jellies, hams and bacon and bottled figs, barrels of pickles and candy, and even pickled pigs' feet — all imported to tempt her appetite and please her child. He had put himself deeply in debt to stock the store with them, and only a generous cheque from his father in England had kept him from foundering.

These luxuries were for us and were seldom bought by the Indians or the trappers. Trappers were satisfied with plainer fare: flour, potatoes, beans, rolled oats, candles and tobacco. This diet though often brought on a craving for tinned tomatoes or fruit and men would sit on the steps of the store upending can after can. Ours were not the inflated prices that had shocked me in Dawson, but of necessity they were high in comparison with prices outside. Ivory soap was 20¢ a bar, a pound of ham cost 45¢, apples and prunes were 25¢ a pound and a gallon of maple syrup sold for $3 — each item about four times the price advertised in Vancouver.

Only one customer, a Mr. Eaton, settled his bill that year, and Ted wrote "Paid" in his ledger with a triumphant flourish that showed it was an unusual event. He sold very little for cash and he gave away hundreds of dollars in supplies to grubstake prospectors and miners who seldom returned to settle accounts. It was the fur trade that kept him going; he was, in fact, more of a fur trader than a storekeeper, and might well have pleased Maude by calling his place of business a post.

We came back to the cabin laden with wooden boxes and bolts of material. Maude liked the soft effect of the muslin which Ted pasted to the walls and ceiling. She decided against wallpaper because it would have to be ordered from outside. Pictures and photographs were tacked up, fur rugs were spread on bed and trunk and floor. Ted placed a box under a mirror, and Maude busied herself with her needle, making a little skirt for the box out of pale blue silk and a gathered overskirt of dotted Swiss. All around the mirror frame she tucked dance programs with slim gold pencils dangling from them, souvenirs of her happy days with Madge and

Ernest. She had even brought up her engraved invitation to Miss Maude Walker to attend the lieutenant-governor's reception in honor of the Earl and Countess of Aberdeen. These were talismans with which she surrounded herself to ward off the wilderness. She opened her trunk one day and showed me a pale green velvet cloak, trimmed with swansdown, that Madge had given her for balls in Victoria, and an ivory fan that had been the gift of one of her beaux, a lovely thing of filigreed ivory and ruffled lace. Remembering the letter I had helped Ted to compose, I felt a stab of remorse when I saw them. God knows she would never use them at Mouse Point.

It was the absence of friendly neighbors that Maude found the hardest to endure; social intercourse was as necessary to her as the air she breathed, but at Mouse Point there was no one who could satisfy her needs. She once crocheted half a dozen dainty lace collars and gave them to Ted to display in his store.

"They are *not* to be sold to Indians — only to clean, respectable white women," she instructed him, and wondered why he chuckled. The little collars lay on a shelf, gradually turning gray with dust and age. Only one white woman besides herself set foot in the village during the years she lived there. On that memorable day a rowboat landed and a white woman climbed ashore. The stranger was a botanist, studying the hundreds of varieties of Alaskan wildflowers. She spent the afternoon strolling with Maude in the meadow beyond the hills sketching dozens of flowers that were new to her, while Maude, indifferent to the plants that excited the visitor, poured out the story of her miserable existence in the Indian village. When the woman rowed away up the river, Maude watched her go with the anguish of a castaway who sees a passing ship sail on, oblivious of signals of distress.

THREE

In earlier times, the Athapaskans of Alaska's central plain were nomadic hunting tribes who moved to new locations when their villages became polluted. Now, many of them found it profitable to stay in one location and make a living from the white men around them. The Mouse Point Indians had ceased to be migratory except during the fishing season, but they kept a nomadic attitude toward their living quarters. There was a time when they obeyed a strict code that forbade river pollution, but the old laws were slipping away from them under the influence of an alien race, and the white man's habit of dumping refuse into the river was not one to inspire sanitation.

Whether or not the white man was to blame, the fact remained that the Yukon Indians for the most part were dirty, decadent and diseased. Maude tried vainly to keep her daughter from them, terrified of infection and corruption. During the summers in particular, she forbade Margaret to wander near the Indian cabins, believing that germs were more potent in hot weather. The stench certainly was more powerful then. Men, women and children relieved themselves outside their cabins, as uninhibited as their savage, shackled dogs. Ted had built a sturdy two-holer near his cabin, and the Catholic priests would point it out to the Indians and urge them to build themselves sanitary privies. The natives found the idea highly comic, and garbage and excrement continued to accumulate around their houses until rain and snow dissipated it to some extent during the winter months. Adding to the foul odors were the corpses of Indian dogs left to rot in the creeks and bushes. We were always running across them.

A few squatters threw up tents during the summer on the bank near the trading post. Most of them stayed only a few days and then sailed on to the goldfields and were never seen again by us. One squatter who returned regularly each year to Mouse Point was Ruby Smith, so-called after he discovered shining red stones while panning for gold. He collected a stack of them, thinking that he had found a bonanza of precious gems, only to learn that they were false rubies, or red garnet, of little commercial value. Red garnet, however, is often concentrated with gold, and its brightness serves as a guide to the yellow metal. Ruby gained something from his find: his nickname was also given to the creek in which he had discovered his red stones.

Ruby always pitched his tent a few yards from Ted's cabin. He was a 'squaw man' who lived with a young, tubercular Indian girl named Ellen. During the first summer that Maude spent in Mouse

Point we would see Ellen standing outside the tent day after day, gazing wistfully at Margaret as she played among Ted's flowers. She was little more than a child herself, poor Ellen. Margaret was forbidden to go near the tent for fear of infection, but sometimes, when solitary play palled, she sat on the cabin steps and stared back with curious interest at the Indian girl.

One day Ruby Smith came to the cabin door and asked Maude's permission for Ellen to take Margaret berry-picking. "She loves that child, ma'am," he said. "She watches her all the time. Ellen's a good girl. She won't teach her anything bad."

Maude's soft heart often got the better of her resolution. She was torn, now, between pity and her protective duty. The sight of Ellen's small, lonely figure lingering shyly by the tent finally decided her. "Run along, then," she directed Margaret, adding distractedly, "but stay outdoors when you're with Ellen, and don't breathe deeply!"

Margaret was with Ellen every day during the berry season. Ellen led her up the bank to the birch groves and showed her how to strip bark from the trees to make long cylinders pinned with twigs and stopped up at the bottom with chunks of moss. They climbed the hills, and Ellen showed her where to find blueberries to fill the cylinders. When they came home, Margaret always took Ellen into the garden and gathered a bunch of flowers for her, telling her their names. Ellen loved flowers. When Margaret was called inside, Ellen would give us her shy smile and walk slowly back to the tent, her hands filled with golden poppies and blue cornflowers.

FOUR

Ted by now had cornered the trade of the Mouse Point Indians. The commercial companies grew aware of this independent trader who had corralled for himself the furs that previously had gone to them. The Northern Commercial Company, an offshoot of the original Alaska Commercial Company, retaliated by sending competition in the person of a young man named Miller. He and his wife arrived one fall and occupied a log building several miles downriver from Mouse Point. It did nothing to lessen Ted's dislike of the big trading companies, and he was fiercely triumphant when, after a brief struggle, his rival admitted defeat the following spring and sailed away with his wife and the violin that he had played to relieve the monotony of his lonely days in the empty store. Despite the fiasco of Ted's dinner party that first Christmas, the Indians had come to accept him as their friend. They brought him their furs and depended upon him for supplies and for solutions to many of their problems.

Maude was less popular with the Indians. They sensed her dislike of them, and they could not understand why Ted and I waited on her hand and foot. They felt she must have some sort of supernatural power that we respected. We did our best to help Maude and keep her happy, much the way one cossets a caged bird, having denied it freedom. But there were times when we had to be away, Ted to market his furs and Jock and I to tend our traps. Maude and her child remained alone in the cabin, making out as best they could.

One winter we were away for a week, and Jock and I got back just as Ted came down the trail with his dog team. We went into the cabin and found Maude sitting at the table. She was wearing her velvet cloak with the swansdown collar and playing idly with her little ivory fan, fanning herself and clicking it open and shut.

"What are you dressed up like that for?" Ted asked her.

"Old Joseph was here this morning. He threatened me." She seemed more indignant than frightened.

"What happened?"

"After breakfast, Margaret went out to play with the boys." (Fred and Neketla, two little Indian boys, had become Margaret's closest friends and came up to the cabin every morning to play with her.) "I was in the bedroom, trying on my cloak when I heard a loud banging on the cabin door, too loud to be the children. I ran to open it, and there on the doorstep was old Joseph. He nearly fell over when the door opened so suddenly. I told him you were away and there was no money for him, and he shouted at me to get out of Mouse Point. He said I kept the rabbits away and all the Indians were hungry and I was to blame."

"There aren't many rabbits this year," Ted agreed. "Was it your fault, Maude? What did you do to them?"

119

"Don't be foolish. It wasn't funny. That dirty old man stood there with his oily hair hanging about his shoulders, threatening me! The children came running up to listen. Joseph was chewing tobacco, and suddenly he spat out a stream of filthy juice, all over the steps and over the front of Margaret's caribou parka."

"The devil he did! I'll cook his goose for that!" Ted tried to hold and comfort her, but she jumped up to show us how she had answered the Indian.

"I stamped my foot, like this, and called him a wicked old man. I pointed with my fan at the hill behind the cabin and told him I would talk to the ghosts in the graveyard up there and tell them to come down and punish him for what he had done."

Arm held high in a menacing manner, she must have looked to him like a female shaman in her cloak of velvet and swansdown, the clicking ivory fan her shaman's rattle.

"He whipped out a big hunting knife from his belt . . . "

"No! My God, Maude, what did you do?"

She lowered her arm and sat at the table again, fanning herself and looking over the top of the ivory sticks at our open-mouthed distress.

"Before I had time to do anything, Joseph leaned over and scraped the tobacco juice from Margaret's parka and from the steps. Then he walked off down the trail."

"Good for you, Maude," I said. "You gave him a worse fright than he gave you."

"He glared at me in such a nasty way as he left," she complained.

"I don't like it, Bill," Ted said, frowning. "Twenty years ago, Indians murdered a storekeeper's wife down on the Tanana because they thought she was bad medicine for them."

Maude shrugged. "I'm not afraid of them."

"Maude, sometimes it's wiser to be frightened and keep out of danger," Ted cautioned.

We stayed close to home for several weeks after this, or took care to be absent only at separate times. Maude showed no concern; she was never afraid of the Indians. But she thrived on affection and admiration. The hostility of some of the natives was a sore point with her. She chalked it up against them as further evidence of their ignorance and bad taste.

One day the next summer a young boy came running to Ted's cabin. He was speechless with excitement and fear, but finally he got control of his tongue and begged Ted to come and help his people because a strange devil had been washed up into the shallows of an eddy, and all of them were terrified to go near it. We ran down the bank and found a young whale that had been washed ashore. It may have been a beluga, for this species often travels up the Alaskan rivers, though not this far, according to the natives, who had never before seen such a creature.

Maude, who had come down with us, suddenly spotted old Joseph among the Indians. Evidently she decided this was a good opportunity to establish her prestige and lessen his hostility, for she sailed over to him and said triumphantly: "You see, Joseph, I bring you luck. I bring you this big whale to eat, so it is a good thing for you that I came here."

"Maude!" Ted beckoned her back. "I wouldn't tell them you brought it here if I were you. They think it's a devil and won't even feed it to their dogs."

Our own dogs feasted on chunks of whalemeat for some time, but the Indians after that looked with redoubled suspicion upon Maude, the bad luck woman who had summoned a devil from the waters of the Yukon.

FIVE

Our nearest white resident at this time was the Jesuit priest, Father Jules Jetté, who had taken charge of the mission and the tiny school at Kokrines, the Indian village six miles down-river from Mouse Point. In the Jesuit tradition, Father Jetté was a literate scholar who was widely read and willing to discourse on many subjects. His research on the dialects of the Athapaskan Indians along the Yukon is widely known. There were so many variations of the dialect in those days that Indians living within a two-day journey from each other could only converse in sign language or in the English they had learned from the white man.

I doubt if there was a single soul up or down the Yukon who did not admire and respect this dedicated priest, including Ted, though he had been so overexposed to revivalist religion in his youth that he now called himself a skeptic. But Father Jetté, though deeply religious, had a realistic attitude toward conversion and allowed the Indians to retain some of their traditional ways. In this he was much like the sixteenth-century Jesuit, Mateo Ricci, who believed that mankind's varied customs should be respected whenever possible and that his own converts in China should be permitted to worship their ancestors. Several times while we were at Mouse Point, Father Jetté was called up to conduct a funeral, and we watched him performing the Catholic rites and then standing by patiently as the Indians heaped the grave with pots and pans, clothing, tools and weapons for their dead to use in the spirit world. Too sudden and complete a severing of their old beliefs often set them adrift, bereft of the old and without comprehension of the new. This was the mistake made by many of the west coast missionaries whose zeal led them to burn totem poles and potlatch masks with no understanding of their true significance.

One day we took Maude and Margaret down to Kokrines to meet the priest and see the schoolhouse. The school had been built for the Indians, but the natives took little interest in it. Margaret was fascinated by the miniature building which had a brass bell on top and a long rope hanging from the bell.

"Pull it," said Father Jetté, "and see what happens."

She made it ring out with a fine clamor and, as the sounds died away, one small Indian boy came running from the village, scuttled inside to a seat, pulled out a book and sat fluttering the pages. It was, Father Jetté said ruefully, about the usual size of his classes here. In the residential schools, of course, where children were separated from the habits and traditions of their parents, the church made better educational progress.

As soon as Margaret got back to Mouse Point, she rounded up several little Indian children and sat them on the floor of the trading post while she recited nursery rhymes and supervised the use of crayons, all in imitation of Father Jetté. She was more successful than he in capturing pupils, perhaps because she began and ended the lesson with a stick of candy from the big barrel beside the counter.

When Ted was absent from the trading post for any length of time, the two young Brothers who worked with the priest were sent up regularly by him with loaves of bread baked at the mission; and whenever clothing and school supplies arrived from outside for the use of his flock, a selection of coloring books, crayons and small religious pictures was parcelled and delivered to Margaret.

Opening a parcel was always a big event at Mouse Point, especially in early fall when boat deliveries ceased and the river ice was still too soft and treacherous to permit local delivery by dog team. We were more isolated at such times than in the depth of winter, and the first sight of the black-robed young men approaching over the snow was heralded with delight. Margaret would hop about in an agony of suspense while Maude sorted the religious pictures judiciously. Those that showed Jesus and Mary were permitted as acceptable to Anglicans, and Margaret went off with them to paste them on the walls of her doll's house, but bleeding hearts smacked of popery and were consigned to the flames of the kitchen stove.

Neketla

6

"IT'S FRED AND NEKETLA!"

Every morning there was a knock on Ted's cabin door, and there on the doorstep stood the two little Indian boys, Fred and Neketla. They were favorites with Ted, who had given them the freedom of the cabin before Maude came to Mouse Point. They were reasonably clean, healthy youngsters, and polite to us, but no Indians were permitted now to set foot in Maude's muslin-draped bower. They stayed outside with Maude's child in the area around the cabin and the trading post to which her play was restricted.

I came up one morning to talk to Maude, as I did whenever work permitted. Ted had gone to his store to take stock. She was standing by the window, watching the three children who knelt by a toy fishrack Ted had made for them, pretending to sun dry minnows that the boys had caught in the creek, and then tossing them to Curly. Curly was a good-natured mongrel dog whom Ted had taught a number of tricks to entertain the children, and he was wolfing down the unappetizing tidbits in an obliging manner.

"Look at them," Maude said resentfully. "Margaret will be an Indian like the rest of them if she stays here much longer."

The children caught sight of her at the window and ran up and stood below it, smiling up at her.

"Bill, come here," she summoned me in an altered tone. "Look there. Look at Neketla's eyes. They're blue — the same light blue as Ted's."

"The Yukon Indians are a pretty mixed race," I explained. "Most of them are half-breeds now. Neketla's brother Fred is the son of a trader up-river."

The trader openly acknowledged his son and came down to visit him sometimes, encountering no animosity from the Indian husband of Fred's mother. We all liked Fred. He was a handsome, dark-eyed boy with aquiline features, quick-witted and even tempered, a shining exception to the usual run of Indians on the Yukon. With Margaret, he was always gentle and patient as he taught her to fish or to shoot the small crossbow that her father had made for her.

Maude opened the cabin door. "Neketla, come in here. The rest of you stay outside." She shut the door after him and went to her sewing basket and took out her tape measure. "Here, you may play with this." He squatted on the floor, examining it with interest and trying to fathom its use.

"Look up, Neketla!" The child raised large blue eyes to hers, and she stared at him intently until he bent his head again over the mystery of the tape measure.

"Maude, you can't think . . . " I began as she took the tape measure from Neketla.

"That's enough. Run outside now." She shut the door again and turned to face me, eyes big with import.

"What else am I to think?"

When Ted strolled in, unsuspecting, the storm broke.

"Maude, what on earth! Why pick on me? They say four white men at the least fathered Neketla's brothers and sisters."

"And Neketla is yours!"

"He isn't, but I wish he was."

"You deceived me once before," she said bitterly. "You told me I was coming to a comfortable home and friendly people. Why should I believe you now?" She disappeared into the bedroom, slamming the door behind her.

"Now, what started all that?" Ted wondered.

For several weeks Maude brooded over her suspicions. I thought them a symptom of cabin fever induced by her loneliness.

"Maude," I told her, "you've got to get this out of your mind.

125

You're making yourself miserable over something that only exists in your imagination."

"It's the name as much as anything," she said. "It would be like Ted to call his child Neketla when all these Indians call their children by their English names."

I never did believe that Ted had fathered Neketla, although it was obvious that he loved the boy dearly. But Ted gathered children about him wherever he went. In time, Maude's attitude softened, but she never again let Neketla into her cabin.

We tried to lead her thoughts away from her grievances. Ted came back from a trip to Tanana with an ancient phonograph that he had bought from an Alaskan who was departing to a kinder climate. It had a blue horn like a big morning-glory from which there emerged a wheezing, squawking version of a dance tune when Edison's old cylindrical record was played. Maude was delighted with her toy. She tried to teach Ted to dance but had to give it up as hopeless. Here, too, Ted showed independence. He preferred to hop about doing an odd solo dance in double time to quavering chords from an accordion hung about his neck. Maude then seized on me as a substitute and often sent for me to come up from the woodcutter's shack to learn the intricacies of ballroom dancing. She was impatient with my slowness, but in time I learned to waltz well enough to satisfy her. The store was our ballroom. Margaret would perch on the counter while we circled the room, whirling and dipping and colliding occasionally with Ted and his accordion as the cylinder turned and the cracked voice sang:

> Waltz me around again, Willie,
> Around, around, around,
> Waltz me around again, Willie,
> Don't let my feet touch the ground.

I played a banjo, but the only place Maude would let me play it was in my own cabin. She said it sounded terrible. I never learned to play more than one piece at all well but got great pleasure from plucking the strings and singing "Tis the last rose of summer, left blooming alone . . . " while Jock Weir smoked his pipe and endured it all without complaint.

126

The anniversaries of childhood always offered an excuse for Maude to relieve the monotony of her life at Mouse Point. On Christmas Eve, she built up suspense by reciting "A Visit from Saint Nicholas," and on Christmas morning the tree was ceremoniously revealed, gayly decorated with paper chains and strings of cranberries. Ted dressed himself in a costume made from red flannel and cotton batting and doled out presents from a flour sack.

Ted was patient and ingenious at constructing these gifts. He bought a lathe from a departing jeweller and turned out all sorts of objects from the ivory of walrus and mammoth tusks dug from the riverbank. Dark brown mammoth ivory was often found imbedded in the Yukon's banks and Ted once discovered an enormous mammoth tooth. (Maude took this with her when she went outside and sold it to a dentist for display in his waiting room.) Fat little billikin idols, rings, manicure sets, chessmen, and tiny dolls' dishes and knives, forks and spoons were carved with painstaking care. Ted made gold nugget rings and brooches for Margaret and her dolls, and Maude sewed dresses for the dolls and trimmed them with bits of ermine fur. Margaret waded in the river shallows beside a toy steamboat propelled by the workings from a clock. Toy canoes were shaped from birch bark like the Yukon Indian canoes, and a wooden pirate, carved from driftwood, wore a wig of black bearskin fur. Ted made bows and arrows and a miniature crossbow and a little metal crown with a round stone of quartz set into it which Margaret believed was a magic star. Maude encouraged talk of fairies and magic, welcoming an escape from the reality of Mouse Point.

Ted dropped in on Jock and me one winter evening on his way back from the creek. "Come with me to the cabin," he said. "Help me to persuade Maude and Margie to come up the creek with me. I have a surprise for them."

Fred and Neketla were playing nearby, and we called to them and took them with us. It was a cold night and Maude protested at first, but when she noticed the three of us grinning, she hurried to dress Margaret and herself, eager as a child for whatever treat we had in store.

Ted led us up the gully through a grove of birch and willow.

"Why, look over there!" Maude pointed ahead to where a rosy light shone through the trees. "Whatever can it be?"

The children sped ahead on their snowshoes, stopping short in awe and rapture when they came to a glowing palace that had risen as if by magic in the gully by the creek.

Ted had made an igloo from big chunks of drifted snow, large enough for a child to enter. Windows cut into the snow were covered with squares of red tissue paper to give the rosy light. He had left a lamp burning in the igloo and the snow, melting slightly in its heat during the day but freezing again at night, had turned the igloo into an ice palace. Inside, a throne carved from snow also glistened with ice. None of the children had heard of igloos, and this shining house was something they never forgot.

Jock and I tried to entertain them, too. Jock came down from a trip to Tanana one day and drew out a bag of peanuts from his pack. "I've thought up a trick to give Maude and Margaret a laugh," he said. "See if you can get hold of one of Margie's dolls for me."

I managed to kidnap a big blonde doll and Jock took a penknife and eased off the wig.

"What on earth are you doing? You'll be in dutch with her if you scalp her doll."

"Ted can glue it on again." He got his peanuts and poured them into the doll's hollow head, replacing the wig loosely on top. "Come on," he said, "let's give them a laugh."

Jock handed the doll to Margaret. "Here's your dolly. I've been looking her over, and I don't think her health is too good, Margie. Her hair is coming out fast. Just give it a little pull and you'll see what I mean."

Margaret gave us a puzzled look, but when she saw us smiling she gave the wig a gentle tug. Off it came, revealing the peanuts. Jock was shaking with laughter, but he sobered up when the child burst into tears and ran to her mother for comfort.

"Look here — peanuts!" Jock called to her, but she refused to look up, keeping her face buried in Maude's lap.

"Well, by golly, can't say I blame her," said Ted, peering into the

128

doll's cavity. "It looks like the creature's brains in here. She thinks you scalped her baby."

"Bill warned me," Jock said gloomily, "but who'd ever believe the wee bairn thought her poppets were alive?"

\Poor little Margaret suffered again when an Indian couple came to the cabin a few days later and begged for a doll to cheer their child, who was ill in bed and restless.

"Choose one of your dolls for Pauline," Maude told her. "Four dolls are more than you need." Maude was less hostile toward Pauline's parents, who led a fairly stable life and seemed devoted to their children. But Margaret was devoted to her children, too. She wept in misery, a mother faced with the painful necessity of singling out one of her little ones for the sacrifice. Daisy, a doll with head and hands of shiny china, was eventually given up amid wails of protest, and the Indians carried her away. One hopes the china doll provided a brief solace for fretful Pauline, but a few days later we saw a number of little Indian boys running down to the river, one of them clutching Daisy. While Margaret watched in distress, Daisy was tossed into the air and fell with a splash into the Yukon. The small boys howled with wicked glee as she sank down to a watery grave.

Ted and Maude vied with each other to entertain their child. Ted amazed her with birds, teapots and boats which emerged from squares of paper intricately folded. On long winter evenings he placed a candle near the muslin wall and amused her by twisting his fingers to form shadow pictures of a quacking duck, or a rabbit sitting upright and wiggling its ears, or an old man with a long beard who gabbled at her soundlessly. Both Maude and Ted had an endless store of rhymes and riddles (I had a few myself, but they outdid me). Ted carried on a continued story for her about two children who sailed up and down the coast as he had done in his youth, but whose wild adventures far outshone his own. Maude enjoyed tricks of dexterity and legerdemain, like weaving complicated cats' cradles of string.

The legerdemain of our brother Harry, who hopped off a passing river boat to visit us briefly, was less to her taste.

It was good to see Harry again. He had a dozen schemes and

projects going and seemed as confident as ever. He brought out three walnut shells and a dried pea and showed Margaret the shell game used to fleece cheechakos out of their savings.

"Watch, Margie! Where did I hide the pea?"

The child leaned on the kitchen table, watching her uncle's quick fingers. "Under this one!" But she was always wrong. She could never pick the walnut shell that hid the pea after Harry had shuffled them about. This convinced Maude that he was a gambler who would bring disgrace to us all. He liked to tease Maude, and she was an easy mark with her passion for appearances. Harry shuffled his walnut shells and boasted of his hectic life and reckless spending.

I daresay some of his wild stories were true, but Harry could work hard if he chose. He studied furs and the fur trade while he was in Alaska, and thought up a scheme of traveling about to different fur traders and collecting first-class skin specimens to send down to the Vancouver Fur Company. He did well at this, but affluence always set him off on a round of pleasure with free-spending friends. "What's the use of money if you can't spend it?" he would say. Then it was all play and no work until he lost another in a succession of jobs. He was never downhearted. He was sure of his ability to win himself new fortunes, and he did win them, only to toss them away as fast as they came.

TWO

Apart from his own business trips, Ted was often called upon to solve problems that no one else wanted to be bothered with. One winter a trapper came to the store for tea and bacon and told him there was a man in a cabin up one of the creeks who had frozen his feet and seemed to be dying of scurvy.

"Why the devil didn't you bring him out?" Ted asked.

"Bring him out? Why should I? I brought word to the post, didn't I?"

Ted harnessed his dogs to his Yukon sled and mushed down to the creek where the sick man had been seen. He had traveled up the creek ice for several hours when he came upon a cabin. This can't be the one, he thought; it's too short a distance from the Yukon. He pushed open the door and was greeted by the stench of rotting flesh and a weak cry for help from the emaciated man lying on a bunk.

The sick man was a cheechako who had tried to master the wilderness without knowledge of either the layout of the land or of simple survival methods. He had no idea that he was only a few hours away from a village, nor that by boiling the juniper needles or the willow shoots that grew outside his door and drinking the water, he could have prevented his scurvy. He had watched the rot growing in his feet, picking off the dead flesh until the bare bones of his toes were exposed. At last he had given up all hope.

"See, there on the table," he gasped. "Letters to my family, saying goodbye to them. Will you mail them for me after I'm dead?"

"Dead? You're not dying, man. I'm taking you back to my post and I'll have you cured in no time."

The poor fellow was in terrible agony, and was sure his end was near. It was snowing hard now, but Ted wrapped him in blankets, carried him out to the sled and hurried the dogs back to the trading post. He stopped at my cabin and got Jock and me to help him carry sled and man into the store while he made up a bed beside the stove and gave his patient a large swig of brandy. Then he motioned me to come with him to Maude's cabin next door. It had stopped snowing now, but it had turned very cold.

"I can't take him to Fort Gibbon in this weather," he decided. "He'd never last that long. There's gangrene in his feet, too. Looks like there's only one thing to do, Bill." He pulled open a drawer and took out a big hunting knife. "Stay with Maude," he whispered to me. He stood a moment as if nerving himself, and then strode out of the cabin.

"What is he doing?" Maude asked apprehensively. I tried to calm her, but a succession of agonized yells from the direction of the store raised our hair on end. Then the cabin door opened and in walked Ted, looking pale and shaken, holding the bloodstained hunting knife.

Maude screamed and sank into a chair. "Brandy! I'm fainting! Quick, give me the brandy!"

Ted cleaned the knife, then sat down beside her, laughing weakly. He pulled the bottle from his pocket and held it high in the air between them. "Which one of us needs it most, Maude?" He compromised by giving each of us a stiff drink and taking the rest back to his patient.

He had cut off the gangrened portions of both feet, but the man survived and slowly regained his strength from Ted's nourishing meals. When the mail team came by some time later, Ted bundled him up and sent him off on the mail sled for professional treatment in the nearest town.

Few travelers called in at the Independent Store, for Kokrines, six miles down-river, was the logical stopping place. Ted's trading post was empty most of the time except when the Indians came down from their traplines to exchange their furs for supplies. Other than these, visitors were mainly those in trouble who struck Mouse Point first when seeking aid, or travelers taking shelter from sudden, dangerous drops in temperature. While Maude was at Mouse Point, the wayfarers were bedded down in the store.

"Every traveler who knocks at a cabin door should be given a bed and a good meal," Ted tried to explain to her. "It's the code of the north, Maude." But the thought of strangers sleeping in their cabin curdled her blood. "They might murder us in our sleep," she shuddered. "Put them up in the store!"

There were times when I sympathized with her. Ted brought home one guest I would not have cared to bring into my cabin. This chap had set out with a hotel-keeper companion to snowshoe from Rampart to Kokrines, and one of those sudden drops in temperature to 50 below hit them. The hotel-keeper told us the story of their experience when he stayed with us directly afterwards.

When the cold spell struck, he had urged his friend to keep on the move, warning him that a pause might be fatal. When the fellow upended a whisky bottle for a good pull, he warned him again, for both whisky and extreme cold were strong inducements to sleep.

They had plodded slowly along, breathing with difficulty. Every so often the one with the bottle ignored his friend's protests and took a hefty swig to warm and invigorate himself. Suddenly, the fatal combination of alcohol and the extreme cold overcame him; he became dizzy, swayed, then fell forward into the snow and lay still.

The hotelman had bent over the fallen man, shaking his shoulder and urging him to get up and walk, but the exertion made his head whirl and when there was no response, he had looked with pity at his companion for a few moments and then had plodded painfully down the trail until at last he reached Mouse Point and told his story.

With dogs and sled, Ted followed the trail back to find the traveler frozen to death. Rolling the corpse onto the sled, he returned to the store and thrust his stiffened passenger into a small, unheated lean-to behind the post where he kept his sacks of beans and boxes of tinned goods.

The hotelman was given a meal and bedded down on the floor of the store. In the morning, he was moved to take a look at the body of his companion. On opening the door of the lean-to, he let out a yell: Ted had shoved the stiff corpse into the cramped space in an upright position, and the startled hotelman was greeted by the sight of his friend standing against the wall, staring glassily at him, one frozen elbow resting on a sack of beans. There the ghostly guest remained until taken away weeks later.

THREE

Jock and I of necessity became good plain cooks, but Ted loved to experiment with unusual ingredients and odd recipes. We were always glad of a chance to sample his dishes, but Margaret was a bit dubious about some of them, and Maude refused to try anything that she considered uncivilized fare.

Ted wanted to try out a new duck recipe, so one morning I climbed the hill to the swampy meadow where melting snow formed a large pond in the spring. Ducks often rested here on their northward journey and sure enough, a dozen of them were swimming about, out of shooting range but mine for the taking if the open ground between birch grove and pond could be covered without startling them. Suddenly strange, hoarse cries sounded overhead: seven white swans were flying in single file over the birch trees, their great wings flapping loudly. They flew in a swaying line like the enchanted princes in the fairy tale, one behind the other. I shot the

133

leader, which tumbled into the shallow waters of the pond, and with my double-barrelled shotgun was also able to bring the last in the line crashing down into the snow. In those days there was no protective law for these beautiful birds. Swans may live to be 100 years old and can be tough eating, but these two were young and tender. Ted was delighted to try out a new kind of game fowl. He told Maude that swans were a favorite food of the ancient kings of England and that he would serve her roast swan and swan pie, which Samuel Pepys served to his London guests. This reconciled her.

Moose's nose she viewed with more suspicion, though Ted considered it a great delicacy. After singeing off the hairs, he boiled the nose gently with herbs, onion, and garlic until the meat was tender. Jellied moose tongue, served in cold slices, was another treat. Ted tried roast porcupine, but it was very fat and he used it only in emergencies. Bear steaks, roasts and liver were always delectable.

The many varieties of mushrooms in Alaska fascinated Ted. He sent for a large illustrated book about fungi and studied it industriously. When he was sure he could distinguish between edible and poisonous varieties, he combed the meadow for the harmless types and served them creamed or sautéed. The close resemblance of some of the dangerous kinds to the edible ones intrigued him, and he would point out to Maude the vital difference in gill color or decorative frill or slight variation in shape. She took no interest. He was the mushroom hunter, and she was content to trust his judgment. She doubted him in some respects, but she never doubted that his knowledge was all-inclusive.

"Your father knows everything," she often told Margaret complacently, and then she would add furiously to me: "But why does he misdirect his talents?"

"Well, Maude, that's a matter of opinion. Perhaps his talents find their best expression up here in the wilds." But that was something she did not wish to hear.

Sourdough was a staple item for us Alaskans. Sourdough starter is a yeast cake endowed with eternal life. We mixed the yeast with a cup of flour and a cup of water and allowed it to activate overnight. Many trappers had no yeast available, and then the starter

134

had to be made from a combination of flour, sugar and water set aside to ferment. The next evening, more flour and water were added, and the sponge mixture was kept warm overnight. Before adding still more flour and water, plus fat and seasonings, half a cup of the mixture was removed and kept in a cool place, ready to start the next sponge. A fresh half cup was thus always available, and the process could continue for years on end provided a baking was done once a week of bread, pancakes or muffins.

A common method employed by miners and trappers to keep the sponge warm overnight was to take the tin to bed with them. Ted's cabin was always so warm, even overnight in coldest weather, that he only needed to wrap the sponge and place it near the stove. His dog Bungo once got hold of a tin that had the remains of a sponge mixture in it and carried it to his bed in the barn. He lay with paw and chin over it and rolled imploring eyes at Ted when he tried to reclaim his tin.

"Keep it then, old timer," Ted told him, tears of delight trickling from his own eyes. "You've proved yourself a genuine Alaskan sourdough!"

Maude came round in time to a good many of Ted's dishes, usually after he had thought up some way to persuade her that they were not barbaric fare. But one time he went too far.

All of us were in Ted's kitchen. Jock and I had been invited up to share the Sunday dinner. Ted was slitting a large roast when we got there and stuffing it with sage and onion sprinkled with seasonings.

> ... pepper in portions true
> (Which he never forgot), and some chopped shalot,
> And some sage and parsley too.

He chanted this helpful Gilbert ballad as he worked, and then popped the roast in the oven. Soon an appetizing odor filled the room, and Maude breathed it in sensuously.

"What is it? Bear meat?"

"No," Ted grinned.

"Moose?"

"No. Something different and delicious. Roast lynx!"

135

"Wild-cat!" Her head came up like an animal scenting danger and readying itself for battle. "You're cooking a *cat*? We can't eat cat!"

"Plenty of Alaskans eat lynx, Maude. It tastes like pork."

"No respectable family ever ate a cat. I won't have it!"

The argument waxed hotter until finally Maude grabbed a dish-towel, pulled the pan out of the oven, and flung the sizzling meat through the doorway into a snowbank. We men gave a yell of outrage on seeing our Sunday dinner sailing away just as we were smacking our lips in anticipation. Ted leapt after it and restored it to the oven.

"Maude," I pleaded, "why don't you try it? I've heard it's excellent."

My sister ignored us all. Tight-lipped, she dressed herself and Margaret in skin parkas, high mooseskin mukluks and mittens and marched with her child out of the cabin, leaving the battlefield to us barbarians.

We sat about, silent and subdued, until Ted announced that the meat was done and served it up, whistling defiantly. I daresay it was a good meal, the meat hot and savory and surrounded by vegetables, but none of us had much appetite.

"Where do you suppose she went?" Ted pondered as he looked outside. "She's nowhere in sight."

"Then she must be up in the hills. She wouldn't go down to the Indians."

"Come on," said Ted. "It's turning cold and dark. I'll take my lantern."

Our search of the hill and the meadow beyond found no trace of them. We continued past the frozen lake where I had shot my swans in the spring. Beyond this, scrub fir and stunted birch formed a wood that thinned out again toward the mountains.

"Damn it all, has she gone into the trees?" Ted worried. "Spread out, and we'll try to find her tracks. If we can't locate her soon, I'll round up the village Indians and string them out across the country. The two of them will freeze to death if they stay out all night."

Finding tracks in the darkness was pretty much of a gamble. Ted had brought along his dog and kept giving Bungo sniffs of Maude's glove while urging him to scent a trail. He swung his lantern as we shouted repeatedly, "Maude! Margaret!" We reached the trees, anxious and miserable.

We had penetrated the wood for some distance when a faint cry answered our shouts. We converged and found them, half frozen, stamping with their snowshoes to keep life in their feet.

Maude had lost her way among the trees. After wandering about, she had found herself on a trail made by two sets of snowshoes and had begun to follow it thankfully, thinking it was an Indian trail leading to their village. In time, the two sets had become four, and to her dismay she realized that she and Margaret had been following their own trail round and round clockwise, in a circle. Darkness had descended, and she had tramped on blindly among the trees, pulling her crying child with her and not daring to stop and rest in the freezing night air.

Ted took off his parka, lifted Margaret onto his back, and slipped it over them both, Eskimo style. Her icy little body thawed out fast from the warmth of the heavy parka and the heat of her father's body. Jock and I supported Maude as we all set out for the village.

Back in the cabin, Ted rubbed Maude's numb hands and feet and brought the Morris chair close to the stove for her. As Jock and I left for our own quarters, he was serving her a civilized meal of pickled pigs' feet.

FOUR

"Now, whatever use will you find for a horse at Mouse Point?" I asked Ted.

He patted the nose of the big work horse. "The Indians here have never seen a horse, Bill. Wait until Neketla gets a look at him! The kids can ride him."

As it turned out, they couldn't. We ended up calling him Old Buck, because he refused to be ridden and threw anyone who tried to mount him. But the Indians came over often to marvel at his size and strength and to watch him hauling loads of hay down from the meadow for fodder. In the winter, our dogs came in by the stove, but Old Buck had to stay shivering in the barn even when the temperature fell to 60-below. Every cold morning as soon as Ted got up, he heated a pail of water on the stove. "Old Buck must have his morning tea," he would always say.

Ted spent much of his time thinking up ways to amuse and amaze Fred and Neketla, but his deepest affection was reserved for the little blue-eyed Indian.

One day, we heard that Fred had taken a shotgun from his cabin in the Indian village to hunt for grouse in the hills, and Neketla had followed him. Fred had let him come; although Neketla was too young to go hunting himself, he could help to carry home the birds that Fred hoped to bag.

As they climbed the hill, Nekelta had suddenly forged ahead, pulling himself up by grabbing at bushes and digging his feet into the dirt, determined to be first to reach the top. This was more than the elder brother could permit. Fred had climbed faster, struggling to regain his lead. Both boys had their eyes fixed on the summit as, panting and stumbling, each fought to get there first. Just then, Fred stepped on a loose stone and fell heavily. His gun went off with a bang and a kick that struck him a blow on the chest. There was a scream of anguish above him, and he looked up to see Neketla tumbling down the steep bank, over and over, until caught in the branches of a willow bush.

Fred had crawled down to the child, who lay still with blood seeping from his side. It was a terrible moment for poor young Fred, and I imagine he looked wildly about him at the distant Kokrine hills, searching for a way of escape. He had tried to lift Neketla, but the limp body was too heavy for him to carry, and he lowered it again to its resting place by the willow bush. Then he stumbled down to the creek and ran, panic-stricken, to break the news to his mother.

She came to Ted and begged him to find Neketla and bring him home. None of us went with him; we knew he would want to find the boy himself. Shortly afterward, we saw him walking slowly back, the dead child cradled in his arms, and as he entered the Indian village we could hear the wailing of the women.

Fred lingered near his cabin until Neketla was carried inside, but when Ted came out to question him he had disappeared. Ted sent an Indian down to Father Jetté at Kokrines to arrange for a funeral service, then went over to his trading post and came out with a thick bolt of red flannel. The Indians loved bright red flannel, but it was too expensive for them to buy in quantity at one time. They would line parkas or ornament mukluks with it, and tie scraps to the fences around the graves. Ted reasoned that a whole bolt of red flannel would be a royal gift for a funeral, unheard of for the grave of a child.

Father Jetté came to read the Catholic service, but Ted shut himself in his bedroom during the ceremony. When it was over, Margaret climbed the hill to view her playmate's last resting place.

"There are clothes and pots on his grave," she told her mother and me, "and I saw the crossbow and the birchbark canoe that Daddy made for Neketla. There was a little wooden man with a paddle sitting in the canoe. I think he's lonely, but I left him there, because you said I must never touch things on the graves."

"Did you see the red flannel?" Maude asked her.

"Yes, it was right in the middle, on top of everything."

"Your father is sad about Neketla," Maude said. "You must show that you love him." She opened the door to the bedroom and eased Margaret inside, then stood by the door, listening tensely, until she heard the murmur of his voice as he caressed their child and found comfort in her presence.

Fred's mother came to us again. She was afraid that her missing boy would never come back to her after the shock of the accident that had caused his brother's death.

"I'll find him," Father Jetté said, "and bring him back."

"I'll go with you," Ted volunteered, but the priest preferred to go alone. If Fred blamed himself for the accident, he might be afraid to come out and face Ted's anger.

For three days Father Jetté searched the Kokrine hills, calling Fred's name and begging the boy to come out and talk to him. At last Fred appeared. "Come home," urged the priest, but Fred shook his head. He steadfastly refused to go back to the village but finally agreed to go with him to Kokrines. Father Jetté kept him at the Mission, along with the two young Brothers, and trained him as an acolyte to help with the services.

139

The priest was quick to recognize the boy's intelligence and un-selfish nature, and in time he arranged to send him to Seattle for schooling — the first Indian from that district to be sent outside for an education.

FIVE

The days warmed into summer. Maude was expecting another child and dreaded the thought of childbirth up here in the wilds.

"Lots of women have children in Alaska," I reassured her, careful not to add that many of them died in childbirth. "Ted will certainly take you to one of the towns when the time comes."

Ted was delighted with her news. He hoped for a son and was full of plans for the child's future. He promised to take Maude well ahead of time to Fort Gibbon where the army doctor could deliver the baby.

The summer was short and hot. Sometimes we climbed the hill to a second vegetable patch that Ted had planted on the heights. He had set a trap among his vegetables to discourage wild animals, and one day we found a little red fox crouched there, caught by a slender paw. Ted had the skin made into a neckpiece for Maude and she wore it for years, but Margaret always shrank from the soft fur, haunted by the terrified eyes of the little prisoner. There were wild roses in the meadow, and we picked pails of blueberries, thimbleberries and black currants. Farther along, in the swamp near the shallow pond, ducks nested in the grass, and we gathered the eggs. Ted candled them and put aside the fertilized ones for the Indians who relished them and couldn't understand why he gave them away.

"You like eat egg," they would say. "You like eat duck. Why you not like eat egg partway turned to duck?"

"Why don't we?" Ted asked me. "I'm damned if our habits aren't as unreasonable as a lot of the Indian ways that we call nonsensical."

Fall arrived, with its swarms of gnats, and all too soon the first ice cakes dotted the river. The waters froze fast; the long, cold months of isolation were upon us. Ted left for Tanana in December on business, promising to arrange a place for Maude to stay during confinement in early February.

The weeks went by. She expected him daily, but there was no sign of him. When not away checking my traplines, I drew water for her from a hole chopped five feet through the river ice and hauled it up to the cabin. We kept a canvas over the hole to keep it from refreezing, but a thin layer of ice always formed and had to be broken before the water was dipped out. In the winter, the water was crystal clear, for the glacial streams were frozen then and none of their silt emptied into the Yukon. Once the breakup came, the river was full of sediment again. With a sudden breakup, we often lost canvas and dipper, as the whole body of ice moved silently down the Yukon.

"Why don't you practice cooking?" I asked Maude, trying to divert her from her fears. "Why not bake us something good?" She had lived in boarding houses for the first five years of her marriage, where she had neither opportunity nor need to learn even the simplest rules of cooking. When she came to Mouse Point and found Ted able to produce delicious meals with ease, she had refused to expose to him her own uncertain efforts for comparison.

"What can I bake?" she asked. "Think of something Ted has never made."

"Chocolate cake," I suggested, since it was one of my favorites.

Maude practiced industriously at the big range, turning out cakes that were flat, lopsided or thrust up in the center like Mount McKinley. Success came eventually, and she relaxed in triumph. Most of her cooking remained haphazard and unpredictable, but she always presented each dish with a dramatic introduction that guaranteed it a respectful reception. Bread baking, however, was still beyond her, and Father Jetté's young Brothers continued to tramp the six miles between Kokrines and Mouse Point, their long black skirts billowing beneath their parkas, bearing gifts of fresh bread for Maude and religious pictures for Margaret.

Near the end of January, Maude grew frantic with fright. I had been away on my trapline for several days and on my return went at once to her cabin. When the door opened, she turned her head eagerly. Her face fell.

"Oh, it's only you!"

"What sort of welcome is that?"

"Don't you understand? Ted hasn't come, and my baby is due two weeks from today. Do you know what my Tacoma doctor called childbirth labor? 'The Valley of the Shadow of Death.'" She shivered. "His wife died in childbirth in a city hospital with doctors and nurses to look after her. What will happen to me, alone in this cabin with no one to help me?"

Late that day the door burst open and Ted stepped inside, his fur-lined parka covered with snow and with icicles hanging from eyebrows, moustache and beard. As he held his wife in a freezing embrace, she shrieked from the cold and poured out her fears and reproaches. But already her panic had subsided. Ted could always be relied on in emergencies: his calm, matter-of-fact way of taking charge was enough to ease hysteria. He built up the fire and defrosted himself while he told Maude his plans for her.

He had arranged to rent a cabin in Tanana, close to Fort Gibbon and the army surgeon. Until it was available, they would stay with sheriff Vortier and his family in Tanana. "We'll leave tomorrow," he told her.

"You must come too," Maude appealed to me. "Who knows, it may happen when we're half way between roadhouses, out in the wilderness in the ice and snow."

The long, cold journey up-river took us several days; we traveled from early morning until reaching a roadhouse at night. The roadhouses were small log cabins, usually with three rooms: a kitchen, the owner's quarters and a larger guest room shared by travelers. Amenities were even more primitive than ours at Mouse Point, and the communal room was generally crowded. But the roadhouse-keepers always tried to help matters when they saw that our party included a woman and child. At each stop, Maude and Margaret were offered the owner's quarters for the night, while he bedded himself down in the communal room.

Maude's short stay with the Vortiers was a happy time for Margaret, who enjoyed her play with 12-year-old Rita Vortier and her brothers. The children were never permitted to play by the shore. The town refuse was left to rot beside the water, and odorous fishracks farther up the bank added to the smells. Fierce huskies were chained to stakes to keep them from the fishracks, and they complained with an endless howling. Margaret mourned the move to the cabin, having grown deeply attached to Rita, a pretty, good-natured girl who escorted her to school, the first school Margaret had attended even though she was now almost eight. Her life with the Indians had left her shy and inarticulate, and she came home in tears the first day that she went to school alone. The Tanana children, neat in low leather shoes, had made fun of her high Indian mukluks.

"Why is it bad to wear mukluks?" she asked us in bewilderment.

A few nights after the move to the cabin, Ted ran down to Fort Gibbon and brought back the army doctor.

"I rooted him out in the nick of time," Ted told me later. "We heard Maude screaming when we were down the road and we sprinted the last yards, getting there just as the baby came. The doctor got busy with Maude. 'Tie the cord!' he snapped at me over his shoulder. His bag stood open, but damned if I could see anything to use. When he'd finished with Maude, she asked me to bring her the baby. She shrieked when she saw it, and covered her face with her hands. 'Doctor,' she cried in horror, 'my baby has a huge growth on its stomach!' He came to look, his face all concern, and then he roared with laughter.

"Well, Bill, I'd seen nothing in his bag to tie the cord with, so I'd gone to the bureau and taken some ribbon that was threaded through the neckline of one of Maude's nightdresses. The growth was pink satin ribbon, tied in an elegant bow."

I saw the baby that afternoon. It was a little girl. Ted concealed any regrets he might have had that there was no son to take trapping and fishing and hunting, to bait a hook without flinching, or to face a trapped animal without feminine tears. They had decided to let Margaret name the baby, and he was highly amused that she had chosen to call it Doris after the heroine of his endless tale of adventure, invented for her entertainment during the long Alaskan winters.

I went back to Mouse Point ahead of the others. When the four of them returned a few months later, Ted looked glum.

"I'm leaving," Maude announced cheerfully. "I'm taking my girls outside to civilization and suitable schools. They shan't grow up wearing mukluks and smoking fish on the riverbank."

There was still plenty of prejudice in those days against the mixing of races, and I hadn't the heart to argue with her. When Ted finally agreed to let her go, she waved a blithe goodbye to us from the deck of the first steamboat to travel down-river to St. Michael following the breakup.

Ted's home in England.

Ted's first home and trading post at Mouse Point, Alaska.

Summit of White Pass, between Alaska and Yukon.

Lake Bennett, Yukon.

City of Seattle leaving Victoria for the Klondike in 1898.

Madge and Maude at Beacon Hill Park, Victoria, 1898.

Joe Fortes, lifeguard at English Bay, Vancouver, B.C.

Maude in her swansdown cape.

Alice.

Miles Canyon, Yukon.

The reindeer herd comes to Spruce Creek.

Bill and Jock, heading for the Novakaket River.

Interior of cabin, Mouse Point, Alaska.

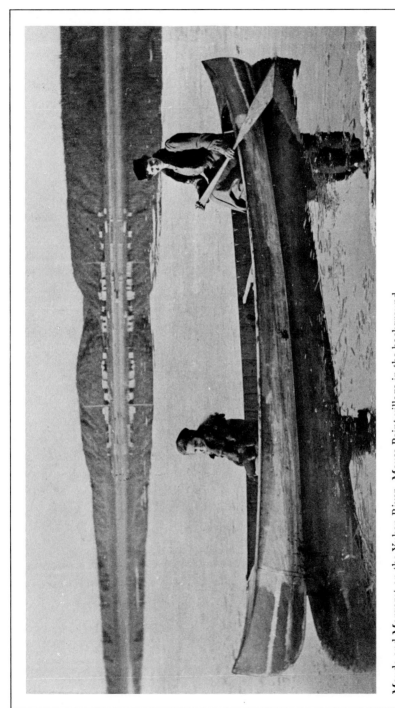

Maude and Margaret on the Yukon River. Mouse Point village in the background.

Indians at Mouse Point, Alaska.

Ted and Margaret, by ice floes pushed ashore by the Yukon River breakup.
Mouse Point.

Margaret in winter clothing; caribou skin parka and moose skin mukluks.

Bill, with Nugget, hydraulic mining at Spruce Creek.

Nugget and his dog. Spruce Creek.

Whitehorse Rapids, Yukon.

Vancouver Public Library.

Innoko Gold

7

ONE

THROUGH WILD LAND lying between the Yukon and the Kuskokwim rivers, the little-known Innoko River pursues its lonely zigzagging course for some 500 rapid-ridden miles, rising far north in the Kuskokwim mountain range and flowing down to the Chageluk Slough, which in turn empties into the Yukon River near Holy Cross.

In 1906, miners prospecting at the headwaters of the Innoko struck gold. News of their find traveled slowly at first, but as one creek after another proved to be rich, there was a stampede with several hundred men crowding in to stake their claims. Finally, word filtered through to us up at Mouse Point.

"Gold in the Innoko," Ted mused. "Remember that fellow I grubstaked when he stopped here on his way down the Yukon? He said he'd pay me for the supplies by staking a claim for me on the Innoko."

"Where's the Innoko?" asked Jock. "Never heard of it before."

"Comes into the Yukon down by Holy Cross, he told me. Never thought I'd hear from him again. Maybe I won't."

"But maybe he did stake a claim for you," I suggested excitedly. "Why don't I take a trip down the Yukon and find out? What was his name?"

"Valentine, he said."

"Well, Bill," said Jock, "see if you can find Valentine. If he kept his promise, he'll be our valentine right enough, and we'll all go down to the Innoko and try our luck at gold mining. What do you say, Ted?"

"I could do with a few sacks of gold dust. Robbie Burns scoffs at gold and all that, but he never tried to support a wife and two children who live outside on the proceeds of a trading post in Mouse Point."

We debated the question: whether or not it was possible to rake in a small fortune and still stay independent. The three of us agreed it was worth a try. It was time to leave Mouse Point. With Maude gone, our bachelor existence had become peaceful, uncomplicated but dull. We even missed Maude's complaints, endlessly spurring us to devise means of allaying her discontent. If my reconnoitering trip proved the feasibility of a move, all of us would pull up stakes and start a new adventure in the goldfields.

I took the old poling boat we had made at Black River. It was still short in the beam and inclined to tilt and wobble, but I had come to terms with its capriciousness. I was unsure of distances, but I was to travel about 500 miles down the Yukon and then fight my way another 500 up the rapids of the torturously twisting Innoko River. Nonetheless, the thought of the long, lonely trip appealed to me, and the possibility of finding gold at the end of the journey gave it added zest. I had hunted and trapped happily enough for almost 10 years, despite little or nothing to show for my labor, but if I followed a rainbow to the Innoko creeks and found a pot of gold, it would be a satisfying climax to my adventures in Alaska.

Down the Yukon I sailed, poling with the current, past the little Catholic mission and the Indian village at Kokrines, past the mouth of the Melozitna River that emptied its clear, brownish waters into the yellow-gray Yukon until, about 35 miles below the Melozikaket, the Yukon turned north to reach the Koyukuk Flats.

This was a storied land, stained by blood and hatred. An iron cross set up on a high rock by the mouth of the Koyukuk River commemorated the death of Bishop Seghers, who was murdered by a half-breed in 1885. Three years later a prospector, John Bremner, was also killed up the Koyukuk by a young Indian. Bremner was popular with the miners who promptly avenged him by hijacking

146

the steamboat *Explorer,* sailing up the Koyukuk and lynching the Indian youth from a pole strung between two trees.

These Indians were impulsively aggressive and caused a good deal of trouble for the early white traders. Twenty miles below their river, at Nulato, a Russian trading post was built at the site of the Indian village. In 1851, the Koyukuk Indians came down-river, burned all the Indian houses and shot down the Nulato Indians — men, women, and children — with a rain of arrows as they tried to escape. Breaking into the fort, they killed the factor and his guest, young Lieutenant Barnard of the British ship *Enterprise.* Barnard had come up the Yukon from St. Michael, hoping to find word of the lost Arctic explorer, Sir John Franklin, in the event that he had made his way out overland, as did Amundsen years later. He found no news of Franklin, only a lonely grave for himself high on the bluffs, far from his homeland.

Except for Kaltag, 40 miles below Nulato, there was not a settlement for 200 miles until I reached Anvik. Great bluffs and mountains loomed close to the river on my right, while on the south side the bank was low and thickly overgrown with spruce, cottonwood, birch and willow. Still the great river wound south. At Holy Cross, an Indian village with a Roman Catholic mission, I poled across to the east bank and into the clear water of the Chageluk Slough which receives the Innoko River 100 miles above the Yukon.

Few white men had ventured up the Innoko before gold was discovered there in 1906. The upper reaches of the twisting river were rough with rapids, the Indians were among the most primitive in Alaska, and for 100 miles up the slough the mosquitoes were vicious. On the Yukon, relief from the insects could be found on the gravel bars where the wind drove them away, but up the narrow slough with its densely wooded banks there was no breeze, and mosquitoes descended in clouds.

Ten boats were pulled up on the bank by the mouth of the slough, and I pulled in beside them. We exchanged news of the gold strike and what information we had about the long trip to its location at the river's source. Suddenly, one of the men exclaimed, "What's that?" It was a queer, slapping sound, coming from up the slough and gradually growing louder. "What the devil?" We got up and stood looking at the bend. "There she comes!" he shouted. A raft swept around the curve, waves splashing and slapping at its logs. Lying on the raft was a man who stood up as he sighted our boats and poled to shore. He was tall and thin, with a beard cascading to his waist. Under his hat he had wound a dishrag about his head, letting it hang down over his face and neck for protection against mosquitoes. Through holes in the dishrag, his eyes peered out. He staggered as he jumped ashore, and we ran to help him tie up.

"I've floated five hundred miles down the Innoko," he reported weakly. "My grub gave out half way down."

After a feed of bacon and eggs, he told us about the strike.

"The best is Big Ganes Creek by the Innoko headwaters, but the first ones up got all the narrow section of the valley staked — that's the part where the gold is richest and easiest to get at. The wider parts of the valley are no good. But they're all crazy for claims; they're staking everywhere, on all the creeks."

"Did you run into a man called Valentine up there?" I enquired anxiously.

"Valentine? That's me."

"You're Valentine?" He was a comic valentine, all right, in that rig of his, but I was delighted to have found him. "You're the man I came here to find! Did you stake a claim for Ted Crompton of Mouse Point?"

"I staked for him on Little Creek. He grubstaked me to get to the Innoko, and I told him I'd mark up a claim for him; so there it is, waiting for him on Fifteen and Fifteen Pup. I'm going back to work my claim as soon as I raise another grubstake to keep going."

With that, he thanked us and drifted off down the Yukon.

The men debated among themselves:

"A month, he said. Valentine said we'll be a month fighting those rapids before we get to the headwaters."

"Fighting mosquitoes, too. They're murder here. Eat you alive."

"The best is all staked. You heard him. We'll break our backs to get there, all for nothing."

Their pessimism moved me to protest, "How do you know? You

148

might find a spot somewhere. One thing certain, you'll get no share of the gold if you don't go up and see for yourselves."

By morning, however, half the boats had shoved off down the Yukon, and only five of us remained to struggle the long way up to see if the pot of gold lay waiting for us at rainbow's end. One of the men came over to me. "Look, my partner has given up and gone back. I've got no transport. Now, you have a boat and I have a dog. I'll make you a fair offer. Take us with you, and my dog will do a man's share of the work." Dubiously, I agreed to form a temporary partnership of two men and one dog.

For the first 250 miles, we found the going easy with the downward current barely noticeable. Later, small steamers were able to get this far with supplies for the miners and traders. The sails of our poleboats would catch a breeze and carry us smoothly along, then we'd round a curve and change direction, the breeze would drop and we'd resort to poles again. A hundred miles later, we passed an island in the slough and came upon the waters of the Innoko flowing into the Chageluk. The lower Innoko was a beautiful river, wide and calm, its rocky banks topped with thick woods of birch and spruce which thinned out occasionally to grassy slopes dotted with single trees. We passed the mouth of the Iditarod, a sluggish, twisting river flowing through swampy tundra land and to whose headwaters there was another rush when gold in quantity was discovered the following year. Now the Innoko, too, began to twist in earnest, often doubling back completely upon itself, so that after a day of travel, if we took a short walk through the trees, we could see the same spot we had passed in the early morning.

The Innoko rapids began at the halfway mark. Poling was difficult even close to shore. We followed the usual method of up-stream travel, one man remaining in the boat to steer while the others walked the gravel bar, hauling on the rope. When the current switched at each bend of the river and the gravel bars alternated sides along with it, we poled across stream and hauled rope on the opposite shore.

"Now you'll see my dog is one damn fine worker," said my partner as he buckled a special harness onto the dog and attached the harness to the hauling rope. The big husky jumped from the boat as soon as we reached a gravel bar and strained his broad chest against the harness. I had to agree that he did a good share of the hauling. He seemed to enjoy the work. He hopped into the boat again when the gravel bar ended and rode across with a wide grin, tongue hanging out, as if he was thinking it a joke that we must sweat and strain to pole to the other side while he rode at ease. But the instant we landed, he leapt out, eager to do his share again.

The river was to become a familiar route by summer's end, but now we were traveling cautiously, apprehensive of what lay ahead in unknown waters: pulling, poling, crossing and recrossing, camping on the gravel bar for a quick meal and overnight rest, and battling the mosquitoes with a smudge fire of smouldering moss. Even the husky crawled close to the smoke to escape the insects, and all of us were badly bitten despite a grease repellent of lard and tar smeared on our faces and hands.

A month after starting, we reached the headwaters and went first to Ganes Creek. "Everything's taken down here," we were told. "You'll have to go a long way up-stream." We trudged for miles up the creek bed. Ganes was a long, winding creek, fed by many side streams as it meandered down.

At last we found unstaked land, but the creek had narrowed here and the valley was wide and flat.

"It's the section Valentine warned us against," I recalled as we stood looking about forlornly, wondering if we should chance it and stake. We were hungry and discouraged, and fearful that our long, difficult journey had been for nothing and that we had arrived too late. So far, I had come across no one who could direct me to Little Creek, and I felt as disconsolate as the rest.

"Look at the mountains," said my boat partner. "They're sure different from the big ragged coastal range peaks around Juneau."

"Glaciers did that," explained a miner who seemed knowledgeable. "The ice grinds them as it travels, tearing out boulders and carrying them down the mountainside. Then the streams carry them farther, breaking them up and washing off the gravel and dirt. You saw that down below on Ganes there were half a dozen creeks joining in; well, they all added their rocks, back in the past. That's why it's richer down there. Not only that, but it's had so much washing and tumbling that what's left is almost pure gold."

"And up here, it's all quartz," said my boat partner gloomily. "Too hard to get the gold out. No use staking. Better cook ourselves some grub and get back again."

I was gazing up the mountainside. Something moved, almost imperceptibly. Fixing my eyes on the spot, I made out a caribou standing motionless among the bushes and scrub trees.

"Who'd like a caribou steak?" I asked, keeping my eyes trained on the animal.

"Who wouldn't? We've had so many beans, they ought to be sprouting from our ears. Well, get out your pots, boys. Let's build a fire here by the creek."

"Hold everything. Since I have the only rifle, it's up to me to provide the steaks," I said, and started off up the incline to the mountain. Behind me, down by the creek, the men could be heard debating: "Did he see something? Nothing up there, is there?" I went ahead quickly but cautiously, determined to provide them with those steaks so rashly promised.

The caribou moved, then stood still and looked back, making me freeze and hope my figure was indistinguishable in the distance from the stunted trees around me. The caribou moved on again slowly. There was no breeze, so the animal had caught no scent of me to cause alarm. Following in the direction it had gone, I caught sight of moving antlers down in a gulch where reindeer moss grew thick and green. Figuring it was within range, I sighted carefully and squeezed the trigger. The rifle cracked and recoiled; the caribou fell. Several shots fired in the air alerted my party, and the men began to straggle up the mountain. By the time they rejoined me, the meat was sizzling on a spit improvised from forked sticks and saplings.

Full stomachs helped to restore our morale. We were hopeful again as we headed north across the flats, jumping the smaller creeks, aiming for the tents of Ophir to spend the night. Some of our party had paused at creeks we passed to stake out claims on the few remaining spots. About two miles north of Ganes we hit Little Creek. I found the lower part taken, but Valentine had staked

Number Fifteen for Ted, and along a little side creek, Fifteen Pup, there was another discovery stake in his name. This was what I had come to find, and I was eager to get back to Ted and Jock with the good news. Legally, Ted had only a month from the date of staking to record the claims; even then he could lose them after a year unless he worked at them for at least 10 days, or paid the recorder $100 assessment fee, or restaked under a new date. He could never make it to Ophir in time, but with luck no one would jump the claims before we got back. This, however, often happened to prospectors unfamiliar with the rules who would come back hopefully to good claims after a year outside working to collect supplies, only to find their properties taken over and lawfully recorded by more knowledgeable prospectors.

I started back for Mouse Point the next morning. Ophir was soon to be marked out as the town headquarters. Houses and stores would mushroom, and a commissioner would be appointed to register claims, but at this time there were only a few tents a short distance from the river bank to mark the site. Although ignored at first, Ophir produced several of the richest claims in the Innoko headwaters. Some romantic soul had chosen for the town and creek the name of that fabulous land of the Far East, famed for its abundance of fine gold. From ancient Ophir, gold was brought to King Solomon, and from it were formed his shields of beaten gold, his throne of gold and ivory and his golden drinking vessels. Gold from Ophir overlaid all within his temple: the altar, the oracle and the carved flowers and cherubim upon the temple's folding doors. The old Biblical verse echoed the wild hope in the hearts of all weary miners who stepped ashore here at the creek:

> And they came to Ophir, and fetched
> from thence gold . . .

TWO

At Mouse Point, I got the welcome that traditionally is handed out to all bearers of good tidings. My enthusiasm whetted Ted's and Jock's appetites, and we decided to leave at once. Jock and I went first and Ted, after arranging for the freighting of his stock, followed us a week later with a new partner he had found for the mining venture, Homer Mezaire. Homer was an American who had worked in mines at Fairbanks. He exuded confidence from every pore and guaranteed to teach us all we needed to know about mining for gold, which was everything from A to Z.

Jock and I made it in good time, but Ted and Homer were slowed by heavy rainstorms on the Innoko. The deluge continued day after day with monotonous persistence. Ted poured a can of water over the bow of his boat and ceremoniously christened her the Ark. She was less crowded with passengers than was Noah's, but she was wide open to the elements, only the supplies being protected by canvas.

Several boats were making the trip up-river, some of them bound for the Iditarod to track down rumors of gold in its creeks. They were as unfamiliar with the route as were Ted and Homer, but they sounded cheerful. Ted could hear music from a gramophone coming from one of the boats, and the barking of dogs. He kept ahead of the Iditarod flotilla, which he called the Chinese Funeral because the boats were rigged with square sails and moved very slowly.

The rain pelted down, but nothing dampened Ted's spirits. The journey was a comedy of errors and absurdity that amused and stimulated him, and when we were finally reunited, he related the details with gusto.

Part way up the Innoko, in mid-July, the Ark came to some cabins, and Ted poled in to shout to the Indians on the bank: "How many days before we reach the Iditarod?" One of the natives held up four fingers. "Odd," Ted remarked to Homer, " I could have sworn we were almost there, from what Bill told me. We'd better camp by that hill ahead. The Chinese Funeral must be miles behind us."

The torrential rain kept them under canvas until late the next day, when they saw the Funeral creeping past. Breaking camp in a hurry, they speedily overtook the boats, shot ahead saucily and camped as usual in the hills that night. Ducks were getting scarce now, but two were brought down for supper and one to share at breakfast. In the distance, the Funeral straggled into sight below them and they set out hurriedly again on their hare and tortoise race. They were now forced to row against a strong wind for several miles until a bend in the winding river gave them a fair wind for sailing once more.

An old man in a peculiar boat bore down on them here. He had constructed a kind of coracle out of canvas and telegraph wire, and it wobbled down-river, bobbing and circling in an uneasy minuet with the waves. In answer to their shouts, the old man told them they had already passed the Iditarod by some 25 miles.

"What the devil did those Indians mean with their four fingers?" Ted muttered. "Four bends in the river?" He hollered after the canvas coracle that was joggling away on the current: "Turn back the boats behind us! They're making for the Iditarod!" The old man raised his arm in assent and drifted on down-river to head off the Chinese Funeral.

While camped that night on the hillside, they were wakened by the noise of a passing steamboat. Tumbling from their tent, they ran down the incline to the riverbank yelling at the top of their lungs. Luckily, a crew member riding on a scow lashed to the steamer's side heard their frenzied shouts above the throb of the engines and had the boat stopped. It was the *Ben Hur*, and her skipper was willing to take on passengers. Ted's supplies were transferred to the scow, and they traveled on in comfort with their boat in tow.

On August 1, they reached Dishkaket, site of an Indian village and a trading post where Ted bought several hundred pounds of flour and sugar.

"I've had a report of a missing man," the trader told him. "He was camping farther up the Innoko, and he's disappeared. Louie Shagair, he's called."

"Where was his camp? I'll stop off there and make a thorough search for him," Ted promised.

Homer nudged his partner. "Hey, don't forget our month is already up. If we don't get that claim recorded we may reach the Innoko and find someone else has done it for us . . . in his own name."

"Lots of time. A lost man is more important than a lost mine." After his years at Mouse Point Ted had begun to feel himself personally responsible for lost men. Uncovering clues and tracking down a missing man appealed to him far more than a timely arrival at the goldfields.

The Innoko narrowed as they worked their way up, and the steamer grounded on one bar after another, finally wedging herself so firmly that no poles or reversed engines budged her. Ted paid off the purser and unloaded his supplies on the beach. He found his boat severely battered from her bouncing ride behind the steamer at the end of a towrope, with the current swinging her like a pendulum against rocks in the shallow water. He and Homer gathered together some makeshift material and tried to patch her.

"Poor old girl, her bottom's been sadly beaten." Ted examined the cracked and splintered boards with a pessimistic eye. "We'll doctor her up, but I doubt if she'll be strong enough to take the rapids."

Their guardian angel materialized just then in the form of an old prospector named Lindenbaum who poled past them, heading upriver. They had talked to the old fellow in Dishkaket and learned that he was on his way to Ganes Creek to try to persuade a friend to take him in as partner. They watched the boat as it made slow progress up the first riffle. But the rapids were too swift for the old man, and he was forced to float down again and landed beside them.

"Can't make it," he said, blinking away tears of frustration. "I'll never get to the goldfields."

"What about the scow?" Ted suggested. "See, they're detaching it from the steamboat. They're going to pole it up-river. There's not room for Homer and me and all our gear, but you're traveling light."

Lindenbaum shuffled over to the scow and begged for passage. The crew agreed to take him, and he climbed aboard, all smiles now, shouting happily: "Take my boat, boys!"

Ted and Homer, happy too, began to load their gear. Heavy rain soon halted them again and they camped for two days. Their grub was getting low, and they eked it out by picking blueberries and shooting and eating a crane. At noon on the third day they saw a

155

boat being poled up-river by two men with a third man sitting amidships.

"Have you heard anything of the lost man?" the passenger called over.

"Just going to look for him," Ted shouted.

"Well, I'm him," the man shouted back, thus abruptly ending the search for the missing miner.

More bad luck was to bedevil them. They hit a snag that ripped a hole in Lindenbaum's boat and were forced to unload at once on the shore and make repairs. Everything in the bottom of the boat was soaking wet and had to be spread out to dry by a fire.

The rain pelted down. The river was rising fast, the rapids grew fiercer, and when they started out again they were able to pole only short distances during brief intervals between the deluges. Finally Ted spotted the old *Fairy*, the short-beamed boat he had built on the Black River and which I had moored in a slough. Seeing her there, he felt they must be nearing the end of their long, damp journey. Torrential rains and boiling rapids halted them for three days when they were eight miles above the North Fork, but at last we were all together again.

"Heard you had a bit of rain down on the Innoko," said Jock.

"Well, one good thing," said Ted, "the rain kept off those bloodthirsty mosquitoes Bill was telling us about."

Jock and I took them over to Little Creek to see Number Fifteen and Fifteen Pup. We had heartening news for them: gold had been found on claims below and above our own. Hills ran along one side of Little Creek, turning where Fifteen Pup Creek branched off and continuing up the steep incline to the higher mountains. There was no gravel on this side of the creek, nor on the near side at the curve, although the land here on our claim was lower. No gravel usually meant no gold, but if it was true that strikes had been made below and above us, we felt that gold must surely be thick in the old hidden creekbed running through our claims.

We built a cabin on Fifteen Pup for the four of us. A lean-to held our own supplies and served as a small store for miners on surrounding claims. Ted had arranged to have some of the stock in his Mouse Point store brought up by boat to the halfway mark up the

Innoko and dumped there at the head of navigation. I spent most of the summer floating down the rapids and poling back up with supplies, a ton at a time. As a result, I soon felt myself familiar with every cross-current and jutting rock in the rapids. Disaster came fast, however, if familiarity was allowed to lull one into complacency. Especially at curves in the river where the current swirled to the banks and pulled boats with a mighty grip, an idle glance to one side was all that was needed to send a boat crashing to destruction.

This was what caused our old, short-beamed boat — so incongruously labeled the *Fairy* — to smash into a snag. The half-sunken roots of a tree in the river ripped a hole in her side and nearly sent us both to the bottom. Fortunately, the current whirled her to the shallows before she could sink, enabling me to pull her onto the bar. I shouted for help to a group of poling boats shooting downstream, but none gave me a second look. My faith in humanity was restored when a boatman, who followed them by a few minutes, poled over to the bar and stayed to help me patch the *Fairy* and make her watertight again.

A measure of immortality came to me after this adventure. Thenceforth, the curve in the river where my boat hit the snag was known as Fairy Rapids by travelers on the Innoko.

Hearts in Alaska were warm or cold in violent contrast, like the extremes of her summers and winters. On one occasion when I arrived at navigation head to load up, there was a party of men camped in tents beside the canvas-covered supplies dumped there by the steamer. There were two miners on their way to look over the goldfields, and four men who were weighing and sorting potatoes into small bags, reloading sacks with the bags and strapping them on packhorses to be taken to Ophir and sold for fancy prices to the miners. The two older men were traders from Fairbanks, and one reason for their trip was to find out if it would be profitable to ship goods overland by packhorse to the Innoko and the Iditarod. St. Michael, however, was the closest and obvious choice for Ophir storekeepers to turn to for their orders. When the town built up, horse-drawn scows brought up supplies at regular intervals from the head of navigation. Nothing came of the Fairbanks idea to bring supplies overland.

This potential alternative may have dawned on the Fairbanks men after their long trip, as they were short-tempered and surly. Their young helpers were two brothers, the youngest about 15 and the other about a year older, whom they constantly nagged: "Speed up your packing! Get a move on!" The boys looked weary and disillusioned with a land that had brought them not wealth nor adventure but only this prosaic toil. When the sorting and saddling were completed, each man mounted a horse and led a string of three or four potato-laden packhorses behind him. The miners were ready to leave in their poling boat and so all of us started out together, the packhorse train traveling up the gravel bars just ahead of me and crossing the river from one side to the other.

On reaching a bar and wading ashore, I was thrusting my arm into the loop tied in my towing rope when I glanced ahead to watch the horses crossing to the opposite bar. The youngest boy, last in line with his string, was starting into the river. I watched his uncertain handling of the reins and decided he must be a novice at fording rapids. He stopped, started up, and then stopped his horse again, looking ahead nervously at the angry white waves. He looked back at his packhorses, scanned the river intently and finally came to a decision, turning his horse to one side and making for a patch of quiet water that looked easier to navigate. I let out a shout, being familiar enough with white rapids by now to know that quiet water in them often meant deep water.

Suddenly, the boy's horse stumbled and dropped out of sight. The boy had time for only one frightened cry to his brother: "Help me, Al!" before tumbling with his horse into the deep hole. He must have struck his head or injured himself in some way, for although the horse reappeared a moment later, swimming and scrambling back into the shallows, there was no sign of its rider. By the time the traders had turned back and got him up with poles, he was blue and lifeless. His brother knelt beside him on the gravel bar, stroking the cold, wet shoulder helplessly, looking up at the men with shocked, bewildered eyes. One of the traders bent down, frowning at the drowned boy. "He's dead." He got up, slapping his thigh with exasperation and snapped, "It's up to you to lead his horses. Rope them to your string. Come on, we can't waste time here."

"But you're not leaving him like this?" Al's voice was shrill with horror.

"He won't know the difference. Come on, get moving! I hired you to pack potatoes!" The trader jerked at the rope of his lead horse, mounted and began crossing the river.

Al fumbled blindly with the ropes, tears streaming down his face. He stood for an instant staring down at his brother, then pulled himself slowly up into his saddle.

The two miners stayed behind by the body. "Don't worry, kid!" one of them called out in sympathy. "We'll get your brother buried."

The boy looked back with a quavering smile and lifted a hand in gratitude as his horse splashed into the water.

As I pulled my boat up to the crossing point and began to pole across the rapids, the sound of the miners' picks could be heard beating out a rhythmic dirge for him on a bank of the wild Innoko River.

THREE

Ted wrote away for a boiler, and when it was brought down the Yukon and up the Innoko to Little Creek, we set to work in early fall to sink our first hole. The thick, two-foot-high turf was dug out over a six-by-four-foot area and laid aside. Then points six feet long, attached to the boiler, were used to steam down vertically. On alternate days, the thawed and cooled muck was shoveled out. It was easy going for several feet where dirt and gravel were not tightly frozen, but further down the permafrost was reached, and this rock-like gravel took longer to thaw. The steam points were a vast improvement on the earlier methods employed by placer miners who were forced to build fires to thaw out the frozen gravel and then, when the fire died down, to dig it out and rebuild the fire in a slow, laborious descent to bedrock.

We laid off in the extremely cold weather but started in again in the early spring. Homer was in charge. At Rampart, Jock had been initiated into the mysteries of drifting and digging, but he had no knowledge of the preliminary setting up. As for Ted and me, the whole procedure was foreign territory, and we turned to Homer for

159

guidance at every step. Confident, forever talking, laughing and joking, Homer instructed us, working hard himself every minute of the day, cutting wood for the boiler, watching the gauge, building a two-by-four wooden bucket with slanting sides to haul up the dirt, and setting up the winch and the poles for the cleated bucket to slide along from platform to dump. We could whipsaw lumber, but he had to show us how to shape the sluice boxes and fit in the cleats and riffles.

Bedrock had shown a reasonable amount of gold in the panned samples. It was 15 feet down, though, too deep for hydraulicking, the mining method by which the waste soil was washed away and the remaining paydirt sluiced. This method only paid off when the gold lay fairly close to the surface on wide, slanting benches. Here we must drift, widening the hole underground, removing waste and pay by softening with steam and hauling it up with winch and bucket to be sluiced on the surface. We widened our shaft so that eight-foot-long points could be used to drift more quickly.

The usual practice around the Innoko creeks was to find bedrock with a good showing of gold and then drift in the direction taken by the paystreak, digging up about four and a half feet from bedrock to allow at least a cramped working space. The first two feet above bedrock were sent up to a pay dump to be sluiced; the ground above, which usually showed little gold in panning tests, was sent up for the waste dump and left in a great pile to defile the landscape and impoverish the soil.

But Homer had learned his mining methods in Fairbanks where the fabulously rich mines produced varying but good yields of gold at all levels, increasing in value as they approached bedrock.

"There's a stack of gold in the big gravel layer above the sand," he told us. "We want to get every ounce of it out. These poor green-horns around here are throwing away fortunes in their waste dumps. Waste? Why, there's enough gold in those waste dumps to make every one of us a millionaire!"

"You're the expert, Homer."

So we began to drift a hole 20 feet wide, when only halfway to bedrock, drifting across the old creekbed instead of exploring its course. On alternate days, we sent up bucket after bucket of dirt which our points had steamed out. "Get the volume up," Homer would encourage us. "We've got it made if we get the volume up." On the surface, beside the shaft hole, the dirt began to pile up, higher and higher, 50 feet across, until it became an oddity that miners from other claims came to stare at and discuss.

But Homer's confidence silenced doubts. A reporter from a Seattle newspaper, who came up to Ophir looking for the story of another Klondike, walked over to see the gigantic pile of drift by Little Creek that was the talk of miners on all the nearby claims. Homer was in his element.

"You've got to know what you're doing in this game or you throw away as much as you take out. You've got to have the old know-how. Yes, you've got to be sharp to get all the gold. Did you see the waste dumps on the other claims? Do you know what they're doing? They're keeping the cream and pouring off the milk. You and I know there's nourishment in milk; doesn't look as rich, but only a fool would throw it away. Now, let me show you how I've run my sluice boxes right through the center of this dump. Take a look at these boxes. See how they're made? I worked out this scheme myself. When I'm ready to wash the dirt, I can unpin sections and let controlled amounts of the dirt slide into the boxes. I'm telling you, we don't aim to lose a penny of the profit in this dump — profit that's being tossed away on the other claims."

The reporter paced off the size of the dump and, basing his calculation on Homer's estimate of the gold percentage, decided we had $80,000 worth of gold waiting to be sluiced out. He wrote this up for his paper, and my uncle and aunt in Seattle clipped out the story. When I visited them two years later, they greeted me with the respect due a young man who had achieved early success.

Ted was chosen to man the boiler so that Jock and I could work steadily with the steampoints, while Homer darted from one job to another with his inexhaustible Yankee energy. A long hose ran from the boiler down the side of the hole, joining a bar to which four six-foot hydraulic pipes were attached for the initial descent and replaced by the eight-foot pipes for drifting across. Each pipe contained a narrow tube that brought the steam out with terrific pressure from the pointed steel ends. The steam pipes were thrust into the frozen wall of the hole at various spots where they thawed out the packed, icy gravel sufficiently to allow it to be broken up with picks. The pipes were left in overnight to ensure a large thawed section, and the following day we worked with pick and shovel, sending up the dirt and gravel in the big wooden bucket. The steampoints, however, had their unpleasant aspect: sometimes the points ran against a large rock, or small bits of gravel worked into the openings in the points, and then the steam backfired, pouring up to the roof of the drift, softening it so that dirt and gravel showered down on us and turned our slickers black with mud.

Ted's job was to keep the boiler well stoked with wood in order to maintain the steam pressure up to the required 60 to 80 pounds. Unfortunately for Jock and me, Ted had bought himself a book of mathematical problems which fascinated him, and he couldn't bear to be parted from it for an instant. He sat beside the boiler, book and slide rule in his lap, figuring out problems with pencil and scratch pad, lost to the world. The fire in the boiler gradually burned low as he scribbled, the pressure dropped, steam filled the drift hole, and then mud and rocks began to splatter our bent backs.

"Hey, up there. Ted! Stoke the boiler! Get the steam up."

"Wait. I want you to alter the valves." Ted's excited voice echoed down the shaft. "I figured it all out in my notebook. With a smaller hole, the pressure will be concentrated and you'll need only 40 pounds to do the same job. Let's try it out."

"The devil we will! We're getting steamed alive like bloody lobsters," Jock yelled back, his equanimity obliterated by a gob of mud in one eye. "For God's sake, stoke the boiler and get up the pressure!" His furious cries sent Ted on the run to the boiler to fill it with wood and get the pressure back to 80.

"Just like that fellow Rex Beach at Rampart," Jock recalled later, his good humor restored as he bore down on the point again. "They're all the same," lumping authors and readers together as impractical thinkers instead of doers.

As soon as ice melted in the creeks, we ran our heavy canvas hose from a dam high up in the hills down to the sluice boxes in the drift. Now would come our reward for the months spent grubbing in the muck, the painstaking work of whipsawing lumber for sluiceboxes, the back-breaking toil digging ditches and a dam to get water with sufficient pressure to sluice the dirt from the gold. Now the $80,000 was to be ours, perhaps with thousands yet to come when we could dig and drift again.

Drift was taken into the boxes through Homer's ingenious removable sections, the water was turned on and run through the boxes, carrying off the gravel, which we shoveled away as it accumulated at the mouth of the flume. After a week of this, Homer decided it was time for a cleanup. Nails were loosened from the cross cleats, and the sets of riffles lifted clear. The fine gravel and gold were always hard-packed in the bottoms of the boxes and had to be loosened with paddles, letting the hose run gently while the gravel was stirred and washed away. Then the signal was given to slow the water still more until the fine sand could be stirred and removed. The water was shut off. Now the gold, mixed with a small amount of black sand that could be blown away, should be revealed as a mass of yellow lumps and fine gold dust. The four of us bent over the sluice boxes to feast our eyes.

"What the hell! What's happened?" From box to box we moved slowly, unable to believe our eyes. Each contained a scattering of tiny gold nuggets and traces of gold dust, the whole not exceeding a few dollars in value. I looked at Jock and Ted and saw my own consternation reflected on their long faces. Only Homer stayed confident. "Just a fluke. Tomorrow we'll start getting it out. We've got the volume, that's what counts."

But tomorrow was no better, nor was the next day. None of the drift was rich enough to warrant sluicing, and we had spent a year piling it up and making preparations to sluice. After two months of sluicing, we took out a little over $200 in gold to pay expenses and share among the four of us. Even Homer found his ready explanations faltering, and his perpetual smile faded away. He boarded a scow that was leaving for the head of navigation, and we never saw him again.

But a large part of the enormous drift remained, a monument to Homer and our mistaken trust in his judgment, and to our own folly in attempting to mine without experience or qualified instruction. Homer had assumed that the creek benches here were as phenomenally rich as those at Fairbanks, which were proportionately rich at all levels. He was smart, energetic and experienced, but experienced only in the mining of bonanzas. He had not been smart or experienced enough to be able to adapt his methods to Innoko conditions.

"Yankees think big," said Ted philosophically. "He wanted all or nothing for us. And nothing was what we got."

FOUR

Having learned at least a little by now, we decided to try another hole farther down, just past Fifteen Pup creek and on the opposite side, on Number Fifteen claim. We panned samples when we were part-way down and found them promising. Schwartz, the elderly miner on the claim above us, came down to take a look and give advice.

"Do it right this time. And don't drift higher than four feet above bedrock. Above four, it's worthless; under, it should pay well. All those rich claims below us are part of the same old creekbed that runs first beside Fifteen Pup. I'm getting out plenty of gold myself; nuggets are rough up here, full of quartz, but the gold is in them. Why is there so much quartz? Reason is, they were trapped in the stream crevices before the water could tumble them smooth. Farther down, the water's had a chance to wear off the quartz."

Excited and hopeful, we continued to work the points and dig toward bedrock. What treasures lay hidden there? We were never to know. Before we reached bedrock, we hit an underground spring. Water filled the hole, sending us scuttling up the ladder.

Ted sent away for a centrifugal pump and when it arrived, we set it up in an effort to check the flow. The small pump, however, proved inadequate to hold back that burst of water that welled joyously forth, clear, fresh and bubbling, drowning our hopes and forming a barricade between us and the gold that lay untouched below.

We were sick of the claims — the great, unproductive dump on Fifteen Pup and the inaccessible bedrock under the spring between the Pup and Number Fifteen. Gold might lie somewhere at bedrock on our land — Schwartz insisted it was there in quantity — but we had no heart to search further for it. Even if we had wished to continue, there was no money left to keep us eating while we worked. Now we could understand the despair that drove a miner to blow out his brains when long months of hard labor and high hopes ended in failure.

One day Jock said: "I was talking to a Scotsman over on the next creek. He's got a Welsh partner, Evan Jones, but they say they need men to work on their claim. What do you say we walk over and see what they have to offer?"

"You and Bill go," Ted encouraged us. "I'll stay on in the cabin and tend the store, and pan the drift for what I can get from it."

Jock and I walked up the flats to Spruce, the next creek parallel to Little, and hunted up the Scotsman. McNaughton was a big, heavy set man who wore a drooping walrus moustache that gave him a look of melancholy. He offered Jock and me a lay in the mine, which meant that the first 25 per cent of each day's takings would go to MacNaughton and Jones, and the remaining 75 per cent would be divided four ways among us all. Jock and I agreed and moved in with our new partners.

We worked the claim all summer, and every week we took out a substantial amount of gold. Spruce was a rich creek. Vinal, below us, took out $10,000 in one cleanup, and MacNaughton and Jones took out up to $3,000 worth at a time when they emptied their boxes.

One day we turned off the water before stopping for lunch. This was always done, since dirt that was washed out of the boxes accumulated in front of the last box and would block up the opening and cause an overflow if someone was not stationed there continuously to hose and shovel away the accumulation. Before leaving, we filed as usual past the boxes to examine them. Should any nuggets become trapped on top, too large to go through the riffles, they were apt to be washed away and lost. MacNaughton gave a sudden yell and swooped up a huge, smooth nugget as big as the palm of his hand and over half an inch thick.

"Look at this beauty! It's the biggest I've seen taken from any of the Innoko creeks!" It was valued later at $260, more than all the gold we had found in two months of cleanups from Homer's mountain of dirt on Ted's claim.

My savings were mounting. I had been in Alaska now for 12 years and began to hanker for a sight of the outside world again. In late summer, with sluicing on Spruce Creek soon to slow down and come to a stop during freeze-up, I traveled the Innoko and the Yukon to St. Michael and sailed from there down the coast to Seattle.

Who Would Inhabit
This Bleak World Alone?

ONE

STEPPING OFF THE BOAT in Seattle after 12 years in the wilds of Alaska was like stepping into a new world. Automobiles, infrequent enough to be novelties on the road when I left the city of Victoria, now roared and rattled through bustling Seattle, as numerous as the horse-drawn buggies. The hurrying crowds and the hard pavements were unfamiliar and exhausting after my years in Alaska's vast unsettled areas with their acres of tundra underfoot. I felt a wave of relief on seeing the familiar home of my aunt Meg and uncle Dick — a tall, white wooden house, its porch and gables lacy with gingerbread trim. I was led through the house to the back garden where tea was laid on a table under the cherry trees, and where the branches of the rose bushes hung down with the weight of their heavy pink blooms.

My aunt was an incurable romanticist. Maude had become engaged to Ted here in her rose garden, and as soon as my aunt saw me, 30 years old and still unattached, she determined to exhibit me to some nice girl and let the roses work their magic once again. I considered myself too old for romance, settled as I was into a permanent bachelor life in Alaska with my partner Jock, but my aunt, loath to lose a moment's time, slipped across the street before pouring my tea to ask a young college student, Alice Mills, to join us and hear about my adventures in the north. I was a bit chagrined by her plotting; I was still bashful at 30 and was sure I had nothing to say that would interest an 18-year-old schoolgirl.

Alice told me later that she had expected a weather-beaten, bearded miner, and it was a pleasant surprise to see a man who was clean-shaven and comparatively young. And I was amazed at her maturity. It was her way of walking with head high and spine straight that gave her an air of dignity beyond her years. In contrast she had a friendly smile that dimpled her cheeks and a lively, frolicsome nature that preferred fun to formality. She was a beautiful girl. I could not take my eyes from her.

"Let Alice sit down for her tea," said my aunt, and I released her hand so suddenly that we all laughed and relaxed.

"Now, tell me about Alaska," said Alice.

What could I say? Alaska, of course had been much in the news. It had been established that year as a U.S. territory, with its own territorial legislature. It had startled the continent, too, with the terrible volcanic eruption of Mount Katmai in June which laid waste the Alaskan Peninsula, darkened Alaskan skies for 60 hours and sent volcanic ash drifting through the air to soil washing on Chicago clothes lines half a continent away. Jock and I, walking through the long grass to our mine on that summer day, had been puzzled by dust on the grass which turned our boots white. When news of the eruption reached us, we realized it was volcanic ash and that the darkened skies and rumbling sounds we had heard had not been warnings of an approaching thunderstorm, as we had first thought, but had also been caused by the eruption. I myself had been in the local news with that item in the Seattle paper telling of $80,000 worth of gold waiting to be washed out of an enormous pile of gravel beside Little Creek.

But with this eager Desdemona hanging on my words, I dredged my memory for stories that would keep Alice wide-eyed: stories about our days up the Black and on the Yukon and our journey up the rapids of the Innoko. I talked on and on, encouraged when my tales made her laugh or shudder. My tea grew cold in the cup, and my aunt Meg looked from one to the other of us with the contented smile of a successful matchmaker.

I lingered in Seattle through fall and winter, seeing Alice daily and pouring forth my mining plans to her as we walked in the park or rode home from the theatre. When March arrived, I knew it was time to head north, for sluicing would start when the breakup released the creek waters. On my last night in Seattle, I went to say good-bye to Alice. I was sitting beside her on the sofa when for a brief moment we were left alone. This happened so seldom in her home that I must have become rattled and lost my head. I heard myself asking her to marry me.

"I don't expect you to go north with me," I told her earnestly, holding her hands. "When I've made a fortune, I'll come out to you. If you'll wait for me . . ."

"Wait for you? I wouldn't dream of it, Bill!"

"No, of course you wouldn't. I was crazy to suggest it." I withdrew my hands and sat with them limp between my knees, wallowing in despondency.

"But you don't understand. I want to go, too."

"Are you serious? You mean, you'll really marry me and go to Alaska?" I was out of the slough of despond and up in the clouds. Then doubts assailed me again. "I can't take you with me. Spruce Creek is all scrub spruce and mud and mosquitoes. It would never do to take you there."

Her parents felt the same way. "How can you support a wife?" they added. "You said that news story about the eighty thousand was all a mistake."

I told them then about Spruce Creek and the claim that Jock and I had staked just above MacNaughton, painting a glowing picture of the steady supply of gold that we expected to get from that rich, buried creek bed. Alice's parents remained unconvinced and adamant. They remembered the volcanic eruptions of Alaska's Mount Katmai the year before and the catastrophe in the same year when the luxury ship *Titanic* collided with an iceberg and sank in the Atlantic with the loss of 1,517 lives. They were reluctant to see their daughter sail to the Bering Sea, whose gigantic icebergs I had obviously described with too much eloquence.

"Go back to Alaska, Bill," they advised with the caution of age. "Add to your savings for another year. Then, if Alice still wants to join you, you'll be in a better position to support her."

"A whole year," Alice despaired. To an 18-year-old, a year seems

169

a lifetime. She threw her arms about my neck. "How can we bear it, Bill?"

"Alice!" commanded her mother. "Restrain yourself."

"But, we're engaged!"

"Nevertheless . . ." Decorum was demanded by parents in those days, even for engaged couples!

MacNaughton's mine was still producing, but I was eager to start work with Jock on our claims just above. "I'm engaged now, Jock," I said, "and I've got to prove to Alice's parents that I'm a man of substance."

It would be prudent to continue the lay partnership during the summer to be sure of enough money to cover both my trip to Seattle and our honeymoon, but when the time came for me to settle down to work again, Jock and I would sink holes on our own claim and divide the profits. We felt by now that we had a good working knowledge of mining methods suitable for Spruce Creek.

Amateur prospectors arriving in Alaska saw a bewildering variety of placer mining methods in operation, depending on terrain and location of the mineral. If gold-laden rocks had been tumbled far down the streams, gradually releasing the gold to a gravel bed near the surface, panning or rocking was the method followed. This gold had been brought down so recently that it could be found on the bars and the bottom or on rims of the present creek, and $5 to $10 a day could be made by prospectors who dumped the gravel into a pan of water and shook or swirled until the gold separated from the gravel and could be removed. For rocking, gravel was shoveled onto a screened section of a cradle-like rocker. A dipper of water was poured over it and the rocker was shaken jerkily to send the sand and finer gold through the screen to a burlap apron below. Some of the gold stayed in the apron, while any that fell to the bottom was trapped in transverse riffles. Sometimes sluices were placed directly in the creek, and gravel from bottom and rims dumped in; $10 a day could often be made in this manner, too. In rich bonanza areas, of course, the take could be up to 10 times as high.

If gold was found on benches above the ancient creek beds and there was a good grade to the bench, hydraulic mining was the best bet. Benches were hosed to wash away the gravel, and riffled sluice boxes trapped the gold. If bedrock was deep down, as at Fifteen Pup, a hole was sunk and drifting was employed. The width and richness of the paystreak was tested and if the gold was too widely scattered to be worth the labor involved, big companies sometimes came in with dredges that could scoop out a scattered paystreak quickly and easily.

Hardrock or lode mining, as opposed to placer, was employed where gold was found in the solid rock, usually far up the mountain sides. Since this gold was entrapped in the rock, often embedded in quartz, it needed to be a rich vein to be worth sending out in heavy rock chunks to the smelter. At Spruce, gold had been found on sloping benches above the creek within 10 feet of the surface, so hydraulic mining was the choice.

When there was time to spare, I worked on a log cabin and had it finished before the cold weather began.

"What do you think of it?" I asked Jock, trying to visualize Alice in those two rooms.

"Sturdy and snug, Bill. Should please her." I was too wrapped up in my own emotions to notice the reserve in Jock's voice. He never talked much. Silently, he listened to my plans for Alice and sat patiently as always during the summer evenings when I plucked the strings of my banjo and sang my favorite melancholy song:

> When true hearts lie wither'd
>   And fond ones are flown,
> Oh, who would inhabit
>   This bleak world alone?

I had thought myself a confirmed bachelor at 30 and was even more convinced of Jock's solitary inclinations at 42. But my partner, quietly smoking his pipe, was shrewdly pondering the possibility that something was lacking in his own life and the need to do something about it in a hurry. A canny Scot, he said nothing when issues were in doubt but searched his memory and came up with a family in his boyhood village in Scotland, a sober, industrious couple with five single, hard-working daughters.

In the fall, before freeze-up, I told Jock and Ted: "I've decided to hike out overland to Seward and sail from there to Seattle. I'll take Alice to Los Angeles for our honeymoon and surprise Maude with my bride." (Maude had settled with her children in Los Angeles near the home of Madge Crompton's brother, Charles, and his American wife.)

"Well, now," Jock said offhandedly, "it just occurs to me I might like to come with you and keep on going to Scotland for a look at my old home."

"If you're going to Los Angeles, Bill," chimed in Ted, "I think I'll take a trip there myself. Maude may decide to come back to Alaska when she meets Alice."

The three of us set out to cross the Takotna Divide, the boggy marshes and the taiga forests. Crossing the Great Divide in the Alaska range, we could see Mount McKinley on our left, the tallest peak on the continent, rising up white and majestic for more than 20,000 feet, standing out clearly against the sky, above the nearer mountains. This time we were traveling before the freeze-up, and we were forced to skirt the lakes and rivers with time-consuming detours, even circumventing the lakeside trails sometimes when we found them blocked by trees that industrious beavers had gnawed and toppled.

That cross-country hike in the crisp autumn air was a treat for us after a summer spent sluicing dirt in the mines, plagued with mosquitoes and weary of monotonous evenings when we were too tired for talk. One day, picking our way among the big tufts of grass in the open areas, Ted and I entertained Jock with Hood's sad poem of Faithless Sally Brown, whose young man came to an unpleasant end when he was shanghaied:

> His death, which happened in his berth,
>   At forty-odd befell:
> They went and told the sexton, and
>   The sexton toll'd the bell.

"Same age as yourself, Jock. Who knows, that might have been your own fate if you'd stayed with the sea."

"Aye, a sailor's life is hard," Jock agreed. "I'm lucky to be out of it, having a soft time up here in Alaska."

Three congenial companions, we tramped those hundreds of miles each hoping to bring back a wife and each oblivious of the possibility that marriage might jeopardize our cherished freedom.

THREE

The chief reason for my having chosen Los Angeles for our honeymoon was the chance that it would give me to show off my bride to Maude. But that year California was a drawing card for thousands. Its widely publicized golden sunshine produced an invasion almost as spectacular as the rush to the golden creekbeds of Alaska and the Yukon. There was a big boom in real estate, especially in rapidly growing Los Angeles. To this cradle of the motion picture industry Maude had come with her children, to a bungalow on Logan Street, off Sunset Boulevard, a block from Echo Park with its reed-choked lake and its walks lined with giant palm trees.

It was an ideal entertainment center for Alice and me with our limited funds. We often walked the short block to the park which motion picture producers used as a location to shoot scenes for cheaply produced reels. We had a ringside preview of Keystone Cops brandishing their guns, chasing each other in circles and collapsing in a heap of entwined arms, legs and popping pistols. Adults and children crowded the park when Charlie Chaplin or madcap Mabel Normand appeared with a crew to shoot a scene. Chaplin stayed aloof from the public, but Mabel was friendly and outgoing, and she often strolled over during breaks to talk and joke with the children. Many of Maude's neighbors were on call for bit parts, and we always had to be on hand to watch their performances.

"Babe is on today," Maude would inform us. "Be sure to be in the park. You'll see Babe jump off the bridge into Echo Lake."

Babe was an immensely plump woman who lived alone with a tiny Boston Bull terrier. On the day that we watched her jump off the center of the arched bridge, her flailing arms and legs became entangled in the slimy reeds that grew thick in the lake. A rowboat was rushed to her rescue, and three men struggled to pull her free and into the boat without swamping them all. Babe shrieked like a banshee as she sprawled half over the gunnel, her arms and legs draped with reeds. We hung over the bridge, fearful and fascinated.

We went to the movies with Maude to watch her red fox fur, brought from Mouse Point, appear in a film. Beautiful Helen Wooten of Logan Street wore it in her part as a wealthy society girl for the big role of her career, lasting a good 30 seconds.

Los Angeles was famous for its air meets, and Alice and I went to several, craning our necks to watch the stunts and marveling as records were broken by the rickety planes with their unreliable engines. The spectacular Vanderbilt Cup auto races were also featured while we were in Los Angeles, and we joined crowds that jammed onto the trolley cars to Santa Monica to watch them.

Maude soon made it clear to all of us that she had no intention of returning to Alaska. She enjoyed the lively bustle of Los Angeles and was popular with her friendly neighbors. She urged Ted to stay.

"How can a miner and fur trader earn a living in the city?" Ted threw up his hands. City life was not for him.

They found no solution to their problem. Ted headed back to the wilderness, and Maude stayed in Los Angeles. Both wished to be together but were helpless to find a way. What spelled freedom for one meant unbearable confinement for the other.

When Ted had left, Maude brought out the silver jewelcase that René Berthon had given her and took from it the tiny letter that Ted had written to her a dozen years before on an inch of thin birchbark stripped from a tree beside the Black River in Alaska. She let Alice decipher the microscopic words:

> ... and if circumstances prevent us from living together, they will not prevent me from always loving you just the same. Sometimes, Maude, I am afraid that you are sorry you married me, because I have been able to do so little for you and you have had such a sorry time since. But you know I love you, don't you, Maude? And I have only done what I thought best for you ...

FOUR

In early spring, Alice and I returned to Seattle where I caught a boat at once for Seward on the Kenai Peninsula. From there I would mush overland to Ophir before the thaw. Our prolonged

174

honeymoon had used up a large part of my savings, and I wanted to be at the mine when sluicing began. Most of my money had been left with Alice, who would follow me to Alaska in comparative comfort by way of St. Michael as soon as the breakup began in the Yukon River.

The weather was warm and sunny in Seward, and the snow had melted away in some of the open spots. My long trip must begin without delay, for the ice on lakes and rivers would soon be melted, and the snow in the mountain passes would turn wet and treacherous, hiding softened ice beneath it that would crack and send a traveler crashing through it to his death. Unless I could go at once, there would be a delay of several months until the Yukon was free of ice, and steamers could take me up the river on the route which Alice planned to follow.

I bought equipment for the trip: a pack, a heavy horseblanket, snowshoes, an axe and a change of wool socks, then asked about trail conditions through the Alaskan Divide up to Ophir.

"Going to Ophir?" a young fellow asked as he leaned on the counter beside me. "I'm Billy Keyes. I'm making for Ophir myself."

Almost everyone in Alaska had heard of Billy Keyes. I said: "So you're the famous Billy Keyes who knows every Alaskan trail like his own backyard."

Billy grinned. "Well, you won't lose your way if you travel with me, I can promise you. How about it?"

"I know the trail; came over it last fall." I still had a compulsion to reject assistance. "Will there be much snow this time of year?"

"Bound to be. It's wise to travel in couples; a sudden thaw could be dangerous. I'd be glad of your help," he added tactfully.

"I'll take you up on your offer then. We can help each other along."

"That's the ticket. I'm ready if you are. Let's go."

For the first 60 miles we followed the railway tracks. It was open and sunny and the ties were clear of snow. We were joined on the walk by five Italians bound for Fairbanks, dapper young men wearing city suits and leather shoes. They were amused at the sight of us two sourdoughs with our heavy wool socks and rubber boots and our five-foot-long snowshoes strapped to packs.

"Springtime! Sunshine!" They waved their arms at the blue sky and the bare trail. "Who needs snowshoes in springtime? You have the seasons mixed up. Why those big blankets? Englishmen have cold blood, maybe!" Laughing and joking, their white teeth flashing, they kept up a running commentary while Billy and I plodded on in silence.

After 10 miles of tramping, the young Italians grew quiet, sighs and groans replacing laughter. By the time they had covered 25 miles and reached the first roadhouse beside the lake, the lightly-shod group were limping painfully. Moaning and commiserating with one another, they removed their city shoes as soon as they got inside and revealed huge, puffy blisters. Dishpans and dogpans were brought out, and they sat soaking their feet in warm water, bewailing a fate that brought them such suffering.

Their troubles had only begun. There was a heavy snowstorm that night, and they woke to find a foot of snow outside. Billy and I were up early, knowing that travel would be difficult. We abandoned our packs with the heavy blankets and tinned food to make fast time between roadhouses. Carrying only our axes, we started out in the early dawn. When we got to the edge of the lake, we looked back and saw the young Italians emerging from the roadhouse, hugging themselves as the cold wind bit at them in their light suits and floundering helplessly in the snow as they searched for the hidden trail. If we felt a somewhat uncharitable sense of satisfaction that the storm had come to prove us no great fools after all, we were relieved to learn some time later that the Italians had managed to reach an Indian encampment where they stayed until the weather cleared. Eventually they got to Fairbanks, perhaps with the aid of snowshoes, which had seemed so comical to them on that warm and sunny morning in spring.

The journey to Ophir took 14 days. The damp snow stuck to our snowshoes, weighing us down so that we sank in it and grew weary hefting up one burdened foot after the other. We took turns snow-shoeing ahead, feeling out the hardness of the trail under its soft covering. After each 50 yards, we changed positions, the second man able to rest somewhat as he followed the tracks of the leader over frozen lakes and rivers, through the spruce groves, and across marshland and tundra. Our plan was to keep going without a pause for food or rest until we had covered the 30 to 40 miles between road-houses strung at intervals along the trail. It would be hard going, but we would be sure of a good meal and warm shelter at the end of each day.

The best laid schemes gang aft a-gley. We were plagued with storms and twice were forced to spend the night in the open. We cut spruce boughs with our axes, dug through the snow with our snow-shoes to make a clearing on the moss and built a fire for warmth, much as the Indians had done years earlier when Harry and I had camped with them beside the Porcupine. The wind bit at us and swept away the heat from the fire. It was painfully cold at night, without blankets for outer warmth or food to warm us inwardly. But it was a bearable spring chill, and the endurance of discomfort and the need for improvisation were challenges we were ready to accept. There was no temptation to linger by the inadequate fire, and we were up at dawn again to slog on over the white, silent land.

One day a heavy storm struck in the late afternoon, and the going was particularly bad. The snow was about 10 inches deep on the trail, making it difficult to feel our way. We kept at it steadily, taking turns as leader, until almost midnight, aiming to reach a small roadhouse operated by a man whom Billy Keyes referred to as the Mountain Climber.

"He's a real crank," Keyes gasped out to me. "I don't know what kind of a reception we'll get, but there's the place ahead."

I saw a large tent looming in the dark and when we poked our heads through the flap, we saw a stove with a fire crackling in it and a set of bunks, one above the other.

"Hello, hello!" we shouted, yearning for the warmth. "Anyone there?"

Two long, skinny legs were suddenly dangled over the edge of the top bunk, and a tousle-headed man sat up and reached for a rifle racked at the bunkhead.

"Get back! What are you doing here?"

"Traveling through to Ophir," said Billy.

"You're no travelers. Where's your dog team? I don't hear dogs."

"We have no team. We're mushing on snowshoes."

"Never heard of such a thing. Can't be done."

"Well, that's what we're doing."

"Never heard of such a thing."

"I'm Billy Keyes. Have you heard of me? I've stopped here before."

"Never heard of you."

We were cold and weary and felt we were making no progress at all toward a night's lodging. "Damn it," said Keyes, "what kind of a roadhouse do you run if you won't take travelers caught in a snowstorm? Are you going to let us in or let us freeze to death?"

Our unwilling host stared at us suspiciously for a few moments and then said grudgingly. "Well, I guess you can stay," as he slid down from his bunk. "But get outside!" he ordered as we moved toward the stove. "You two will sleep in the other tent." He pulled on some clothes and came out to point to a small tent a short distance away. "That's where you'll bunk."

Our hopes for a warm and comfortable night's sleep faded as we saw two bunks with only a thin blanket apiece and a very small stove that never in this world could hold off the penetrating cold. During that miserable night we used up every stick of wood in the tent in our battle to keep warm. Before we retired to our hard bunks, the Mountain Climber brought us each a plate of beans and a pot of tea, but that was the extent of the room service. In the early morning we got up and quitted our spartan lodgings, glad to get away without another sight of our host's surly, suspicious face.

It was still wet and cold when we got through the spruce woods and started the long climb through the divide in the Alaskan Range. Storms here were always fraught with danger. One hit briefly when we were part way up and I thanked my stars that this time I had sacrificed independence for Billy Keyes, who led the way with no sign of panic until at last we reached a roadhouse atop the divide.

We were always up at dawn to start again, fighting to finish the journey before the spring thaw brought disaster. Our discomfort formed a familiar pattern now; it became a habit which we organized and controlled, mushing doggedly in the damp, sticky snow, snatching a few hours of sleep by a campfire if our progress was too slow to allow us to reach shelter before our tired bodies demanded

178

rest. We got down through the steep canyon, crossed the flats, following the Kuskokwim River for 100 miles, mushed through the divide in the Takotna Mountains and came at last to Ophir. There I said goodbye to Billy Keyes, who had guided me so well, and continued on to Spruce Creek.

On nearing my claim, I was surprised to see a new log cabin not far from my own. When I got to it, the door opened and Jock stood there with a plain, neat little woman beside him.

"My wife, Meg, from Scotland," Jock announced briefly, relishing my amazement.

He had traveled to his village in Scotland, looked up the old couple and brought back the eldest of their five unmarried daughters, now in her early thirties.

"Welcome to Alaska, Meg!" I shook her hand, thinking her an odd, reticent little person. "Jock, you sly old fox, you've given me the best possible wedding present: good company for Alice, right next door. When Alice comes here this spring, we'll have some great old times together." I spoke heartily and hopefully, but as I looked at the rough cabins on the flats with the bare hills rising behind them, the clutter of boilers, boxes and ravaged earth before them by the creek and thin scatterings of stunted pine and spruce stretching away beyond the narrow stream, I wondered uneasily what would be the reaction of a gay young college girl after leaving family and friends and arriving here to join a husband whose only assets were hopeful prospects.

Alice in Alaska

9

THE ICE WENT OUT in the Innoko. I was anxious to get word to Alice so she could leave at once for St. Michael on the first lap of her long journey to Spruce Creek. There were two methods of sending news. A letter would take a good two months to reach her by scow, steamers and coastal boat. On the other hand, she could be contacted quickly if I could find my way across country through 90 miles of wild land to Iditarod where a wireless station would send out a message in a matter of hours.

My plan was to follow the hills that stretched all the way from Spruce to the Iditarod creeks, climbing the steep incline behind my cabin and making my way along the trail left by the caribou as they wandered across the saddles of the mountains. It was a two-day trip. The first night was spent in the open, down in a wooded draw to escape the wind. Mosquitoes were bad here, but I put up a fly tent with mosquito netting sides and lay watching the insects swarming over it thickly and listened to them whine in frustration.

I rose as soon as it was light and walked steadily, taking advantage of the 20 hours of daylight. Sometimes the trail would veer off, and I hesitated before following it, but always the caribou had turned aside for good reason as they searched for the easiest grade.

Fog rolled up the second day, forcing a halt. I made out a giant boulder bulking up through the mist a short distance ahead and groped my way over to its shelter to wait for the fog to lift. Long wisps of gray mist drifted past, touching me with cold, wet fingers. I shivered, straining to see through the fog which increased in density until visibility was no more than six feet in any direction. A feeling of claustrophobia came over me, a sense of panic at being shut in and unable to escape. The danger was real: a young man who worked in a store in Ophir had died the previous year in the fog on these mountains. When the trail turned aside he left it, thinking it would lead him astray, and continued straight ahead. Then the fog came. By the time it lifted, he had wandered blindly far off the route. To escape the cold winds, he climbed down into the wooded valley and became hopelessly lost. Struggling up and down the saddles, he grew weak from hunger as the days passed; and when at last he stumbled on the trail again he collapsed. Several days later, a man came up from the Iditarod over the caribou trail, discovered him and hurried back to the town to round up a rescue party. But help came too late: the young fellow was found dead on the mountainside.

Remembering this, I stayed put until, after a few hours, the fog shifted, sections of the mountains loomed through breaks in the murkiness, and eventually it cleared enough to reveal the winding, erratic route of the caribou and I got up to follow it once again. At last I saw black dots moving about on the flats far below me and knew these were miners working the creeks. Then I cut down the hillside and took the miners' well-beaten trail in to Iditarod.

On approaching Iditarod, I thought of Dikeman, a morose fellow who lived down-river at a place that was later named for him. He was one of the first to discover gold on the Iditarod River. He had one close friend — the little gray-bearded Schwartz who was located just above Ted on Fifteen Pup. Dikeman had staked on the Iditarod for himself and Schwartz, and warned his friend not to tell anyone about the strike. "Don't let word of it leak out to Ted Crompton," he said bitterly. Ted, after a series of fruitless grubstakings of hopeful prospectors, had refused a request from Schwartz. He had softened his refusal by giving a rifle to Schwartz, who was pleased and bore him no grudge. Dikeman, however, took up his friend's cause and would pass by Ted's cabin on his way to visit Schwartz without acknowledging Ted's greeting. This was unusual behavior in the Alaskan wilds where cabins were left open for stranded travelers to take refuge and where strangers always spoke when they met. Schwartz was torn between his two friendships, but resolved his dilemma by secretly entering Ted's name in an association claim on the Iditarod so he could share in the profits.

Claims were often staked for Ted by friends and well-wishers who struck it rich and who tried to share their luck with him by offering him claims which, by all rights, should have proven even richer than their own. In time he became a fatalist, however, convinced that wealth was not for him. Paystreaks turned at right angles and circled his claim or they petered out to a token yield between his stakes. Schwartz's generous gesture, too, was unproductive. The association group made nothing, though many individual claims on the Iditarod produced rich yields.

In Iditarod, I sent off my message to Alice, 2,000 miles away. RIVERS CLEAR. COME AS SOON AS YOU CAN. Back came her reply: LEAVING IMMEDIATELY. ALL MY LOVE. I trod the 90 miles through the mountain saddles back to Spruce Creek as though on winged feet to await the coming of my bride.

TWO

I knew when the steamer would arrive at St. Michael and the approximate time it would take for Alice to travel by large steamboat to Holy Cross and then by small steamer up the Innoko to the head of navigation. From there she would come up by scow. Sailing down the Innoko in my poling boat to meet her, I almost collided with the scow as it came round the bend.

"Here's your husband!" I heard one of the scowmen shout to Alice. "Looks like he couldn't wait for you to get to Ophir."

That first year in Alaska was an exhilarating adventure for Alice. She thought the two-roomed cabin with its muslin-draped walls ingenious and unique. Everything had the charm of novelty for her and, like the rest of us, she valued the freedom she found there. She had come to Alaska aware, to some extent, of the difficulties and discomforts that might lie ahead; but with the confidence of youth, she was prepared to face them.

I told her about our neighbors. Jock and Meg were nearby. On the claim below ours, MacNaughton and Jones mined without help from us since Jock and I were now working our own claim. Below MacNaughton was George Baker, a talkative chap with a library consisting of a single book, which he misquoted continually. "According to the Riverside Laws . . . " he would begin every conversation, which puzzled us until the day he produced the book to reinforce a statement and we saw that it was titled *Revised Laws*. George Baker left Alaska with a fair-sized fortune and met a woman in Seattle whom he promised to marry. Shortly afterward, he thought better of his promise and told her he had changed his mind. Furious at being bilked of his wealth, she promptly shot him to death to prevent him from enjoying it without her.

Below Baker's claim, the Vinals had pitched a huge tent beside their diggings. Vinal had come from Nome to be the gold commissioner at Ophir, on the creek above Spruce. He and his wife had a big log cabin there, but he had staked a claim on Spruce just where a side creek ran into it. The tiny side creek may have had something to do with the richness of his claim, for it yielded so heavily that he soon became a wealthy man. His lively, black-haired wife was much younger than he; short, plump, and incredibly active, she bustled about the camp, wearing a large cowboy hat, cooking meals for the half dozen men who helped them to mine, and often panning the stream herself. "I get my pocket money out of my gold pan," she told Alice. She was a cheerful little woman, tough as nails despite her small size, determined to see every possible ounce of gold wrested from their claim. When they left for the outside and a life of ease, the sturdy Mrs. Vinal fell ill and died. Vinal outlived her by only a few years. Just before he died, he remarried and his young bride fell heir to the fortune the Vinals had worked so industriously to amass.

Vinal was an amiable fellow, and he and his wife became good friends of ours despite the frequently strained relationship caused by the savage dog team he drove. They were all small mongrels, fast running but noted for attacking any dog team they met on the trail without warning or provocation. It was the resultant tangle of traces as much as the danger of injured paws that roused the wrath of other drivers. The first time I met Vinal on the trail, the fierce mongrels swerved their sled to my side and tore into my dogs, snapping, snarling and yelping, a hopelessly tangled mass of enraged dogs and twisted harnesses. "Get those mutts off my team!" I yelled, but my voice failed to penetrate the hellish clamor. Vinal and I pulled and kicked at the dogs and were bitten on arms and legs. In desperation, I grabbed my rifle from my sled and aimed a vicious blow with the butt at Vinal's dogs. At that moment the mass shifted, and I laid my own lead dog out cold on the snow.

After this humiliating encounter, I always made a wide detour off the trail whenever I met Vinal and his team during winter travel. Vinal would wave cheerfully and sweep past, grinning complacently as he rode away behind his aggressive mongrels.

Two creeks below Spruce, on Ganes, were Jim Pitcher and his wife. Jim was a small, thin man half the size of his Mabel who was a big, raw-boned woman with muscular arms and a deep, booming voice. Despite her masculine appearance, Mabel Pitcher showed a motherly solicitude for her husband as well as for anyone who fell sick and called for her help.

In Ophir, on the creek above Spruce, were Dr. Martin and his attractive wife from Toronto. They were a middle-aged, sociable couple, popular with everyone. Several times during the winter I would harness my dogs, and we would travel to Ophir, a half-hour run, to visit the Martins and watch entertainments staged by the townsfolk in a little hall. It was a longer trip, across the Takotna Divide, to visit Dr. Green and his wife. Dr. Green made a fair living by doubling as doctor and dentist. Takotna was much smaller than Ophir during the latter's peak days, with only half a block of stores and houses and a two-room roadhouse. There were few bunks available in the roadhouse, and it was a case of first come, first served. Once when we arrived there with the Vinals and found most of the beds taken, plump Mrs. Vinal wrapped herself in a blanket and rolled underneath a bunk like a large ball. "Snug as a bug in a rug," she insisted to Alice, who had prostrated herself on the floor to peer under the bunk and urge her to come out. She slept soundly all night, snoring peacefully, with Alice and me resting uneasily

above her, and her husband sharing a bunk with an elderly
prospector.

THREE

Despite the general good will that existed between sourdoughs and
cheechakos, the British were inclined to mingle more freely with one
another. Soon after Alice arrived at Spruce Creek, I took her to
Ophir to visit the Vinals. On the way we passed a group of tumble-
down cabins housing several families of Russians who shared a mine
beside one of the creeks. The cabin doors were open, and some of
the men were sitting on the stoops talking.

"Come on, Bill," Alice exclaimed impulsively, "let's get to know
these people." She grabbed my hand and pulled me off the trail
and over the grass clumps toward the cabins.

"Wait!" I held her back. "These Russians are a rough lot," I
cautioned her, "and the women speak very little English. They're
not the sort for a young girl like you."

"Bill!" She was shocked and disappointed at this urban attitude
in her new pioneering world. "All of us must be friends up here. We
don't want to be thought stand-offish!" With that, she darted away
from me and ran to the cabins, waving a greeting.

Reluctantly, I followed her and waited while she spoke to the
men and smiled and nodded at the women who came to their windows to look out at her. But, back on the trail, brushing at the
muddied hem of her skirt, she admitted ruefully that the Russians
had seemed more puzzled than pleased by her overtures. Like the
British, they were inclined toward clannishness.

Undiscouraged, Alice urged me to think of some neighbor living
alone who would enjoy a dinner with us, and finally I suggested a
man who was batching in a shack on Ophir Creek. Alice sat down
at once to plan her menu.

"I'll bake a pie," she said.

"Not a pie, Alice," I advised hastily, remembering Maude's cooking disasters at Mouse Point. "This Frenchman on Ophir Creek was
once a professional cook in a big hotel back East. Until you've practiced a bit, keep to something simple."

"I'll bake a simple pie," she laughed.

I soon discovered that Alice was an excellent cook. She produced hearty, delectable meals with ease and dispatch despite cramped quarters and limited supplies. What she had, she used with imagination; and she said there was more variety than she had expected in this wild land beside the bald hills.

There were plump little ptarmigan, for example. There were the bitter-fleshed spruce hens, and ruffed grouse whose sweeter meat was due to a diet of willow buds, nuts and fruits. There were no salmon so far up-stream, but there were whitefish and grayling. Thousands of grayling packed the river in the fall, preparing to drift down to the Yukon. They were, unfortunately, well down to the Yukon before freezing weather, so they could not be kept frozen and remained a seasonal dish.

The mountains yielded treasures besides the gold that tumbled down to us in the icy streams. In the berry season, we climbed the hills to find masses of low-growing blueberry and cranberry bushes, luscious wild raspberries and wild red currants. We took with us wooden pickers made from cigar box lids slit into long fingers. These we ran along the branches, dislodging the berries and letting them shower into tin pails. Some of the fruit Alice made into jam and jelly, the rest was put up in barrels between layers of sugar. Summer and winter, hot fruit pies bubbling with fragrant syrup were taken from the oven of the big iron cookstove.

"Is this up to French chef standards?" Alice would ask with feigned anxiety.

"Can the French chef reach your standard? That's the question," I would answer, prepared to eat crow as long as I could eat her pie along with it.

We planted a vegetable garden of lettuce and peas, turnips and kale. Potatoes were seldom grown successfully here because of the short growing season; thus they were a luxury. The heartless trader who had abandoned his lifeless young helper had known this when he pushed on so relentlessly for Ophir, leaving the boy's body on the riverbank. No doubt he reaped a rich profit from the potato-hungry miners, soon after that day when I followed him up the Innoko, hearing the measured beat of the miners' picks as they dug a lonely, unmarked grave.

In the spring and summer, traders occasionally traveled to Ophir and Takotna and then over to Iditarod to fill the needs of the isolated miners. Reindeer, imported originally from Norway for stock raising, were brought down from Nome or St. Michael to sell as meat. Their herders kept to the mountains for most of the journey so the animals could feed on the short greenish moss growing on the shaded slopes and in the gulches. This was the only food they fancied, and they would paw off the light covering of snow to get down to the rich, brittle plants. The first sight of the herd was a succession of antlers showing above the small, sparse trees as the reindeer were guided down the bank of the creek. Since they came in early spring or summer, meat could not be frozen and kept for any length of time. An animal was killed at the first stop and the miner there would take a part of it, the next claim took more, and so on until it was time to sacrifice another reindeer from the mobile meat shop.

FOUR

The winter parties in Ophir were organized by married couples. Though Ophir seemed big in comparison with Takotna's size of half a block, it was still a very small town, and its population steadily decreased in size as miners left with bulging pokes or shattered dreams of riches. The rush was over, and few new arrivals came to compensate for the steady exodus. Ophir's social evenings were not the elegant affairs of boom-time Dawson nor the unique oddities of squaw dances at small towns like Rampart and Forty Mile, where Indian women and miners jogged about in a silence enforced by language barriers and taciturnity, separating at the evening's end exhausted and still speechless. In Ophir, if someone turned up with a fiddle, there might be a dance or two in the hall, but entertainment for the most part was an impromptu amateur night with performances by anyone who could be prevailed upon to take to the platform. Someone sang, another told jokes or acted out a monologue. The audience was never critical, however inept the artist, and applause was always generous.

"Bill, why don't you do something?" Alice nudged me one night during a lull when it seemed that all talent had been exhausted.

"Alice, you know I can't act. I'd rather face a firing squad than get up on that platform."

"You could recite verses."

"Never! I couldn't force out three words with all those faces staring at me."

Alice jumped up. "Bill Walker will now favor us with a recitation." Everyone clapped and cheered and swiveled about on their hard chairs to examine me expectantly.

"Alice!" I pulled her down beside me, crushed by so unexpected a betrayal.

"Walk up to the platform. You can do it, Bill. Don't be afraid; we're all friends here." Giggling heartlessly, she pushed me into the aisle.

I found myself on the stage, reciting all 23 verses of Gilbert's *Yarn of the 'Nancy Bell'*, a gruesome tale of an elderly naval man, sole survivor of a crew who drew lots to eat each other one by one to escape starvation. The survivor thus became:

> ...a cook and a captain bold
>   And the mate of the Nancy brig,
> And a bo'sun tight, and a midshipmite,
>   And the crew of the captain's gig.

I received much kindly applause from my audience, and Alice exclaimed triumphantly: "See? I knew you could do it. You were the hit of the evening." But from then on, I rested on my laurels and never set foot on the platform again. Any ambitions my performance may have roused in me found their dramatic outlet in a game that we carried on in the privacy of our cabin. It started one day when, while repairing a section of the cabin roof, I looked down through a hole to see my wife combing her hair. I put my mouth close to the hole, and she gave a startled squeal as I remarked suddenly: "Most extraordinary female this!" I was quoting the words of Dickens' Mr. Pickwick, who parted his bed curtains one night and saw an unknown, middle-aged lady combing her hair. "Ha . . . hum!"

Alice looked up, taking her cue. "Gracious Heaven! What's that?"

"It's . . . it's . . . only a gentleman, Ma'am," I faltered, and Alice's piercing scream brought Jock running from his cabin.

That set us off on a series of amateur, impromptu dramatics. We would spend a day being Dora and David Copperfield, or the Micawbers who were forever hoping "to live in a perfectly new manner, if . . . in short, if anything turns up." And, on Christmas Day, inevitably we were the Crachits. There was nothing unusual about our familiarity with the books on our whipsawed shelf. Many dwellers in small cabins in the north read and reread the few volumes they possessed until they knew every phrase by heart. There was seldom a chance to vary reading material up in the wilderness, though not all readers were as limited as George Baker, who seemed satisfied to stick to his sole book, Riverside Laws.

FIVE

Anyone who mined was necessarily a gambler, and it followed naturally that betting in one form or another became a popular form of entertainment in the north. Bets on the date of the ice breakup were held at various points along the Yukon, the Tanana and other rivers, with Nenana on the Tanana organizing one of the largest. The dogteam races at Nome attracted huge crowds who bet on the outcome of the 400-mile cross-country race to Candle and back. First held in 1908, this race became a yearly event. Men trained their teams for months in advance, carefully grooming them and supplying them with special diets of fresh meat and eggs. During the race, the dogs were fed hamburger steaks, their feet were protected with moccasins and they wore blankets to shield them from the intense cold. Camps along the route provided food and water during the three or four days of the race. Fantastic bets, totalling up to $200,000, were laid on favorites, and the prizes for the winning teams ranged from $1500 to $10,000.

Jock's mail-carrier friend, Harry Lawrence, never raced his own dogs, but he knew Scotty Allan, and he told us a good many stories about this famed and frequent winner. Scotty spent large sums of money on the upkeep of his kennels, outfitted his dogs for the races with collars, harness and blankets to fit each one individually and provided them with several sets of flannel moccasins to protect their feet from sharp chunks of icy snow. His dogs drew laughter from the crowds as they raced by, fitted with goggles covered with green mosquito netting to guard their eyes against snow blindness. Drivers never rode on the sleds during the races, but ran behind holding the handlebars. They ran up to 50 miles a day, often over icy tundra and through blizzards of fine, blinding snow. Scotty Allan lost one race to a competitor who was ingenious but unethical. This man won by concealing horses in two sheds along the route and letting his dogs conserve their strength by riding over part of the course, going and coming, in a horse-drawn sled.

In Alaska, we celebrated American holidays. Independence Day, the fourth of July, was one of the most popular, with fireworks, parades and sporting matches. Up to 300 miners came in to Ophir each year from their claims to enjoy the restaurants and saloons and any other entertainment being offered. There were no dance-hall girls to solace a miner for his long months of isolation and toil; claims were not rich enough to attract them. Some form of lively entertainment was needed, and one summer it was suggested: why not a Fourth of July race up the Innoko rapids?

Two men from Dawson who had experience as boatmen on the Yukon announced that they were willing to show up amateurs reckless enough to race them in a 100-yard dash up the riffle. The race course was up one set of rapids that began in front of the town, and though the boats would stick close to the bar where the water was slacker, it was still swift enough to make the going difficult. Things hung fire for awhile with no one taking up the Dawson team's challenge, but finally two more men signed up. The Ophir store offered a prize to the winners.

Competitive sport had never attracted me except as a spectator, but this race up the Innoko was something that seemed tailored-to-measure for me. Battling the rapids so many times, ferrying Ted's supplies from the half-way mark to the headwaters, had made me familiar with every inch of the route.

"With a faster boat," I said to Alice, "I might have a chance in that race myself."

Alice was all for it. "Why don't you enter? You know the Innoko as well as any man up here. You could win the race."

"Not with our old patched-up *Fairy*."

"Team up with someone who has a good boat. What about Frenchy? The two of you would make an unbeatable team."

She spurred me on until finally I walked over to Ophir Creek and asked Frenchy to partner me in the race, using his shovel-nosed poler. He readily agreed. He was a middle-aged man, in his forties, but he still had a taste for the daring that characterized so many of the Frenchmen who explored and opened up Eastern Canada. Back east he had been a champion log-roller and canoe racer, and in the west he became an expert poler. He was a fine fly fisherman, too, and, to round out his versatility, he was famous for his excellent French cooking. A race up the Innoko appealed to him. We formed the third team, and the race was on.

The contestants lined up at the lower end of the bar, six men and three poling boats. The river was narrow up here near the head-waters, and in midsummer the water was low. Only one boat at a time could get up, so men were stationed at the starting and finishing lines to clock each contestant. Harry Lawrence, Jock's old friend from sailing days in the British navy, down from Nome to celebrate the holiday with us, was positioned at the upper end of the bar to clock the finish. Crowds lined the bank, bets were placed and all stood ready to cheer and heckle.

The Dawson men went first, setting off at great speed to make good their boast, plunging in their poles, the poles sliding through their hands until the top was reached, then one quick step forward, up with the pole, hands sliding down, and a plunge again into the water. Cheers at the start indicated they were favorites, and more cheers came at the finish when they slammed to the shore. "Try to beat that time! Can't be done!"

When the second boat started up, we could see that its handlers were long on spunk but short on skill. They began with a great show of action, thrusting down their poles, running several steps, lifting the poles up awkwardly and swinging them in a wide arc. All

191

this only wasted time and energy. For no apparent reason, sometimes they crossed sides to pole. Supporters urged them on at first, but the racers soon tired and poled so feebly that the fickle fans were hooting and catcalling. Three-quarters of the way up, their boat hit a partly submerged rock and halted with a sudden jolt that sent both men sprawling. Before they could get to their feet, the current pulled their boat backward, a wave knocked the bow sideways where the center current caught it, and the next minute they were speeding down-stream to the starting point amid a mixture of howls and jeers, hysterical laughter and hearty cheers. They regained control in time to land on the bar, disgraced as polers but highly popular as slapstick comedians.

Frenchy spat determinedly on his hands. "Come on, Bill. Now we show what we can do."

With Frenchy in the bow and me at the stern, we made a good team, working well together with a steady, co-ordinated poling. The mood of the crowd switched again; here was stiff competition for the Dawson men. Cheering and shouting, the crowd encouraged us with "Come on, boys. Give them a run for their money!" We could tell by the mounting noise that we were making good time, and the cheers spurred us on.

The floorboards in the bottom of the shovelnose were loose, so they could be lifted when the boat was washed out, and one of these had been laid down carelessly at a slight angle, leaving a ridge. I crossed over, eyes on my lifted pole, and tripped, went off balance, and almost fell overboard. For a few seconds we lost momentum, and the stern swung wide as the spectators whistled and groaned. Then I got my pole down and we were off again, shoving and straining. At last the end was in sight, and bedlam met us at the top of the bar as we grounded on the gravel.

"Bill and Frenchy win the race!" Harry Lawrence yelled the official announcement above the cheers of our fans and the roars of disbelief from the Dawson crowd. Prizes were thrust into our arms: a ham, a big slab of bacon and a sack of potatoes.

"Best Fourth of July I've seen in Alaska," said Harry. "It was worth a trip from Nome. This race had everything a good show needs: action, suspense and comedy."

Harry Lawrence, the sailor who became a mail-carrier, ran one of the fastest dog teams in Alaska. His dogs were not huskies but short-haired hounds that had been brought up from Seattle to be sold as sled dogs. Harry was devoted to his hounds. Because of their short hair, they were never left to sleep outside in the snow as was usual with sled dogs. He kept them with him in his cabin at Nome and took them inside whenever he stopped at a roadhouse or wayside hut on his route. They made a swift, smart team, running 50 miles a day with him, and he rewarded them in a manner that was the talk of the district. Besides their sleeping privileges, they enjoyed a diet that had to be seen to be believed. No chunks of frozen fish were tossed to Harry Lawrence's dogs for their stomachs to battle with in an effort to defrost and digest the rock-hard hunks; they were fed on bully beef at $5 a can. Many an Alaskan watched with wide-open eyes and mouth as the mailman emptied tins of the expensive meat into the dogs' dishes and then bedded them down close to his bunk.

Most dogs on the mail teams received preferential treatment compared to the cruelties suffered by many of the northern sled animals. Mailmen picked the best possible for the long and arduous trips across the snow in bitter weather, their dogs being regarded as valuable equipment needing special care. Strong, willing sled dogs were at a premium, however, and fetched high prices. Most men could not afford such costly teams and were forced to make do with any available animal shanghaied from the streets of the big cities and shipped up for the Alaskan trade.

These were the dogs that suffered most. With thin coats that gave them no protection from the storms, they were left outside to endure the cold blasts of winter. Others were tormented by lumps of ice that formed on the hairs between their toes and chafed their skin to open sores. When a dog was too weak or lame to pull his share of the load, he would lie down in protest. The following dogs would overrun him, resulting in fights, tangled traces and a savage beating for the exhausted dog by his wrathful master. It was a common sight to behold an enraged driver forcing open the jaws of a dog that had collapsed and stuffing his mouth and throat with handfuls of snow. The tortured beast would leap to his feet, maddened with agony as he tried to spit out the choking gag.

To such owners, dogs were solely a cheap means of transport, to be run hard until they wore out and were discarded. But, like Ted and myself, many men regarded their dogs as friends and companions and usually freed them between trips. They were seldom chained to stakes, as were most of the Indian huskies on the Yukon, a practice that fostered the vicious nature of the native dogs.

Much as one may sympathize with the human beings who suffered and were defeated in that harsh land, the plight of the animals forcibly taken there seems more poignant still. Trapped as they were, unable to escape their enforced life until death released them, the horses and dogs of Alaska and the Yukon were utterly at the mercy of their masters.

SIX

In Seattle, Alice had resisted the temptation to tell her parents that she expected a child. She knew what the result would be if she weakened; to them, the only sensible course would be to postpone the trip until after the baby was born in December. It would then be impossible to travel until the arrival of milder weather. In the end, she might never get to Alaska.

She broke the news to me when she got to Spruce Creek. I was apprehensive for her at first, thinking of our isolation from city hospitals, but then remembered that Dr. Martin was close by in Ophir. With an experienced doctor from Eastern Canada at hand, I was satisfied that Alice would have the best of care. As it happened, the Martins left Alaska before our baby arrived.

Ophir was too small to offer a medical man a large enough practice to support himself. The Martins, always pleasant and uncomplaining, were actually living from hand to mouth and were desperately concerned about their future. Everyone liked them and had only good to say of them, but more than kind words were needed. They enjoyed their life in Alaska and felt they were contributing an essential service to the community. The time came, however, when they faced the fact that not enough money was coming in to keep them in groceries.

They talked it over and came up with a plan. They wanted to stay in Ophir and would do so if everyone in the district would agree to pay a few dollars a month in return for free medical service. The plan, an early forerunner of health insurance schemes of today, was an excellent idea for that isolated community but too new and revolutionary for the people. No one wanted to shell out for a service they might never utilize.

It was a heavy blow to the Martins. Aware of their popularity, they had assumed that their modest proposal would be readily accepted. The doctor was prepared to work hard and long to minister to every health need of his patients; now the only alternative was to leave.

"They don't want me," he told us bitterly.

"Of course they want you," Alice tried to reassure him. "We all do."

"We're not wanted," he repeated hopelessly, disillusioned with friendships that had failed the test. The Martins joined a party traveling overland to Seward and sailed for Seattle. They settled in the country, a short distance from Seattle, and there they eked out a humble living, too old by then to establish themselves successfully in a new community.

Before leaving Ophir, Mrs. Martin sold her heavy fur coat of wolfskin to Alice. It covered her warmly from neck to ankles, and she was glad to have it when the cold winds of her first Alaskan winter swept across the flats. Bundling herself into it, she braved the icy air for brief, brisk walks. Despite her assurances that she felt well, I worried increasingly as the months passed, remembering Maude's panic at Mouse Point and aware that the nearest doctor now was in Takotna, across the mountain divide.

Early in December, I took my dog team and sled and went to Ophir, then through the divide in the mountains to Takotna. Dr. Green stepped into the other half of his dual role and filled the cavities in my teeth before he started back with me. Dentistry was his true profession. He had taken courses in first aid and midwifery to prepare himself to cope with emergencies in the far north, but his knowledge of medicine was rudimentary.

The plump little dentist struggled after me through the icy divide and down the snow-covered flats to our cabin on the creek. He was thankful to reach its warmth and the hot coffee Alice had ready for us. "Any day now," he told her after his examination. "You'd better put me up until the time comes." He slept on a cot in the kitchen and a few nights later delivered our son.

Dr. Green trudged away on his snowshoes, and big Mabel Pitcher came from Ganes Creek to care for mother and baby until Alice could manage for herself. Huge and hearty, Mabel seemed to fill the cabin with her booming voice and heavy tread. It was pathetically ironic that rough, masculine Mabel was richly endowed with a motherly instinct that could only find expression in coddling her husband and nursing the babies of other women. She had never borne a child of her own.

"Mind you take care of that baby," she instructed us. "He's worth more than any nuggets you'll get from the creek."

While we lived in Alaska, little Billy was always called Nugget. I made him a sled with a box nailed on top, and he rode about in it over the snow, pulled along by a huge dog twice his own size, part husky and part St. Bernard.

SEVEN

Jock and I worked our first diggings on Spruce Creek for two years. Creeks had sometimes altered course several times down through the centuries, and a succession of holes had to be dug near the existing creek as miners probed for evidence of the original waterway. "Time to move house again," Jock would decide after we had dug down for a distance. "No washed gravel here." Gravel that was washed smooth usually indicated an old creekbed below it, and further digging was a worthwhile gamble. With luck, traces of gold would show among the gravel, increasing in richness as the descent continued, hopefully to a rich layer at bedrock. Unfortunately, one could never be positive about the richness of the ultimate yield, and years were sometimes spent following the gold traces that came and went like an elusive will-o'-the-wisp. Men might gain enough to pay expenses but never strike a rich pay streak.

"Washed gravel and signs of gold here!" cried Jock one day as he pointed to exposed bedrock on the rim of the creek. We got Ted's boiler from Fifteen Pup, dug a hole about 10 feet up the bench from the stream and tested the gravel at regular intervals until we got down to bedrock. "Looks good. Let's try again, farther up the bench." We found gold again. "Bedrock's only ten feet down, and we've got a good slope on the creek bench. Seems right for hydraulicking."

We needed a strong force of water to wash away gravel and expose the bedrock as much as possible. The powerful hydraulic machines used by large companies were inaccessible to small miners, whose method was to dig a series of ditches at right angles to the creek through which water could rush down from a dam built up in the hills, sometimes several hundred feet away. Strips of the long tundra moss were put on the sides of the ditches to hold the water until they deepened. Large canvas hoses, 18 inches in diameter, were connected to a gate in the dam and run into the ditches, the force of water melting the frozen ground and deepening the ditches to bedrock. Care had to be taken to maintain the proper force, as too rapid a flow would break down the sides of the ditches. The gold-bearing gravel was then dumped into sluices, which were cleaned out about once a week.

Trees had to be felled and lumber for the sluices whipsawed. The boxes, eight feet long and twelve inches wide, were narrowed from back to front to provide increased water pressure. In each box we fixed two sets of three peeled poles lying an inch and a half apart and held rigid by crosspieces. The gold, separated from the gravel by the force of the water, became trapped in these riffles and fell through the poles. The lighter gravel was carried away by the water. Periodically, the water was turned off, the poles removed and the boxes cleaned out, following the same procedure used at Mac-Naughton's mine and at Fifteen Pup.

"May we have the good luck of MacNaughton," Jock said devoutly, "and never the miserable luck of Homer Mezaire. That lad's cleanups, you might say, were washouts in more ways than one."

The yield was good for over a year but by no means as rich as on the claims below. When the gold petered out, we tested again farther up and sank a new and deeper hole.

Ted came up from Fifteen Pup to look over the diggings at Spruce and offered to help out for a day.

"Where's that mathematics book?" Jock grinned as he remembered our mudbath when Ted had lost himself in calculation at Fifteen Pup and let the boiler cool.

"No book nearer than my cabin at Fifteen Pup."

"Well, then, maybe we'll appoint you windlass worker up here under the heavens, and we two poor devils will descend into the bowels of the earth."

We were sinking our new hole, promising so far but a long way to bedrock. This time we planned to dig and drift. We climbed down the hole and began to work with shovel and pick axe. We shoveled the muck into the big wooden bucket, then yelled to Ted, who wound the rope to haul up the bucket, swung it to one side and let it slide on its cleats down peeled poles to the waste dump or to the pay dump. There he tipped out the load, hauled the bucket back and then lowered it again.

Ted had no book to distract him, but whenever I looked up the shaft to shout at him to haul, he would be leaning against the windlass, gazing at the clouds and wrapped in thought. I knew he was weary of Little Creek. He missed the Indians of Black River with their gentle courtesy and generosity; the pathetic Mouse Point Indian children; and the Mouse Point adults who had amused and touched him with their childlike speech, their wonderment over the ways of the white man and their dependence on the help of the trader. There were no Indians up here by the Innoko headwaters. No salmon came this far up to provide them with food. Game, too, was scarce, except for bears that raided the blueberry patches in the summertime and plump little ptarmigan whose brown, white-spotted feathers turned completely white when the snow came. The nearest Indians were at Dishkaket, about 100 miles down the Innoko. It was a dull life for Ted, serving his infrequent customers and panning the big drift halfheartedly. He had never succumbed to the gold-fever bug; he was a victim only of wanderlust and the lure of the wilderness. He could never stand for long the grubbing in the dirt among the hideous debris of sluices and mounds of muck. The whole idea was as foreign to his nature as was sales work in the city, where men compete feverishly to rouse desire for unessentials. He had tried that briefly to please Maude, but signed orders and lumps of metal could never give him the sense of personal achievement that he felt when bringing in a string of fish or a moose for his cache, or when building a snug cabin with his own hands.

"I feel something calling to me," he had told me. "It's like the migrating urge that birds and animals feel, but the instincts of human beings have dulled, Bill. I hear the call to leave here, but nothing tells me where to go next. I'm left floundering like one of those poor damn animals the scientists experiment with to make them clueless as a man."

"Waste coming up!" At my shout, I saw Ted wake with a start from his dream and begin to wind the rope. Slowly the massive bucket, heavily encrusted on the outside with frozen rock and muck, rose above our heads. Jock and I took up our pick axes and swung at the hard-packed gravel, loosening it for the next load. When Ted appeared at the shaft head again, reattaching the bucket's rope handles to the winch hook, I bent down to exchange my pick axe for a shovel and heard Jock yell a frantic warning; simultaneously, something struck my back like a thunderbolt. It laid me out flat, dead to the world.

With returning consciousness pain hit at me. I was still flat on my stomach but my head was turned sideways, and a coat had been slipped under my head to keep my face above the mud. I opened my eyes to meet those of Jock and Ted a foot from mine, Jock's looking pale in his blackened face, Ted's pupils white-rimmed with alarm.

"He's coming to," said Jock.

"Bill, are you all right?" Ted asked anxiously. "I gave the bucket a kick to center it and the damn thing lifted itself off the hook and went plummeting down the shaft. Thank God you were bending over. If that brute of a thing had hit your head it would have crushed your skull like eggshell."

They carried me up the ladder and made a seat with their clasped hands, supporting my back with their arms, and got me over the flats to my cabin and into bed.

"Aye, Ted's like that fellow Beach," Jock joked. "No good on the windlass."

Alice made tea, and I began to feel better, though the flesh on my back was swollen and rapidly turning from red to yellow to purple.

"Has Ted left without tea?" asked Alice. "I'm so sorry for him."

"What do you mean, sorry for Ted?" I demanded, outraged.

"Oh, sorry for you, too," she laughed. "But sorry for Ted, alone up there on Little Creek. Has he gone back?"

"He said he was going to Ophir to look up Harry."

My brother Harry and family had come to Ophir, where he was working for a mercantile company. For a number of years he had been a devoted family man, proud of his wife and his bright, lively children.

"With Bess's health and my brains and good looks, my children should be exceptional," he once wrote to Maude, making her bristle at his conceit.

"But it's true," Maude admitted to me. "Harry is handsome and smart. He could make a big success; in fact, he has, over and over. But he tosses it all away."

Harry had fallen desperately in love with Bess, an office clerk, when he met her in Seattle. Back in Alaska, he showed me one of the letters he had written to her, and I was amazed at the passion and poetry that this girl had roused in my devil-may-care brother. On meeting her later, I was even more amazed to see a plain, rather awkward young woman totally unlike the pretty, stylish girls Harry had wined and dined in Victoria when "in the chips." But Bess represented something steadfast and stable which had been lacking in his life since early childhood. Unfortunately, such was his nature that he could never hold for long the things he valued. Possessions if cherished too dearly became responsibilities that robbed him of his freedom. He wanted money, but frittered it away; he loved his family, but eventually abandoned Bess and his children. While the Walker relatives debated glumly what could be done for her, Bess surprised both them and herself by suddenly becoming an heiress. A distant relative, whom she had never heard of, died in Europe, leaving her a legacy that made her independent for life. Bess divorced her husband and devoted herself to her children. Harry, wandering back some years later, found that in this case love, unlike the money he made, could not be thrown aside and earned again. He had lost forever his good, plain Bess and his exceptional children.

A few hours after Ted had left us, he was back again, bursting with excitement. "Great news!" he announced. "Harry and I have decided to enlist. We're going overseas to kick the Germans out of France and let the French people come back to their homes and their farms. Who's coming with us? Bill?"

"Nothing doing," I said. "I'm in no condition to fight after the way you bombarded me. And what's the war got to do with us? America's not in it. We're hitting gold here, Ted. There's a lot of it somewhere on the claim. I want to make good before I go outside."

"Ted, are you leaving because you're lonely at Little Creek?" asked Alice. "Why don't you visit us more often?"

"I'm sick of Little Creek, all right, and all this grubbing in the muck. It's not like it was at Black River or Mouse Point. Here, we do nothing but work with a pick and shovel like a bunch of prisoners on a chain gang."

"Have you thought of going back to the Yukon or the Black?"

"There's no use going back. The past chafes at you. It's never the same. Jock, what about you? You were always one for adventures."

"In the forces? Not me! I had my fill of do this, do that and aye, aye, sir, in the navy. Keep out of it, Ted. Sign the oath and you'll sign away your freedom and find yourself a slave."

We were so isolated at the headwaters of the Innoko that news of the war's progress only trickled through to us. It all seemed so far away. Ted was still a British subject, and his many years in Canada gave him a proprietary pride in the Canadian troops when he heard of their stand at Ypres in the face of a poison gas attack. It may have been the blood of his French grandmother that roused in him so much sympathy for the ravaged land of France. Still, he was in his mid-forties, and the war was being fought on a distant battle-field. It was his talk with Harry that tipped the balance scale. Harry, restless with routine work, had fired him with his own enthusiasm to savor danger and conquer it with daring.

Big, placid MacNaughton was the only one at Spruce Creek who was inspired to go with Ted the 3,000 miles to Vancouver to enlist and many more thousands of miles across land and sea to help to drive the invaders from French soil. But peppery little Harry Lawrence, Jock's old companion of seafaring days, heard of their plans and gave up his mail route, boarded out his dogs and came from Nome to the Innoko to join them.

Maude left Los Angeles and came north to be with Ted in British Columbia before he went overseas.

We shook our heads in disbelief when we heard the peculiar decisions of the recruiting officers. "Don't know where they're to," said Jock. Ted, an Englishman, found himself attached to a Seaforth Highlanders regiment; MacNaughton the Scotsman ended up in an English regiment; and Harry Lawrence, who ran 50 miles a day over the Alaskan snows with his team delivering mail, was refused admission to the army on the grounds that he had flat feet.

News of our soldiers came to us now and then. My brother Harry was mentioned in despatches and won a medal for gallantry; Ted was wounded by shrapnel and even more shattered by trench fever. It was ironic that Ted should escape from the muddy ditches of Alaskan goldfields only to find himself trapped in muddy trenches in France. It was not adventure as he had known it, sailing the seas and rivers. It was mud and monotony, with a faint hope that the senseless, seasawing battles for a few yards of dirt would eventually permit the French to return to the ruins of their homes.

Disillusioned with the larger tactics of war, he concentrated on immediate problems, leading refugees to a vacant house, collecting rabbit heads discarded by the army cook for the women to stew, and exchanging his tobacco ration for chocolate to give to the children. He wrote to us by candlelight as he lay on a bed of chicken wire in a damp, rat-infested hole.

But his letters were still full of his bizarre humor and sense of the ridiculous, and he still had his interest in unusual foods. He crawled from the dugout one day and picked stinging nettles; the young plants do not sting once they are boiled, and he ate the greens with gusto as his fellow soldiers watched in dismay, expecting him any moment to fall victim to an itching, internal rash. He kept his thoughts off the horrors of war by mending their watches, a trade he had taught himself in Alaska to while away the long winters at Mouse Point, and by plugging the rat holes and combating the smells and swarming flies with disinfectant.

Maude had moved to Victoria. Her letters told of picnics on the beach, boat trips up The Gorge and walks in Beacon Hill Park among the golden broom bushes on the ridge above the sea.

"It seems a long time since I was on a beach," Ted wrote wistfully from the mudholes of France. "I do so love the sea."

Three Holes in the Ground 10

HARRY LAWRENCE RETURNED to Alaska seething with indignation at the recruiting office that had refused to accept him and his flat feet. He came to Spruce Creek to tell his troubles to Jock and persuaded his old friend to go with him to Rampart to have another try for gold.

While Jock was away, I had an urge to experiment with something new. Our present mine was petering out and did little more than keep us in supplies. Wandering some 300 feet above my claim, I looked at two old holes that had been dug long before by some unknown prospector and abandoned when no gold was found in them. The holes were opposite each other, 40 feet apart, at right angles to the creek. This, then, should be unproductive ground. Standing between the holes, I could see down the creek and the incline of land that sloped to the Innoko. Boilers, or the smoke from them, were visible on claims far down Spruce. These were claims that were all rich or had produced well at some time.

Suddenly it struck me that the boilers were all in a parallel line. My line of sight ran through every boiler, some working, some abandoned. This might mean nothing at all, but my heart began beating fast with hope, and I made up my mind to stake land up here and sink a hole on this spot between the old holes, directly in line with the boilers.

The first six feet went easily, using the pick on half-thawed ground, and took me two days of steady work. Then I hit hard frozen gravel and was forced to work with fire, the boiler and points being down on my old claim and too heavy for one man to drag up. I stacked shavings and dry sticks in the hole, with green logs over them, lit the shavings and hightailed it up the ladder to escape the flames. Banked by the green logs, the fire burned all night and melted the ice from the gravel for six inches in depth. In the morning the gravel was shoveled out and the fire rebuilt. As the days passed and bedrock neared, I liked the look of the sediment adhering to the gravel. It was gritty or sandy in texture, not a slimy muck which usually meant a poor yield, and the sight of it gave me the thrill that always came with a hopeful sign.

The next morning I took my dogs and sled with me, my sled holding two large gold pans. By mid-day I had struck bedrock. I filled one pan with dirt from the top of the bedrock, the other with gravel taken 16 inches above it, and took them to my cabin. Now would come the test.

The half-frozen gravel from the layer close to bedrock was emptied into a washtub and set on the stove to thaw. When the mass was melted, I began my panning, swirling gravel and water around in a gold pan and tipping out the gravel that came to the surface. The bottom of the pan was yellow with gold!

"Alice! Come here! See this!" I held out the pan and let her see the gold, which ranged from streaks of fine dust to fat nuggets.

"We've made it!" Here, surely, was proof. We were to be numbered among the chosen few who struck it rich and left Alaska with improbable dreams come true.

When Jock abandoned his profitless venture in Rampart and came back to Spruce, I greeted him with the good news: "We've hit it at last!" He looked at the samples and whistled. A shovel and a half of gravel in the pan produced about $2.65 worth of gold, rich by Innoko standards, and the same type of smooth, well-worn gold that had been found all down Spruce. We had struck the same rich creekbed. We staked more ground, farther up, and got to work.

It was early spring. The boiler was brought up from the old claim, and we crosscut the ancient creekbed to find the width of the streak. We progressed six feet at a time compared to six inches with the hand-built fires. Panned samples indicated the streak was 15 feet wide, and word soon spread along the creek: "Walker and Weir have struck above stream, up beyond all the pay claims, right by the holes that were abandoned as useless."

Jock and I could hardly believe it ourselves. Before we began the long, hard chore of laying half-mile ditches up the mountain to get a fast enough flow of water to work the sluices, we dug another hole 60 feet down-stream from the first. Samples showed it rich. Still doubtful, we dug our third hole yet another 60 feet down-stream, all three in line with the boilers strung out down the incline. We panned our samples and jubilantly shook hands when we saw the yield. My hunch must have been right: the pay streak ran straight down, and we were on it.

We began digging the long ditches, lining the rims with moss, collecting and stacking wood for the boiler and whipsawing lumber for the boxes. We worked all summer and fall until the cold weather halted us. When subzero temperatures kept us cabin-bound, we made plans for a future in which money would no longer be a problem.

Alaskan winters are long, however. No mining work could be done for five or six months of the year, and the enforced wait kept us on pins and needles. Nothing was 100 per cent certain until we had the gold in our pokes. We were like men receiving word of a sweepstake win: plans were still classed as daydreams until the money arrived.

"You must regret you ever came here, Alice," I said glumly, looking out at the snowcovered flats.

"I wouldn't have missed the years up here for anything in the world," she assured me. "I'll never forget the northern lights dancing and writhing like green snakes across the sky, and the masses of wild flowers we found on the hills: the larkspur, bluebells, violets, poppies . . ."

"And the mosquitoes?" Here on the swampy flats they bred by the millions. We kept a coal oil can beside the door, with a banked fire of damp wood in it that poured forth a thick cloud of smoke. Before entering the cabin, we'd stand in the smoke until the blanket of mosquitoes dropped from our backs, then make a dash for the door and shut it behind us before the enemy penetrated the strong-hold. I remember a hunting trip in the hills with Jock one summer, when he was frying bacon for our dinner over an open fire. Swarms of mosquitoes descended on us, suffocated in the smoke, and dropped so thickly into the frying pan that Jock threw it aside in disgust and served out cold rations.

"I could do without the mosquitoes," Alice admitted.

Spring came, and the ice in the creek melted. We began to widen the first hole and pile up waste and paydirt on the surface. Bedrock was too deep to wash off the gravel and uncover it, so we were forced to dig and send up the dirt in buckets. Every morning I climbed down and sent up a panful from a newly dug area for Jock to test, and he would take it away and thaw off the gravel and pan it for gold. Always he came back and called down to me: "Looks good. Carry on." We were still tense with excitement, but every day we allowed ourselves a little more hope that our luck lay in the area surrounding those three holes.

One evening that summer, Alice said hopefully: "If we hit the paystreak soon enough, we could be out of here before freeze-up and our new baby would be born in Seattle."

"There's no need for you to wait. Why not go to Seattle this summer?" I urged her. "Dr. Martin has gone, and Dr. Green is on the other side of the divide. The baby's due in February and the weather's unpredictable then. If a heavy snowstorm came on, I might not get him here in time. You must plan to go out, long before freeze-up."

"I married you to be with you," she told me firmly, "and I'll stay here until you're ready to leave too. Don't worry, I'm an old hand at this now, and Mabel has promised to help me when the time comes."

I went on with my digging. Jock's reports stayed good, until one morning when he took longer than usual to come back with the pan. I looked up to see him standing at the brink of the shaft.

"Well, how did she go today, Jock?"

"Pretty light this time, Bill."

Foreboding struck at me. I climbed the ladder and looked at the miserable gleanings from the morning's sample.

"That's strange, Jock. It's the direction the paystreak should take. There seems to be no gold outside of a narrow radius around the shaft."

"Better leave this and start on the next hole," he suggested.

We moved the boiler down, and I descended the ladder the 16 feet we had dug down to bedrock. I thawed out sections around the hole and sent up the buckets of gravel and the morning samples. Again the gold coloring was meagre outside of the shaft. We looked at each other, brows furrowed with anxiety. What did it mean? Doggedly we moved to the third hole, widened the base and took samples in all directions. It was the same gloomy story. Gold was promisingly rich at bedrock in the hole, but beyond it there was nothing at all.

TWO

The four of us sat round the kitchen table that night, debating the mystery and what should be done. Later we learned a possible explanation. Bedrock just here was formed of decomposed slate, too smooth and gummy to trap the gold nuggets. Where we had dug, crevices had held back a heavy deposit, but elsewhere the gold had been scattered widely and thinly all over the creekbed. How we had come to pick for our digging three isolated spots with cracks in the slate was a coincidence that baffled us.

"Do we give up, Jock?" I wondered.

"Give up? Not me. There's gold there somewhere."

"Alice expects a baby this winter. She should go outside before freeze-up, and I should go with her."

"You're not to go out because of me," Alice protested. "I know you don't want to leave yet. What about you, Meg?"

"Leave now?" she cried. "We'd be mad to leave now. There's gold down there; ye saw it yerself in the pans, Bill, over and over again. Let the men keep diggin', Alice, and we'll all be rich."

She had echoed my thoughts. I hated to give up and admit defeat when we had been so close to triumph, but further search was a gamble requiring a backload of savings to keep us going.

"Cold weather will be here soon," I reminded them. "If we're

208

going to try again in the spring, we'd better work a few months for wages, Jock, to grubstake ourselves."

I went up to a claim on Ophir Creek, and Jock went up a side creek from Ganes to where a big hydraulic company wanted preliminary testing done on a high bank. Both of us were hydraulicking. I was hosing and shoveling dirt accumulation at the mouth of the boxes while Jock worked alone, holding a big canvas hose and directing a heavy pressure of water at the bank to soften the frozen dirt and wash it away to form a ditch down to bedrock.

On arriving home one night, weary and muddy, I found Meg in the kitchen, crouched in a chair with Alice bending over her and urging her to take a cup of tea. She refused. "I canna, Alice."

"What's wrong, Meg?" I asked.

"It's Jock. He isna home, and it's past the time."

"It's not so late, Meg. I'm only just home myself."

"It's late for Jock. He's no late, ever. I fret if he's away when it's dark, so he knocks off early to get back in the light."

"He'll be along." It was dark, all right. Nights were cold now. It was close to freeze-up, and the dark came early. By the time I had washed up and changed into clean clothes, Meg was peering out the kitchen window at an impenetrable blackness.

The good smell of my dinner tempted me as it simmered on the stove. "Will you have a bite with us, Meg?" I said.

"I'll get back now," she said distractedly. "I dinna want his supper spoiled."

Alice urged her: "Stay here, Meg, if you're worried," but she would not stay.

I walked her over to her cabin and stood with her by the door, both of us staring into the dark and shivering in the chill air.

"Look, Meg," I said suddenly. "What's that?" A tiny light flashed on and off. Just as I thought myself mistaken, it came again, a little light that flickered for half a minute and then disappeared again.

"What is it?" Meg cried, trembling. "Is it Jock?"

"Looks like a firefly hovering. It's a long way off. There's no telling what it might be. But see here, Meg, I'll go down the creek to Pete's claim. He owns a horse. The two of us will ride over and have a look, and if Jock's in trouble we'll have the horse to bring him back. You go inside and keep warm." But she was still there, shivering on the doorstep, when the two of us rode by.

We had ridden a long way, and the lights had ceased to shine out and guide us, when we heard a faint cry for help. We rode up, and I swung my lantern. There in the light of it we saw Jock lying, his leg twisted and his face sharp with pain. We got him into the saddle, half unconscious from the torture of our inexpert handling, and I rode with him to hold him upright while Pete led the horse as it stumbled over tussocks and splashed in and out of creeks, jolting Jock unmercifully.

He had been hosing the frozen bank when the ground, less hard-packed than he had realized, suddenly trembled under tremendous water pressure and launched an avalanche that slid down with a roar. It knocked him flying and pinioned him with rocks and gravel to his armpits. As he fell, a large rock struck his leg and he lost consciousness.

When he came to, he worked his hands free and threw off the rocks and dirt, moving carefully to avoid another landslide. His leg was broken, and by the time he had dragged himself a short distance he knew he could never make it across several creeks to his cabin. He needed some sort of flare to make a distress signal, and he fumbled in his pocket for matches and lit one, holding it high, at arm's length, until it flickered out. It was a feeble substitute for a flare, but he kept on lighting one match after another until the box was empty; then he lay in the dark and cold waiting patiently, like the gray wolf by the Novakaket headwaters had waited in the snow, for whatever must come.

When we got him home to Meg, he set the broken leg himself with rough splints. "We're not licked yet," he told her. The bones healed in time, but poorly, leaving him with a pronounced limp. After a few months, he was back at work again.

We wished more than once that some of us had been foresighted enough to take on Dr. Martin's offer of medical insurance. Mac-Naughton's partner, Evan Jones, had stayed on alone in the cabin below us after MacNaughton left to join the army. During the winter he fell ill, and one evening we found him dead in his bed. We buried him behind his cabin.

That Christmas, we decided to put aside our worries and be merry. I had gone hunting and run across a band of five caribou, a rare sight in these hills, and brought one down.

"Caribou for our Christmas dinner!" said Alice. "We'll ask Jock and Meg over, and we'll get the Vinals down from Ophir and all celebrate together."

On Christmas Day, we made a hearty meal of the caribou and then sat back to wait for the big pudding, the only item on our menu that suggested a traditional English Christmas. Alice unmoulded it onto a plate, poured brandy over it and lit the liquor. Blue flames flickered as she lifted the heavy dish to carry it to the table, and we all clapped and cheered.

It had become a family joke between Alice and me that I always quoted Bob Cratchit at this point: "A wonderful pudding! The greatest success achieved by Mrs. Cratchit since our marriage!" Alice as usual replied with Mrs. Cratchit's doubts about the quantity of flour. Suddenly she closed her eyes and swayed. The hot brandy spilled onto her hand and she cried out and dropped the dish. The pudding broke into a dozen fragments among the sticks and shavings in the woodbox.

"Alice! What's wrong?" I jumped to help her.

"I'm all right now." She looked down in dismay at the mess of crumbs, chunks of pudding, broken china, and sauce. Tears of embarrassment welled into her eyes, and Nugget broke into howls of anguish to see his mother weeping and his pudding lost.

Little Mrs. Vinal came to the rescue. "What's all the crying about? There's nothing wrong with the pudding. We were all set to spoon it into helpings in another minute; now Mrs. Walker has broken it up for us in one fell swoop. Who wants plum pudding? Come and get it!" She scooped up a big chunk from the woodbox, brushed off the shavings, and carried it to the table. "If it tastes as good as it smells, I'll want another helping."

We made a point of returning to probe among the shavings for second helpings. It became an excuse for much prolonged hilarity, more hearty than witty, but our nonsense made Alice and Nugget laugh again. I found our Christmas dinner emotionally exhausting, but Jock said it was a smashing success.

We lost our second child. Death of mother or baby in childbirth was common enough in the northern wilderness where expert medical help was seldom available should complications arise, but one's personal tragedies loom large and are always hard to accept.

I got some of the lumber I had whipsawed for sluiceboxes and sawed and hammered out a coffin. When I had nailed down the lid, I carried the box out to the shed. Since it was impossible to dig into the frozen ground until spring, the coffin would have to lie there until the thaw came.

Big, gruff Mabel from Ganes Creek nursed Alice and she recovered, but she was quiet and subdued. She would rouse herself to care for Nugget but seemed obsessed with a guilt complex that she had caused our baby girl's death by staying with me in Spruce Creek. In desperation, I dug out a book my aunt Meg had given to me in Seattle which she told me she had begun to study after the death of her first child. I hunted out phrases in Mary Baker Eddy's *Science and Health* that might offer help to Alice: "Lamentation is needless and causeless ... there is no death ... God does not employ drugs or hygiene ... "

"Bill," she asked hopefully, "does that mean I wasn't wrong to stay here?"

"Of course you weren't wrong. You must never blame yourself."

Optimism and energy were natural to her. When spring came and I took the small coffin from the shed and buried it under the moss and gravel, her grief and sense of guilt lay quiet too. She said she had come to regret our search for material gain for ourselves. "Is that what we really want?" she asked me earnestly. "I feel it's time for us to leave Alaska and begin a new life that has real meaning for us."

"But what can I do outside? I'm not trained for city work. If I stayed here with Jock until we made a strike ... "

"You might be here for years — for long, wasted years. When we get out, I know you'll be shown the work you are meant to do."

"You go, Alice; go this summer by boat. I'll stay here one more year and make enough for a start outside."

Alice left in July. She seemed refreshed and alert, eager to begin her new life. But she made one mistake: on leaving, she turned for a last glance at the cabin she had come to as a bride and saw beside it the wooden cross that marked the grave of her child, soon to be abandoned to the wilderness. Despite her resolution, she could not hold back her tears.

She traveled down the Innoko on a scow in the company of a number of outside-bound Alaskans who represented as ill-assorted a group as would any typical cross-section of citizens in the gold towns. There were several bearded miners (one, call Hobo Frank, was renowned for living exclusively on porridge mixed with boiled onions); a trapper; an optometrist and his wife, and a shifty-eyed character known as Billy the Rat.

They had tents on board and enough food to last them until they reached the head of navigation at the half-way point. From there the steamboat *Florence S.* was to take them to St. Michael. They expected to see the steamer tied up and waiting when she got to the gravel bar halfway down, but there was no sign of her when they arrived. The scowmen congratulated themselves on a fast run that had beaten her, set their passengers ashore and headed back up the river.

The little party of travelers walked up and down the gravel bar, slapping at the mosquitoes and peering hopefully down-river for a sight of the *Florence S.* As the hours ticked away, the mosquitoes harassed them beyond endurance, and the men built a smudge fire to drive them off.

The optometrist, a friendly and willing soul, was eager to do his share. He had gone to Ophir hoping to start a roaring trade, but everyone in Ophir, it seemed, had excellent eyesight; besides, the population was too small to support him. Nonetheless, he was philosophical about his mistake. He borrowed an axe from Billy the Rat, who was happy to take over the lighter task of gathering up twigs and chips.

"For the love of Mike!" shouted one of the miners. "Hey, take a look at the spectacle seller!"

The optometrist stood with both feet in a big washtub while leaning over awkwardly in an attempt to split a bleached trunk of driftwood. "So I look foolish? I would look more foolish with no feet!" Undeterred by their jibes and guffaws, he stayed in the washtub, refusing to expose his toes to the energetic but erratic blows of his axe.

For Alice, that picture of the neatly dressed professional man standing in a tub and making ineffectual swipes with an axe impressed her as being symbolic of the thousands of ill-equipped and inexperienced men who had been lured by the prospect of quick riches to this harsh and uncompromising land.

"Looks like *Florence S.* won't keep her date with us today," said the trapper. "We'd better set up tents for the night and get some sleep."

They went to bed supperless and tried to settle down to sleep, hoping to see the boat early in the morning. Alice, who shared a small tent with the optometrist's wife, lay on her side on the gravel, brushing away the occasional mosquito that hovered over her slumbering son. She sought patience for the delay, putting from her mind a vision of the steamer's clean sheets and its shining washstand with hot and cold water; and beyond that, so far away, in another world, slanting shadows on the cool green lawn of a Seattle garden.

There was no sign of the steamer throughout the following day, so the miners went hunting for game and returned with several porcupine. Porcupine were seldom killed as game, for they were very fat and slow-moving enough that they could easily be disposed of with a club; thus the hunting of them was considered unsporting. They were, however, lifesavers for miners or trappers lost in the wilderness without a gun to bring down fleeter animals. The miners skinned them, starting at the stomachs where there were no quills and the flesh could be grasped, and then stewed the meat. No one complained of the excess fat, though Hobo Frank talked wistfully of porridge laced with onions. They lived on porcupine and beaver for a week, gradually coming to the conclusion that they had missed the steamer and were left stranded on the gravel bar without hope of rescue until an accumulation of freight at St. Michael warranted another up-river trip.

On the seventh day they debated a course of action. The only solution seemed to be to build a raft from logs and tent ropes and then float down to the Yukon. It would be a long, hungry, mosquito-ridden journey, and they would have several more days of porcupine stew before the raft would be ready.

Suddenly they heard a faint, throbbing sound in the distance. They all fell silent, listened to the putt-putt of an engine from downstream, and then broke into cheers as a small launch came chugging against the current. The helmsman was Mac Simmel, a trader who ran a small store farther up the Innoko, and he told them that the *Florence S.* had come and gone from the navigation head.

"Stuck here, are you? Well, you can't swim down, can you? Building a raft? Forget it. I have a better plan. See if you can all crowd aboard my boat, and I'll turn around and run you as far as Holy Cross."

At Holy Cross, one of the big steamboats was preparing to cast off as they neared the north bank of the Yukon, but a chorus of shouts from the launch made her draw in again and the passengers boarded her, all of them weary, grimy, welted from mosquito bites and eagerly anticipating a menu that offered a change from stewed porcupine.

The optometrist built up a successful practice in Seattle and in later years, Alice would drop in and relive with him that uncomfortable week on the gravel bar. Alice became, for a few years, head of a branch of the Seattle Public Library. But she couldn't rest until she had fulfilled the promise she had made to herself beside the Innoko River: she became a reader in the Christian Science church and a practitioner to those distressed by mental, physical, and spiritual problems.

FOUR

There was a deserted look to Spruce Creek that fall. Many of the miners had abandoned their claims, and idle steam boilers rusted beside gaping excavations and mountains of dirt. My cabin was sadly silent without Alice and Nugget. I missed both their welcome at the end of my day at the mine and the hot meal that Alice always had waiting for me. Sometimes I dined with Jock and Meg, but

Meg's meals were a far cry from Alice's inspired cooking and she seemed resentful when Jock would bring me home.

"We canna waste our money on fancy food," she told me, her face screwed up with anxiety. "Them that saves today won't see want tomorrow." Fearful of the future, she had begun hoarding tins of food. Jock spoke confidently of gold on our claim, and she believed in him implicitly, but she grew more frightened daily as the miners around us decreased in number and drifted off down the Innoko to the Yukon. Jock told me that Alice's departure had been a shock to her and that she lived in dread of a day when only Jock and she would remain on the empty flats, still searching in vain for the elusive gold.

I became increasingly conscious of the atmosphere of grim determination that had replaced the spirit of adventure we knew in the early days of our partnership. I sickened with the loneliness, the mud, the endless frustrations and the feeling of desperation that surrounded me, and looking ahead to a whole year of this, the time seemed as interminable as it had to Alice at 18 years of age while she waited for her wedding day. I began to fear that even a year up here might not produce the needed cash. Every cent put aside had been spent shipping Alice to Seattle, and now part of my earnings went down to her at regular intervals. My savings were re-accumulating at a very slow rate.

On Yankee Creek, below Ganes, a dredging company restaked some unrecorded claims and called for men to do the required assessment work on them to establish their right for the year. I went over to the pool hall in Ophir where men were congregating to be hired. Jock and I still needed a few more months of work with an assured income to provide funds for a renewed search on Spruce.

A young Frenchman, Paul LaFollette, was one of the unfortunates who had neglected to record claims and found themselves in a quandary when Yankee Creek began operations. The dredging company with within its rights to take over, but to Paul, who came to the pool hall and saw the men receiving instructions to dig on his staked land, it was out-and-out robbery. He came up to each of us in turn and advised us to stay off his property if we valued our lives.

"I understand you plan to dig on my claim?"

"Well, yes, but . . . "

"I wouldn't do it if I were you. I'm warning you."

His fury left us uneasy, but we knew he had forfeited his rights, and the next day five of us reported for work and began to sink holes. There was no sign of the Frenchman and as the days passed without incident, I began to breathe easier.

It was early October. The first snow had fallen but the ground could still be penetrated by a pick axe for eight to ten feet before hard frozen gravel was reached and steam or fire was needed to go further. After removing the turf and digging for 10 days, I had a hole four feet across by eight feet deep and would start taking samples to test in a few days' time. Working below ground, I became aware of a crunching sound in the snow above which sounded like footsteps approaching the hole. I straightened my back and looked up, right into the muzzle of a rifle. Behind it was the face of the young Frenchman, his black eyes burning down at me.

For a long moment it was a frozen tableau while the grim thought struck me that I was suitably situated if LaFollette intended to fire his rifle: my grave was already dug, and I was standing in it. Swallowing with difficulty, I smiled stiffly, and was surprised to hear my voice sounding natural: "Good afternoon, Paul."

There was no answer, but the rifle moved slightly with a menacing hint. Desperately searching for a topic to continue talking, I said brightly: "I'm hoping to make enough at this job to grubstake Jock and me at Spruce for another try. You see, Paul, I need something for a start outside with my family."

Silence from above. I leaned on my shovel. It was difficult to carry on a one-way conversation. I knew Paul LaFollette fairly well and felt sure he had no serious intention of pulling the trigger. On the other hand, the rifle was probably loaded; and besides, he had it pointed right at my head. One wrong word, and it would only need a convulsive squeeze of his finger to send me slumping into my self-made grave.

Suddenly a wave of revulsion swept over me. "Paul," I cried, "what are we doing? What has this gold-grubbing done to us? We're good friends, and there you stand with a rifle trained on me, while I'm grubbing up dirt and gravel, a thousand miles away from my wife and child. What kind of a life is that? I've changed my mind, Paul. As soon as my fare to Seattle is saved, it's goodbye to the Innoko creeks. A man and wife should be together. I can do nursery work and landscape gardening, work that I learned as a boy in Victoria, planting things and bringing life and beauty to the land. No more digging in the dirt with nothing to show for my labor but an ugly wasteland. I'll go out before spring. You must call on us, Paul, when you go outside. Come and see us if you ever get to Seattle."

The rifle had slowly lowered during this impassioned speech, and now man and rifle abruptly disappeared. Crunching footsteps on the snow grew fainter and faded away. When I ventured a look over the rim of the hole, Paul was nowhere in sight. Maybe so much of my talking had exhausted him. Also, no doubt it's difficult to shoot a man who invites you to visit his home and confides his longing for his wife, especially if you belong to a race as sympathetic to love as it is zealous in its demands for justice.

That night I told Jock of my plan to leave Alaska early in the new year.

"You won't be here in the spring then, to work Spruce?"

"No, Jock, I want to get back to Alice. We've been chasing a will o' the wisp for nearly ten years, and all we ever got for our pains was just enough to encourage us to keep on digging, digging, digging. I've had enough. Why don't you and Meg come out with me, Jock? The three of us could go down together."

Jock shook his head. "Not us, Bill. We've got something here, and we're sticking with it. What could I do in Seattle at my age? Seafaring is my trade, and I've grown too old for that. My job is here in the mine."

"Can you work without a partner?"

"I'll get one. There was a fellow named Bob Jacima who wanted to come in with us awhile ago. He's still around."

Bob Jacima came to see me a few nights later. He was a slow-speaking, earnest sort of fellow. He had a paper for me to sign, relinquishing my partnership. "I told Jock Weir you should be paid something for the sale," he said, "but he says you don't expect payment. That doesn't seem right to me. I've put down two hundred dollars on the agreement, and you can have it now if you think that's a fair price."

I signed the paper at once and pocketed the money. It would be set aside to take home with me as soon as my fare was raised.

About a month later, Meg came over to my cabin. I was surprised to see her. She had little to say to me these days and never came to call on me, or on anyone else for that matter.

"Come in, Meg," I said. "Is anything wrong?"

"It's Jock," she said, not moving from the step. She was almost incoherent with fright. "The logs went over him. His back might be broken. He's on the sled, out front of the cabin. I canna get him in."

I got a folding cot to use as stretcher, and we carried Jock indoors. He opened his eyes as we were covering him up and tried to speak. He was shivering, and his lips trembled so that we had trouble understanding him.

"Don't worry, Meg," he finally got out in a weak quaver. "I'll soon be in shape to work the mine again. Stick with me, Meg."

"Ah, Jock," she said, tears spilling down her cheeks, "ye know I'll stick with ye. Ye'll make it yet." But she turned to me, desperation in her face.

"What happened, Meg?"

"He was late," she said. "When he was late home, I knew there was trouble again. He went up the draw to bring down the logs he'd been cutting, but he didna come back on time. I ran up the trail to the draw, and there were the dogs lying in the traces in the middle of the trail. The sled was loaded with logs and Jock was lying under the runners. He runs astride the traces, behind the dogs, ye see, when he has the Yukon sled, to steer it with the gee pole. And he must have stumbled and fell. It's that bad leg of his that keeps him limping; he's not steady on his feet now. He fell between the dogs and the sled, and the runner went over his shoulder and neck and pinned him down. The dogs stopped when they felt the bump; that's all that saved him from having the whole load drawn over him." She wiped her eyes, reliving that moment of panic. "I untied the fastenings on the logs and they rolled off into the snow, and then I got him on the sled and drove him home. Bill, do ye think it hurt him, lifting him up?"

Jock said feebly, "Nothing wrong with me."

"Meg," I said, "I'll stay at Spruce until he's able to travel, and then we'll all go down together."

Jock was up on Christmas Day, pottering about his kitchen. He had suffered a slight stroke at the time of the accident, with a brain damage that resulted in a worsening state of palsy. His head and hands trembled constantly. He was 52, but he looked like an old, shrunken man of 70. I had brought over some ptarmigan I had shot, and Meg roasted them. I made a pie, too, from the berries Alice had left packaged in sugared layers, so we had a Christmas dinner of sorts.

"When do you think you can travel, Jock?" I asked.

"Travel? Who's traveling?"

He was still determined to stay in Spruce Creek when I came over on New Year's Eve to greet the new year with them. Meg felt the same way, and at last I gave up trying to persuade them.

It was close to midnight when Meg asked Jock, "Do ye mind the discovery stake on the claim above ours with the three holes? Did ye no say the date on it was running out?"

"You're right, Meg, it ran out a week ago." The claim she referred to was deserted. No work had been done on it in the required time by the original stakers, and it was now available for anyone who wished to relocate it by restaking.

Meg stood up, hands clasped in dismay. "A week ago, ye say? It needs a stick with some new writing, quick, before someone gets ahead of us."

Jock shook his head. "Don't fret now, Meg. It's 50-below-zero tonight. No one is turning out in this freezing cold to take the claim."

She stood wringing her hands. "It's the verra time they'll pick to do just that, Jock, when it's not expected and there's no one to see. Do ye want the dredgers to grab it, like they did La Follette's claim?"

"They'll not be looking for claims tonight, Meg."

"Jock, it's our chance to get more land right in a line with the paystreak. It's maybe the verra spot that has the gold in it. The wind's too sharp for you, Jock, but let Bill go and put up the sticks. He'll not mind, will ye, Bill? It's to save it from the dredgers, ye see."

I waited hopefully for another protest from Jock, but he got up and collected the stakes he had prepared and a marking pencil. The icy air and fine snow blasted us as we stepped outside. It was painful to draw the freezing air into our lungs.

"Let me go alone," I said, but he shook his head. "I'm fit as a fiddle, Bill."

We struggled slowly up to the discovery stake, and Jock drove his own stake into the deep moss, leaning it against a scrub spruce for added support. His heavy mittens made it awkward to hold the pencil firmly while he wrote, so he pulled off the right mitt and began scribbling shakily: 'I, Jock Weir, claim 20 acres of ground . . . ' He moaned in agony and thrust his frozen hand back into shelter. I took the pencil from him and added, 'for placer mining purposes.' We alternated, snatching off mitts and thrusting cold hands under armpits to thaw, until we completed the declaration with 'December 31, 1918.'

"That's it until tomorrow," Jock gasped. "If we try to set up the rest of these stakes tonight we'll be as stiff as they are. Let's get the hell out of this cold." He clutched my shoulder for support, and we staggered back to the cabin to drink in the new year with hot tea. Jock had no money for whisky, and I had promised Alice to give up liquor, this being counsel she had taken from Mary Baker Eddy's book.

As we celebrated with our mild stimulant, I volunteered, "If there was a chance you would come out, I'd wait until spring and go down on the first boat with you." When he shook his head, I gave up. "Then I'll plan to leave in about two weeks' time. I'll hike out overland to Seward."

"Alone? This time of year? Vinal is going out in about a month, traveling with a big party. Go with him. Don't risk it alone."

"I can make it. The mail team leaves a trail."

"And what if a storm blows up and snow buries the tracks? Storms blow up fast in the mountains. Men have died on the trail. Wait for Vinal's party."

But stubbornness was one of my traits, too, and I would not wait.

I saw little of Jock and Meg in the next two weeks, being busy with trips to Ophir to pay bills and sell some of my household goods.

When ready to leave, I took my big white dog, part husky and part St. Bernard, over to Jock's cabin. Meg answered my knock, opening the door just a crack, and seemed about to close it in my face, but I called out, "Is Jock there?" and heard him say: "Hold it, Meg, I'm going out." As he came to the door, she said anxiously: "Be careful." I thought she was referring to the icy steps and offered my hand, but then she added: "Be careful of what you say." Jock closed the door, and she watched us out the window as we walked down to my cabin.

I was leading my big dog and handed the rope to Jock, saying, "Take him as a farewell gift from me."

"But he's your best dog in harness and he's Nugget's pet."

"I'll manage with three dogs. I'll be traveling light. And I want to leave you something."

He went over to look at my team. The three dogs were all huskies, hitched to a light sled that carried axe, tarpaulin and blanket, and dried fish for the dogs. Lead dog was my white Siberian husky, smallish but energetic, and my wheel dogs, running abreast, were a black and a gray.

"Don't let Meg know that I told you this," Jock said nervously, "but I sold the claim last week to the dredgers."

"No! Congratulations! So Meg was right, after all. It's lucky we went out on New Year's Eve and staked it."

"That's not the claim I mean; it was your claim I sold, the one with the three holes we dug."

"The claim with the three holes?" He must have seen shock in my face, for he looked away, his trembling fingers jerking at the rope. "They think the gold is there, but too scattered for anything but dredging. We got a lot for it, enough for Bob Jacima to go home to his own country, and for Meg and me to live easy from now on. Bob thought you should have a bit of it, but Meg said no." He looked at me piteously. "Don't be hard on her, Bill. She's not been the same since my troubles came to me. She's been scared sick, wondering what would happen to us next. If there's someone in charge of all this, he's got a dirty sense of humor, playing with us like a cat toys with a mouse, letting our hopes rise up again and again before hitting us with the final blow, crippling my leg and leaving me with the shakes. Meg could never understand, you see, that men could grow rich just below us, that our own three holes showed promise and then, over and over, when success seemed there in our grasp, it slipped away and left us empty-handed. And now, the dirtiest joke of all, when things look hopeless, the money drops in our laps. The shock's been too much for her, Bill."

His anxious, quavering voice was so unlike his former easy drawl, and there was no trace of the sly humor that was always there in the early days of our partnership. If only he could realize my aversion for the gold that had brought us so much suffering and sorrow.

"Jock, stop fretting. Bob paid me for my share in the claim. I signed an agreement and took his money; and there's time ahead for me to make a new start outside. It was your future that worried me, but my mind's at rest now that good luck has come to you and your troubles are over. Take Meg some place where things will be easier for both of you."

We grasped hands, studying one another and exchanging a few final words. Each knew it was the end of a long partnership, a unique companionship without a day of friction for almost 20 years. We had shared the misery of gnawing pangs of hunger and the delirious rapture when a successful shot ended weeks of famine. We had explored strange rivers together, pitted our wits against the cunning of the wild furbearing animals, thrilled to the discovery of gold and experienced the shattering moment of dismay when our rich streak petered out. Now it was ended. Our paths would diverge, and whatever lay ahead for the two of us would come to us separately.

I turned away, shouted "Mush on!" to my dogs and started down the trail by the creek. A dull ache permeated my body, as though a part of me had been cut away.

The Long Journey Home   11

ONE

ABANDONED DIGGINGS and rusting boilers lined the trail. The place had a ghost town atmosphere. Ophir was emptying fast, and most buildings stood vacant. On the flats outside the town there rose up the rock that miners had christened The Sphinx. It was strangely shaped with jutting ledges and resembled a giant human profile. Its eyeless, enigmatic features faced the creeks that concealed the secret of their hidden gold from so many of the men who sought it. It was a relief when the trail branched off through the divide and down to Takotna, and I could turn my back upon the diggings for the last time.

Once away from them, my spirits lifted. The air was brisk, just cold enough to be invigorating, and the sun was thinly veiled in cloud with none of its dazzling brightness reflected from the snow to blind me. The long journey, my last test in the harsh wilderness, had begun.

I kept the dogs at a good pace, aiming to cover 40 miles a day, the distance between roadhouses. At the first one there was news of the mail carrier. He had stayed there two nights earlier.

"I'll have his fresh trail to follow all the way," I said thankfully.

"Sure, if no snow comes to cover his tracks."

"Well, I'll have to put on speed and overtake him."

"Not much chance of that, is there?"

"Why not? I have a good team here."

I saw amused and skeptical expressions on the men in the road-house and had to admit to myself that my dogs were a pretty motley looking trio. My lively little white Siberian was much smaller than most huskies; my black was a long-legged, ill-natured brute, forever snapping and snarling at his gray wheel mate. I forgave the poor fellow his ill disposition since he had plenty to try him. He had tender feet that needed constant care, and he also had a crafty mate who was an expert at avoiding his proper share of the work. The gray had been sold to me at a bargain price by a passing mail carrier, and I realized after the sale had been made that no mailman would part with a good dog for a song. Good sled dogs were too hard to find. This one was smart, but only in avoiding work. He had evolved a clever method of running just fast enough to keep his traces taut, without exerting any pull on them. All effort was left to the leader and to the unfortunate black. That gray had to be watched continually to make sure that his muscles were straining; and, if he was trotting along relaxed and easy, must be prodded until he buckled down to work again.

The dogs ran well at first, which pleased and surprised me. We crossed the frozen Kuskokwim River on schedule. I kept looking ahead hopefully for a sign of the mail carrier, but the trail wound on, mile after mile, with no other living creature moving over it. Still, if my dogs maintained this pace, and if anything happened to delay the mail team, I might close the gap between us sufficiently to be sure of clear tracks to guide me.

At last I approached the Great Divide. My greatest danger lay in crossing this divide through the Alaska Range. The way led up through a narrow, canyon-like pass where fierce storms came up without warning. The open areas of the mountain approaches on both sides of the divide were dangerous too, and men had perished there when sudden storms and snow buried all traces of the trail.

My black was limping, and I stopped to examine the dogs' paws and remove lumps of frozen snow that might cut their pads. There was an icy wind blowing that afternoon, and as the dogs struggled up the steep incline I kept my head bent low against the wind, pushing hard on the sled handles to help them along. Suddenly the dogs stopped short, and I almost over-ran my wheel dogs, unaware of the halt. The sled bogged down as the reins slackened, and I looked up to find the black and gray immobile in the snow.

But where was my lead dog, my little Siberian? He had disappeared. I climbed around the two and saw that the traces in front of them were hanging straight down. Taking a cautious step nearer, I looked to see where they had gone, and there was my Siberian, hanging suspended in the air over a mountain creek. He had veered off the trail and broken through thin, snow-covered ice. The water below it had dropped to a shallower level after the ice had formed, and he hung in this gap with his toes just touching the water. He was held up by his harness and by his two team mates whose paws were dug into the snow as they shivered and strained to keep from following him down through the hole.

How close could I venture without breaking through ice myself? Slowly, carefully, I inched near enough to seize the traces, then backed away hastily, hauling up my dog, and got back onto the faint markings of the trail.

The dogs were nervous now. I called to them: "Mush on, mush on!" using the old Alaskan command, a western corruption of the French Canadian "marchons." I shoved steadily at the sled, urging on my weary animals, my own legs ready by now to buckle under me. We had to get through the canyon while the weather stayed clear, for any moment a sudden storm could blow up. There was a roadhouse on top of the saddle, and I wanted to reach it before nightfall.

When we reached level ground at the top, the dogs seemed to catch a scent of the roadhouse. They came to life, pulling with new vigor, and I took off my snowshoes and rode the runners to catch my breath and let strength come back to my shaking legs. It was too dark to see the trail, but the dogs raced along, sniffing the wind, and late at night I saw the soft glow of light from the window of the log cabin spilling out onto the snow.

The roadhouse operator repeated Jock's warning the next morning. "Don't travel alone through the divide," he urged me. "Wait here and join up with the next party coming through." He shook his head pessimistically as I continued to harness my dogs.

"How far ahead is the mailman?"

"He stayed here two nights ago."

It had been the same story at each stop. For all my running and shoving, I had made no progress at all in narrowing the gap between us. "Bad luck! I'm trying to catch up with him."

"Trying to catch up with him? You'll never do that, man. The carrier has a full team of fast dogs familiar with the trail. You have only three dogs that don't look fast to me, and they're amateurs, like yourself."

"Amateurs?" I was highly insulted. "I've been eighteen years in Alaska."

"Well, suit yourself, but I know the storms in this pass. You're a fool to travel alone."

I waved a jaunty farewell to my gloomy host and started off along the mountain trail, my dogs eager and willing after their hours of rest. Descending the saddle, they sped down the steep grade, forcing me to ride the runners and brake continually to keep the sled under control. The weather was clear and calm in the early morning, with no wind nor sign of an approaching storm.

Now the steepness changed to a gradual incline. The divide here was very wide, with no trees to afford shelter from a storm. Some distance ahead, the gentle incline became flats, and far off, beyond these, a dark line showed where the timber began. There lay safety. I was confident that I could reach it with the co-operation I was getting from both weather and dogs. The air was clear, crisp and invigorating; the huskies continued to run with enthusiasm. I felt that I could run for days without tiring, especially with the dual incentive of proving myself and of reaching my family at the end of the journey.

The skies grayed around noon, and a few minutes later something soft brushed my cheek. I jerked my head up, staring at the dull clouds. How rapidly the sky had changed its character! Snowflakes drifted down lazily and then a sudden gust of icy wind hit my back. It was the danger signal, the first warning of peril. My heartbeat quickened. The catastrophe that had been prophesied for me all along my route was almost upon me. I had looked for a test and would get one right enough before my trip was over.

The storm approached rapidly, the wind increasing in velocity

227

and sending clouds of fine snow into my face and into the dogs' eyes. It covered the trail and set us adrift to stagger blindly through the storm. The dogs were off the trail almost at once, floundering in deep snow. I halted them, located firm ground, then dragged my lead dog over to it. Before I got back to the sled, the three dogs were lying flat on the trail, whimpering and whining, afraid to move. I shouted: "Mush on!" at them and shoved at the sled, but they lay huddled in the traces, noses buried in paws, trembling in their terror of the blast that howled about them and penetrated to their skin. I, too, was suffering. My parka proved inadequate to keep out this icy wind which stabbed through my clothing and set my teeth chattering.

"Mush on!" We would freeze if we stayed here in the open during the storm. It was imperative to keep moving, but my dogs lay inert. I plodded again to the front of my team and hauled at the Siberian until he rose and moved a few steps, encouraging the other two to struggle up. I stayed in front, feeling out the trail with my snowshoes, and the dogs slipped and staggered after me, willing to follow a leader who sounded out the way.

The fury of the storm eased for a few moments and the timber line showed up, stretching across the horizon. It was farther away than it had been before the storm began, much farther than it ought to be by now. I must have strayed onto another trail, too far left. The carrier's trail should be over to the right somewhere, but a search that involved floundering in this freezing storm could lead to exhaustion, collapse and death.

Forcing myself to stay calm, I backtracked a way on the trail, pulling the dogs behind me, then zig-zagged across it in an ever-widening reconnaissance until firmness was found far to the right, leading toward a closer timber line.

The carrier's trail was located just in time, for the storm worsened. Snow whirled down thickly, shutting out everything, beating at my eyes and choking off my breath. Stumbling off the trail again, I tripped and fell, and lay still. Too numb to feel the cold, I responded to my body's plea for rest, my mind a blank, knowing only an overwhelming need to yield to the storm, to close my eyes and sleep.

I thought Alice cried out to me, whimpering in pain, and knew I must go to her quickly. She sobbed again, and I forced myself painfully back into consciousness. My dogs were huddled about me as we lay half buried in snow, and my little Siberian was crouched on my chest with his muzzle close to my ear. His moans and whimpers had wakened me.

Dragging myself upright, I got back on the trail, paused a moment to stamp my feet and slap my body with my arms to get my circulation going, and told myself sternly to keep calm, endure the agonizing cold with stoicism and continue to feel out the trail patiently and methodically. Only then was there a chance of survival. A surrender to panic would finish me as it had finished so many others on this wide and treacherous divide. Concentrating on the trail, losing it, zigzagging to relocate it and then resuming my snail-like pace, I forgot time and my ultimate destination. The world narrowed down to this open area and the storm that must be battled and overcome. Every ounce of energy was expended on the one task of finding and following the long trail down the divide to the timber line.

T W O

Staggering at last into the shelter of the trees, I was still on the trail and the dogs were behind me. We collapsed and rested, I on the sled and the dogs sprawled in front of me on the snow, all of us feeling more dead than alive, too exhausted for a time to move but thankful for the chance to catch our breath again. Now that we had reached safety, the storm ceased as suddenly as it had begun. But it continued cold, with the temperature about 30-below.

Some distance ahead I could see an open trail cut through the timber, and knew it should lead to the roadhouse tent of the Mountain Climber. Remembering the churlish reception Billy Keyes and I had received from the inhospitable host, I doubted that my welcome this time would be any warmer. At least there were dogs with me, something the Mountain Climber had seemed to feel was the trademark of a legitimate traveler.

The dogs pricked up their ears as a man came down the side trail, riding a sled behind his team. He paused to ask where I was from and said he was the Mountain Climber's partner. "You'll see him back in the tent, if you can make it there. You must be crazy to travel the divide alone in this weather."

"Has the mail team been by?"

"Mailman stayed with us two nights ago. I'm off now, to get us a moose." He shouted at his dogs and rode on.

While debating my next move, the thought struck me that bypassing this unpleasant stopping place and continuing to the next roadhouse would cut a day off the handicap and give me a better chance of overtaking the mail team. About 42 miles separated the roadhouse in the Great Divide from the next one. I had about 20 miles still to cover and could make it by nightfall with fast travel.

First my dogs had the snow and ice cleaned from their paws, and then they were each fed a portion of fish. They lay down when I took hold of the sled handles and urged them to start, but my shouts forced them to stagger up one after the other, whining in protest. My three unhappy huskies were no stout-hearted heroes; they had no devils driving them on to prove their endurance. As strongly as they could, they showed their disapproval. It was as hard to persuade them to co-operate as it was to break trail and keep to the right path. In the shelter of the trees, the trail was lightly covered and they kept to it without much trouble. I took off my snowshoes then and went more quickly. But whenever we entered an open area we lost time as the Siberian wandered off the trail and sank deep into drifts that filled holes and hollows. My snowshoes must be replaced, the path searched for, the team dragged onto it, a stop made to clean off paws and the laggards urged up and on. It would have helped if the mail carrier had been a tobacco chewer. I knew of one carrier whose trail was always plainly marked by dark brown blobs of tobacco juice.

When darkness fell, the dogs lay down once more, refusing to budge. "Time to follow the leader, eh? Up you get, then!" I sighed, resigned to their inadequacies, and went ahead, feeling out the trail, leaving a trodden path for them, and they got up without enthusiasm but willing as before to follow my lead.

Around 10 o'clock that night, we turned in at the roadhouse. The exhausted dogs were taken to quarters specially provided for them where I groomed and fed them before sitting down to a hot dinner. It seemed to me a good omen when my favorite dessert was brought in to top it off: a big slice of chocolate cake. And, for the first time, the news was encouraging. I had gained a day on the mailman. He had left the roadhouse only that morning.

The cold spell ended, and travel was no longer torture. It was pleasant to slide easily over the frozen lakes and rivers. Crossing them had a dreamlike quality as we sped silently over the smooth, level ice. I rode the runners, the sled sliding without noise or effort, the land hushed and quiet, the snow-burdened tree branches unmoving, no breath of wind disturbing the calm. There was no sign of life as we made our runs between the roadhouses, except for tracks of wolverine that were on the prowl somewhere and had crossed the lakes and gone into the timber. The peace about me flooded my soul. The long struggle to prove myself was now ended. I felt calm and confident, sure of my capability to cope with the wilderness.

I never caught up with the mail carrier but ceased to worry. Having made it thus far, overcoming the worst the divide could blast at me, there was nothing more to fear. I reached the railway tracks and caught the train for the last 75 miles to Seward. The journey from Spruce Creek to Seward had taken 12 days. I found someone there who would accept my black and gray huskies as a gift but took my Siberian with me on the Seattle-bound steamer.

As the ship sailed down the Alaskan coast, I saw the entrance to Lynn Canal where 18 years before, a boat had turned in and docked at Skagway to let an excited boy passenger set foot on Alaskan soil for the first time.

Most of the passengers were on deck, gazing up the canal. One of them nudged my arm. "That's the place. Terrible tragedy."

"What happened?"

"The *Sophia*. Three months ago. You didn't know? Where have you been?"

"Up the Innoko headwaters. Not much news gets to us."

"The steamship *Sophia* went down here. She was sailing from Skagway, over three hundred passengers and crew aboard, and ran onto rocks in the canal."

231

"That's strange. Weren't there ships in the canal to save her? There's lots of traffic here."

"There were ships all right, but the captain refused all offers of help. He was sure he could refloat her at high tide, but during the night she suddenly slid off the rocks and went down. There were no survivors. Everyone drowned, right there in the canal. I have a list of the missing, here in my pocket."

Reading the list, I was distressed to see the names of several friends and acquaintances.

"Been here long?" he asked.

"Eighteen years."

"Piled up plenty in eighteen years, I dare say?"

"I've got two hundred dollars in my wallet. That's the lot."

"No luck, eh?"

"Yes and no. We had some good times in Alaska, hunting and fishing and trapping. We were free and independent, and that was something we prized more than money. We did try mining, though, and came mighty close to fortunes several times. There may be gold waiting for us yet on one of our claims. Samples were rich, but the mine flooded out before we hit paydirt."

"You'll be going back for it, then?"

"No." I hesitated, hearing for a moment that siren song that sounds at intervals for every prospector who almost struck it rich. "No. I'm going to try landscaping."

"Certainly be a change. You may find it dull after life in Alaska. But what else can you do? If a man's unlucky up here, there's no sense in beating his head against a wall. Best to give up the struggle and admit he's licked while still on his feet."

I made my way to the bow of the boat, to the spot where, 18 years before, with the salt wind biting at my face, I had breathed in the smell of adventure. There was no feeling of defeat in me now as I sailed for home. My main purpose had been accomplished, for my strength and endurance in Alaska had been proven, at least to my own satisfaction.

Not licked, I thought in silent answer to my fellow passenger. Adventure in the wilderness may be finished, but a new adventure, for Alice and me, is just beginning.

So I was back where I had started as a kid of 16, in the gardening business, content with my landscaping work and fairly successful, a team of men under me, and pictures of some of my gardens appearing in the glossy magazines. We had two daughters in the years that followed. We considered ourselves fortunate. But every so often a craving came over me to leave the city and get back to the wilderness.

Then I would sail up the British Columbia coast 100 miles or so to Quadra Island off Campbell River, where Ted and Maude lived in an old white farmhouse by the sea. Ted had found the best of two worlds there; his house was close to a little creek that ran down to the beach, and it faced a calm blue sea circled with green islands backed by a range of snow-peaked mountains.

Ted had a rowboat fitted with sail, and we would go to distant bays, then climb the hills to hunt deer. In the early dawn we rowed out among the islands, watching the sun rise from behind the purple silhouette of the mountain range to flood the dark sky with red and gold. I knew again the thrill of a sudden tug on the line and the satisfaction when skilful playing brought the leaping salmon to the boatside to be netted. Ted had built a kayak, long and narrow, with a skeleton of slender wooden ribs covered with canvas which he had painted forest green. I often paddled it on the waters of the bay, shooting lightly and effortlessly over the waves. In the kayak I felt young again, swift and free as the wind.

Ted's livestock made me think of our days at Mouse Point. Here, too, they were more entertaining than useful. He had an old cow called Annie, a bad-tempered beast who would lower her horns and run bellowing at anyone coming near. Ted dodged her horns like a matador and distracted her with a box of pea pods, while he pulled at her teats. Half the time she kicked over his pail as soon as he filled it, but he was satisfied if he saved a jug of cream for Maude, who was like a little cat with cream, drinking it up with shameless gluttony.

He had two goats, one white, a pretty, shy creature that gave delicious, mild-tasting milk; the other a rowdy little brown animal whose milk was strong and unpalatable. Ted kept the brown goat because her impudent, affectionate ways amused him. She followed him about the garden, along the trails and down the beach, hopping onto a log beside him when he sat, butting him and nuzzling his ear. He had a russet spaniel, too, that went with him everywhere, brought his slippers to him and slept at the foot of his bed.

The chickens provided daily drama. They were left to run loose by the creek, and most of the hens hid out in the ferns when they grew broody and had to be hunted down and robbed of their eggs. Hawks were attracted by the little colony, especially when hens that had successfully outwitted Ted brought their families of chicks back to the creek. There would be a sudden uproar, a frenzied squawking and clucking. "Hawk in the chicken-yard!" Maude would scream, adding to the clamor. Seizing his shotgun, Ted would dash for the creek and blast away at the villain. When he thought the hawk was routed and not biding its time in the top of a giant cedar, he would calm the hysterical mothers and coax the young ones out of the bracken and down to the creek again.

Ted experimented with grafts, growing three or four varieties of fruit on a single tree. He planted grapes, and the vines on his trellis produced large purple clusters. He set up beehives and, protected by veil and gloves, pursued the swarms tirelessly from tree to tree. The bees clustered in a heavy, writhing mass that often dispersed and swept upward in a black cloud as he crept near. Patiently he trailed and stalked them until the moment of capture when he carried the pulsating mass to a vacant hive.

Jock and Meg had come to live on the island, buying a house and land not far from Ted's property. Ted was shocked when he first saw our old partner crippled and weak, with all his daredeviltry, generosity and dry humor gone. Jock limped over the rough road every day to visit Ted, but he never stayed for long. He would grow uneasy after a few minutes and pull himself painfully to his feet and limp back to Meg in her kitchen. Meg seldom left her sparsely furnished house and opened her door to no one but Jock. When he died a few years later, she sold the place and rejoined her spinster sisters in the little village in Scotland.

"Poor old Jock," Ted reflected sadly. "I never thought to see that independent Scot a slave, but that's what he became — a slave to gold. It broke his body and his spirit. He told me he got a windfall in Alaska, but it brought him no joy; the money came too late and the cost was too great. It was an evil star that led the three of us down the Yukon River and up the Innoko to those miserable creeks."

We had some good talks, though, when Jock was still around — three old partners sitting in Ted's large, panelled kitchen where deer heads and gun racks hung on the walls, and the huge wood-burning range sent out a glowing heat on cold and blustery fall days.

"We had a fine time in Alaska, up the Yukon and the Black," Ted would reminisce. "The way people are moving in here and crowding out the island wilderness, the three of us may find ourselves heading back to Mouse Point some day."

"Aye, Mouse Point," Jock would agree with a far-away look in his eyes. "Those were the days, Ted."

Long ago, Ted taught me to love growing things, and I'm happy enough now, working with my plants and shrubs. But sometimes when I look at a placid, man-made pool of my own creation, ringed by a formal grouping of scentless hybrid roses, I dream of the wild rivers of the north breaking free in the springtime, up-ending the ice cakes and hurtling them about like ninepins. And I think, too, of the hundreds of different wildflowers that carpet the Alaskan hills and flats all summer to gladden the eyes after the long winter has ended: masses of rosy fireweed, bluebells and larkspur, tiny golden tundra roses, the wild pink roses on the bank above Mouse Point, and the blue forget-me-nots on the Kokrine Hills.

For once the wilderness gets into your blood, you are never wholly free of it. It's there to stay.

Bibliography

Adney, E. T. *Klondike Stampede of 1897-1898.* Fairfield, Wash., Ye Galleon Press, 1968.

Amundsen, Roald. *The North West Passage.* London, Constable, 1908.

Andrews, C. L. *The Story of Alaska.* Caldwell, Ohio, Caxton, 1938.

Anzer, R. C. *Klondike Gold Rush.* N.Y., Pageant Press, 1959.

Baird, A. *Sixty Years on the Klondike.* Vancouver, Black, 1965.

Bartlett, G. W. "The Diary of Robert Campbell," *Canadian Magazine,* Aug.-Sept.-Oct. 1915.

Becker, E. A. *Klondike '98.* Portland, Ore., Binford and Mort, 1958.

———. *A Treasury of Alaskana.* Seattle, Wash., Superior Publishing Company, 1969.

Berton, P. *Klondike.* Toronto, McClelland and Stewart, 1958.

Burke, C. H. *Doctor Hap.* N.Y., Coward-McCann, 1961.

Carpenter, F. G. *Alaska Our Northern Wonderland.* N.Y., Doubleday, 1923.

Dawson, M. *Klondike Mike.* N.Y., Morrow, 1943.

Devine, E. J. *Across Widest America*. Montreal, Canadian Messenger, 1905.

Dufresne, F. *My Way Was North*. N.Y., Holt, 1966.

Gruening, E. *The Alaska Book*. Chicago, Ferguson, 1960.

Heller, H. L. *Sourdough Sagas*. Cleveland, Ohio, World, 1967.

Hinton, A. C. *The Yukon*. Philadelphia, Macrae Smith, n.d.

Jacques, F. P. *As Far as the Yukon*. N.Y., Harper, 1951.

Lokke, C. L. *Klondike Saga*. Minneapolis, Norwegian-American Historical Association, 1965.

Lucia, E. *Klondike Kate*. N.Y., Hastings House, 1962.

Machetanz, S. *The Howl of the Malemute*, N.Y., Sloan, 1961.

Martin, J. *Canadian Wilderness Trapping*. Toronto, Fur Trade Journal, 1944.

Mather, B. *New Westminster, the Royal City*. Toronto, Dent, 1958.

Mathews, R. *The Yukon*. N.Y., Holt, 1968.

Michael, H. N. *Lieutenant Zagoskin's Travels in Russian America 1842-1844*. Toronto, University of Toronto Press, 1967.

Morgan, M. C. *One Man's Gold Rush*. Seattle, University of Washington Press, 1967.

Murie, M. E. *Two in the Far North*. N.Y., Knopf, 1962.

Nadeau, R. *Los Angeles, from Mission to Modern City*. N.Y., Longmans, 1960.

O'Connor, R. *High Jinks on the Klondike*. N.Y., Bobbs-Merrill, 1954.

Partridge, B. *Amundsen*. London, Hale, 1953.

Place, M. T. *The Yukon*. N.Y., Ives Washburn, Inc., 1967.

Romig, E. C. *A Pioneer Woman in Alaska*. Colorado Springs, Romig, 1945.

Schwatka, F. *Along Alaska's Great River*. N.Y., Cassell, 1885.

Springer, J. *Innocent in Alaska*. N.Y., Coward-McCann, 1963.

Stuck, H. *Ten Thousand Miles with a Dog Sled*. N.Y., Scribner, 1914.

———. *Voyages on the Yukon and its Tributaries*. N.Y., Scribner, 1917.

Underwood, J. J. *Alaska, an Empire in the Making*. N.Y., Dodd Mead, 1928.

Victoria Historical Review. *Centennial Celebrations 1862-1962*. Research and writing by James K. Nesbitt, Victoria, 1962.

Wharton, D. *The Alaska Gold Rush*. Bloomington, Indiana, Indiana University Press, 1972.

Willoughby, B. *Gentlemen Unafraid*. N.Y., Putnam, 1928.

Wilson, C. "Surrender of Fort Yukon, One Hundred Years Ago." *Beaver Magazine,* Autumn 1969.

Arctic

Brooks

Siberia

Bering Sea

CANDLE

Koyukuk R.

NOME

NULATO

KALTAG

Norton Sound

Stuart I.

ST. MICHAEL

ANVIK

HOLY CROSS

ANDREAVSKI

Yukon

Innoko R.

Iditarod R.

OPHIR

TAKOTNA

Nowitna R.

KOKRINES

MOUSE R.

TAN

Mt McKin

Kuskokwim R.

Alaska

Bristol Bay

Pacific

MAPS: drawn by R. A. Court